W9-CBA-534

KELLY YANG

Private
LABEL

KATHERINE TEGEN BOOKS
An Imprint of HarperCollins Publishers

Katherine Tegen Books is an imprint of HarperCollins Publishers.

Private Label

Copyright © 2022 by Yang Yang

All rights reserved. Printed in the United States of America.

No part of this book may be used or reproduced in any manner whatsoever
without written permission except in the case of brief quotations embodied in
critical articles and reviews. For information address HarperCollins Children's
Books, a division of HarperCollins Publishers, 195 Broadway, New York,
NY 10007.

www.epicreads.com

Library of Congress Control Number: 2021951495
ISBN 978-0-06-294110-7

Typography by Laura Mock

22 23 24 25 26   PC/LSCH   10 9 8 7 6 5 4 3 2 1

First Edition

To my mother

1

Serene

MOM OPENS FORTUNE cookies from the only Chinese restaurant in town—Lucky Szechwan—one after another, until she gets the fortune she wants.

"Look, Serene! This one says 'A pleasant surprise is in store for you!'" Mom smiles. She crumples up all the bad ones and adds the lucky one to her collection of good fortunes, housed in a glass jewelry box. "Better be true—or the investors will have my head on a clothes hanger!"

I roll my eyes. I wish Mom would stop worrying about the investors and just soak this in. It's New York Fashion Week! Her big moment. She's been working so hard, staying up late for months sewing her couture pieces. This time next week, all of New York's elite fashionistas will be oohing and aahing over her creations. I'm only an intern, and even I can tell she's outdone herself.

"You're going to do great, Mom," I tell her. I reach for

the copy of Mom's fashion week catalog and trace my finger over her name: LILY LEE. Someday I want to have my own label like my mom, except I won't have my creativity choked by a bunch of money-grubbing investors. And it'll be my real last name on the tag, Li.

Mom says Lee looks better. More American. So that's what she goes by professionally.

"It's a name white people could have," Mom had explained when I was little.

"But we're not white."

"They don't know that. All they see is the label."

It had been Julien's idea, I'm sure. Julien Pierre, Mom's first angel investor, and the person she credits with opening the door for her in high fashion, has many opinions. His family started a famous line of handbags back in the day, which then got bought out by LVMH, leaving Julien and his siblings with twenty million dollars each. His brother and sisters took the money and snorted it, drank it, and Instagrammed it. But Julien, he was smart. He invested in my mom.

And now he's the chairman of her board and a constant hemorrhoid in her ass. It'd been his "suggestion" that Mom use Lee, just as it'd been his suggestion that Mom start getting highlights and honey-brown eye contacts. Lighten, lighten, lighten. It was all part of his rebranding of Mom—an all-American designer for all Americans—which started when I was twelve and never stopped.

I guess you can never be too American.

"Have you decided what you're going to wear when you come out after the show?" I ask.

Mom purses her lips, thinking, as she serves the beef noodles from the takeout container. Beef noodles are her favorite, but she suddenly wrinkles her nose. Lately, she hasn't been eating as much—I think it's the stress of prepping for New York Fashion Week. Instead, she takes out a piece of ginger from the fridge and dices it up fine. Mom's always adding extra ginger to everything. And I'm always taking it out, hoping my friends and my boyfriend, Cameron, don't smell it on me later.

Guess Mom's not the only one trying to become more American.

"You should wear that silk high-neck piece we designed," I suggest. The other day in the office, my mom and I were messing around with silk. She was trying to teach me how to sew the delicate threads, and we ended up designing this stunning dress, cinched at the neck, made of flowing satin that draped all the way to the floor.

"I liked that too. But it looks too much like a Chinese qipao," Mom says, then sighs. "You know what they would say if they saw me photographed in *Vogue* wearing that."

I look down. "It's not all about the investors, you know. . . ."

Mom puts her chopsticks down and reaches out a hand.

"We all have to make compromises if we want to make

it big mainstream," she says. "That's how this works. Julien and the others, they *know* mainstream. That's why they're here."

I frown. And we don't? Because we're Chinese? I stare down at my own pieces of discarded ginger sitting next to my noodles.

Mom puts her hands on my cheeks and looks into my eyes.

"Hey. We've made it. We're here. We got in."

I smile back at my badass, trailblazing mom, a beacon of hope for all Asian American girls who dream of doing something different. Even if she can't use her real Asian last name.

That night, I add Mom's New York Fashion Week catalog to my collection. It's not a fashion collection, but a collection of reasons why my dad shouldn't have deserted us. He split when I was still in my mom's belly, and she brought me with her swollen feet to America, where she didn't know a soul. I imagine him out there, reading of Mom's success, his regret painful. I hope it's excruciating. Which is why every time something good happens to us, I add it to my box. It's filled with Honor Roll certificates, Excellence for Artwork awards, and every single VIP invitation to Mom's fashion shows.

I just wish I knew where to send it to.

I picture my dad, walking around in Beijing, opening

the box and going *daaammmn*. Ruing his decision not to chase after my mom, not to chase after me. I wonder, if he knew the box would be so big, would he still have left us?

It makes me mad that I'll never know (my mom doesn't know how to get in touch with him—nor does she ever want to). And he's never once tried emailing her, even though she is literally the most googleable person I know.

Most of all, it makes me mad that I'll never know what's in his box.

On Saturday, I drop Mom off at LAX. She has three full suitcases stuffed with clothes and two purses strapped to her body—and this does not include pieces from the collection, which have already been FedExed. These are her personal clothes.

I had stayed up late with her, helping her categorize and label her outfits, putting pieces together for *cocktail party*, *interview*, and *major press*. New York Fashion Week is so crazy and hectic, there's no time to decide anything. So I preplanned, prelabeled, and presorted.

"What am I gonna do without you for a week?" Mom kisses me as I put the suitcases onto the luggage cart. "You sure you don't wanna come?"

"I have a test for AP French," I remind her. I'm taking French as my foreign language. I had wanted to take Chinese, given I can barely speak it and don't know a single character other than my name, but Mom had felt it was more important for me to know the language of the great fashion houses.

Marcia, her personal assistant, runs up to us. Behind her, Julien is pulling up in his Porsche. He dumps his luggage by the first-class curbside check-in, doesn't even bother to put it on the scale.

"Oh good, you're here, we gotta go! *Harper's Bazaar* called—they want an interview as soon as we land," Marcia says.

"*Harper's Bazaar*! That's huge!" I squeal.

Julien walks over, overhearing, and adds, "It's not *Vogue*, but . . ."

I frown at him. He's always doing that, reminding Mom of some higher goal, as though what she's currently achieving is not good enough. Like she needs reminding. He knows how long Mom's been chasing the *Vogue* dream. It's the holy grail for fashion designers. So far, they've featured a few of her dresses and mentioned her name once or twice but never done a full-blown interview.

"Don't worry, Mom," I assure her. "After the show, *Vogue* will come knocking—just watch."

Mom flashes me a nervous smile as she turns to her senior designers. As is customary for New York Fashion Week, the entire senior design team is going, leaving the junior designers and me to hold down the fort (cue wearing flip-flops to work!). Jonathan, one of the senior designers, walks over.

"Oh, Serene," Jonathan says, "can you do me a favor while I'm gone? It's really important."

"Absolutely!" I unlock my iPhone to take notes. "What do you need?"

I tiptoe on my feet, hoping to be trusted with an important email that needs to be sent. Or a meeting with a buyer that needs to be scheduled asap. Or a dress that needs to be FedExed—

"On my desk, next to my rulers and notebooks and fabrics"—he lowers his voice—"is a box of chocolates. Dark chocolate almonds. Can you put it away so no one eats it while I'm gone?"

Oh.

"Sure thing," I say, trying to wipe the disappointment off my face. I wish the senior designers would see me as more than just a coffee order taker. I've been interning now at the company for months! I can handle *more* than chocolate lockups. I want to be trusted with *real* responsibilities—how else can I learn the ropes?

But I remind myself I'm lucky to have this job . . . considering. Everyone in the company still remembers what happened last year. It's going to take people time to forget. But they will. I just have to keep proving myself to them.

You'll get there, I tell myself.

When the last of Mom's bags have been checked in, Mom turns to me.

"You gonna be OK?" she asks, suddenly a little misty-eyed. She always tears up when she's leaving me. "Can't I bribe you to come? A little New York pizza?"

"I'll be fine," I assure Mom. She hugs me hard. "Break a leg. I'll be watching on Twitter!"

Julien reminds me as he walks away, "But don't be tweeting anything. And stay away from One Oak."

I flush at the not-so-subtle reminder of that horrible night. My phone dings as I shake my head—never gonna happen again—and I wave. It's Cameron, my boyfriend.

Hey, Luke and I are having a debate. Settle this for us—what's the plural of penis? Is it peni???

I laugh out loud as I walk to the parking lot.

Are u seriously asking me?? 😂 I text. **It's penises u dope.**

R u sure? What about octopi? 🐙

I don't have time to get into an octopus/penis debate with Cameron, so I text back **At the airport. Just dropped off my mom.** I hop back into my car.

Why?

Hello, does he not remember anything I say? **My mom's going to New York, remember? She's showing at New York Fashion Week.**

I attach links to Mom's show but Cameron's more interested in something else.

8

So you have the whole house to yourself?? 🐙 🐙 😃

I blush. Even though we've been talking about it forever, we still haven't done it. My friends keep telling me to seal the deal already. "You're not going to get hotter than Cameron." Which is probably true. Cameron is very **hot**. As in perfect body at the beach and multiple girls looking like they're going to stab me hot.

Still, I wonder if there should be a more compelling reason to have sex with someone than "probably can't get someone hotter." I remind myself that Cameron is *fine*. I'm seventeen. Maybe biological attraction is the only reason I'll get at this stage in my life.

Maybe. 😃 I text back.

2

Lian

MY PHONE VIBRATES and I reach for the dreaded thing. Ever since we moved to America, the only people who text me in the morning are my parents and telemarketers. My friends in Beijing are all snoring due to the time difference. Sure enough, it's my mom, already on my case at eight a.m. on a Saturday.

You up??? You should be studying!!! she texts.

I shield my eyes from the blinding sun—why is it in America the sun is so bright, it feels like you're waking up in a tanning booth? To make matters worse, our house, the color of mustard, has these bright blocks of glass in the wall, which you can't cover with curtains because they're too small and all over the place. This is the result of Mom getting the house off the internet. No joke, she just ordered a house like a pizza.

My dad got the call from work that he had to move to LA

to help with the operations of his company. And my mom googled "Need house in LA ASAP." And then I think she must have eenie-meenie-miney-moed it because there's no way a lactose-intolerant person would have picked a house that looks this much like cheese.

My phone vibrates again with increasing intensity.

I groan. Texting back only encourages her. It's kind of like when I accidentally clicked on an ad on Instagram for "sexual wellness products," just out of curiosity, and all of a sudden I get fifty-eight ads for dildos and they keep coming and I can't stop it even when I scream into my phone, "Water bottle. Computer. iPhone. Lawnmower. Anything!" So I don't reply.

No sooner do I put my phone down and stare into the glassy mouse holes than I hear her angry footsteps stomping up the stairs.

I grab my phone and quickly text back, **Yeah I'm up! I'm studying!** before the FBI-style door pounding begins.

The footsteps stop. I let out a cautious exhale.

Remember, Mom texts back. **ECEP test coming up. You need 800!!!**

ECEP stands for Early College Engineering Program. It's this new program at MIT my parents are obsessed with, partly because it would allow me to enter college early (next year), and partly because they think I might end up like those guys from *Silicon Valley*. It's the one American show they watch. Never mind the fact that the only Asian guy on the show is a squatter who might or might not have murdered his landlord (it's not even confirmed, another reason why I can't stand the show or the thought of being an engineer).

"LIAN!" Mom shouts, banging on my door. "I know you read my text message. Why you not reply me?!"

"Sorry! OK!" I snap back to reality.

I quickly reply 👍 👍 👍, but it's not enough for her.

She wants to know my exact schedule for the rest of the day, how I intend to bring up my score from a 680 to an 800, and whether the pimple I had on my face yesterday has gotten any smaller. She was like this in Beijing too, even though I had gone to a bilingual English school, which in theory was supposed to be more chill, but it just gave my mom more reason to stress out about me. I bury my head under the pillow. If my parents keep this up, I'm going to have to go home in one of those Amazon boxes the size of human bodies. Which I *know* they have.

Later, I'm watching Ronny Chieng's show on Netflix—*Asian Comedian Destroys America!*, taking a break from the ridiculous ECEP test. So far the best part about this move to America has been the ability to watch Netflix. And Ronny Chieng, he makes America sound pretty good; not like fake-as-shit Instagram good, like listening to my lao ye talk about the Cultural Revolution good.

My lao ye, he can talk your ear off about the Cultural Revolution, and how he got his big toe stuck in a fence and the only way to get it out was to rip the flesh through the metal. Damn depressing, but you had to respect him.

I think about that sometimes, when I'm feeling really depressed about the fact that I'm the only Chinese guy in my school and half the people there mispronounce my name Liam, not Lian. Maybe America is my Cultural Revolution.

There's a knock on the door and I respond instinctively, "WHAT! I'M STUDYING!"

But it's just my sister, Amy.

"Hey," she says, opening my door and carrying a vase full of blue delphiniums into the room. Mom must have asked her to put them in my room. My mom used to do the floral arrangements for big weddings in China. She had her own shop in Guomao, one of the biggest shopping malls in Beijing. That is, until the landlord's daughter decided *she* wanted to be a florist. They kicked my mom out and took over her shop. For a while, Mom hung on to all her vases, hoping she'd open another shop, but there was never a right location or affordable rent. So she sold the vases. Now she just rearranges our house . . . and our lives.

Amy sets down the flowers and points at my laptop. "Can I watch dance videos on your computer?"

"What's wrong with yours?" I ask.

"Mom looks at my history."

I shake my head at my sister, just twelve years old, already getting spied on by my parents. And not letting it get in between her and her dance videos. Respect.

"Go ahead," I tell her.

She giggles. "Ronny Chieng?" She presses Play before I can stop her. She covers her mouth, laughing as Ronny rants. I try to pry it away, but my kid sister insists on watching. And hey, it's America. Land of the free, right? Get up there and say whatever you want. That's the best part about this country to me.

As my sister takes my computer to her room, I close the door, making sure it's shut all the way (unfortunately, my parents do not believe in locked doors). I go to my desk and pull out THE NOTEBOOK.

I walk to my bathroom, look into the mirror, and take a deep breath.

"What is it about American high schools . . ." I open my notebook and say, mimicking Ronny, "You have a note for everything. Teacher, can I get an extension? My pet spider died. I smashed my finger yesterday. Or my favorite—I don't have an excuse, but can you cut me a break? In China, you say that, the teacher will come over and give you an excuse!"

I'm not nearly as poised as Ronny. My elbows poke out awkwardly as I hold my Sonicare toothbrush as a mic. But it's fun being able to say my truth, even if it's just to myself. After five minutes, I'm on a roll, smiling, pointing to the mirror, when Mom barges in.

"What you say?" she asks.

"Nothing!" I press on the electric toothbrush and pretend to be brushing my teeth. Except it's upside down.

"You were in here talking to yourself."

"No I wasn't," I say, right-side-upping my toothbrush. I pretend to gargle.

"I heard you say something," she insists.

"Just going over formulas for ECEP while I'm brushing my teeth," I lie, pointing the vibrating toothbrush at her, while dropping my secret stand-up comedy notebook behind me on the floor (and hoping it doesn't land in the toilet).

The worry lines between her eyebrows temporarily disappear as she praises me for my diligence—studying *while* brushing my teeth! Now that's a gui Chinese son!

"Discipline!" she praises. "Keep it up and you'll get an eight hundred. Remember, that's only six questions wrong. And if you get a seventh—"

"I know, I know," I say. "You'll enlist me in the army, where it's legal for me to get shot."

"I'm serious," she says. "We go straight from test center to army office. I fill out application."

"OK, Ma."

At long last, I get her out of my room the only way I know how—telling her I'm hungry. As she makes dinner, I sit back down at my desk. And I start laughing. It's the only way to process the messed-up way my parents talk to me. Which is probably why I love comedy so much.

And at the same time, I know with mathematical certainty that of all the things that will land me in the army office, stand-up comedy's definitely number one.

3

Serene

ON SUNDAY NIGHT, I invite Cameron over for dinner. I make us grilled chicken and sautéed spinach with roasted Marcona almonds that I got from Bristol Farms. I spent all afternoon slicing them perfectly, savoring the thought of our night together.

By the time Cameron arrives at seven forty-five, shirtless, an hour later than we agreed to, the roasted almonds sit soggy on top of the bed of wilted greens.

"Sorry, babe, the waves were sick today!" he says, kissing me. I turn away, fighting the urge to call it a night, if it were not for the sight of his bare surfer abs.

Still, he should have called. Cameron reaches out a hand to my skirt, cups my butt, and pulls me in toward him. "Hey . . . don't be mad."

"I'm not . . . it's just, I made dinner."

I try and lead him toward the dining room, where the

plates are set and the food is ready, but Cameron stays glued to the floor, his hands traveling up the small of my back. He's hungry for something else.

"You didn't ask me what I was in the mood for," he says breathlessly as he kisses me. First on my mouth, then on my neck. Lower and lower.

I know what he wants. But I don't want it like this. I want it special. In my bedroom, where I have candles all set up . . . after we've stared into each other's eyes during dinner and had a real conversation.

I can hear my best friend Quinn's voice in my head: *God, Serene, this isn't a John Green novel! JUST DO IT!*

I close my eyes and I let Cameron kiss me, breathing in the ocean salt in his soft, blond hair. He always smells like a pretzel. Still, I moan and kiss him back. Quinn says guys like it when girls moan. One of his hands finds a way up my shirt.

"God, your boobs are so nice . . . ," he mutters into my ear, massaging them.

I feel myself glow with pride. There was a time when I was younger when I was legit scared I wouldn't have boobs. I was one of the last girls in my grade to develop. The anxiety every day, coming to school and seeing everyone else changing into sports bras for PE, I thought I would be stuck with my two pale mosquito bites forever, but then one summer, they came in. Overnight, I had a cleavage that even some of Mom's models don't have. Quinn says they're my greatest assets.

I just wish I knew how to handle them. Some girls, they call the shots with guys, and don't let their body get in the way of anything. They know exactly when to turn it off and turn it on. Me, I'm always struggling at the wheel. It's like I can only be at zero or one hundred, never a safe sixty-five miles an hour.

Cameron and I move to the couch, making out in front of the fireplace.

I look down and see his other hand is unzipping his fly— WHOA.

"What are you doing?" I ask.

"What does it look like I'm doing?" he asks, digging into his pants.

I look around at the living room. "Not here!" I tell him. This is the couch where my mom and I go over designs late at night. Where Mom hugged me after I confessed what I'd done last year, after I'd snuck out with Quinn to go to 1 Oak. Mom had every right to be infuriated, but she held me and told me it was going to be OK. Where we plan each other's birthdays and Mom unwinds from her Julien anxiety with a glass of wine. Cameron can't be whipping out his penis in here!

"Why not?" he protests. I try to block my view but it's too late. He's already got his hand on his, um, octopus.

I've seen plenty of dick pics before, mostly from jerkoffs in my school who declare at parties they would *never* date me, and then secretly DM me close-ups of their pubes.

But it's one thing seeing it online and IRL. It looks so . . . pink.

"You want to touch it?" Cameron asks.

Thank God my phone rings.

I jump up from the couch, grateful for the distraction.

"Hello?" I answer, taking my cell and walking into the kitchen, trying to catch my breath.

"Serene? It's Marcia."

"Oh hey, Marcia," I greet my mom's assistant. "How's New York?"

"Not great. Your mom just had an accident. We were at a fashion awards dinner and she just . . ." Marcia's voice cuts out for a minute and my mind races, trying to fill in the blank. What kind of accident? Are we talking wine-spilled-on-dress or something worse?

"She fell," Marcia finally says. I exhale in relief. Falling is totally recoverable. Hayden Panettiere fell at the Met Gala. Heidi Klum at the Emmys. If anything, it's trendy to fall.

But Marcia's next words suck the relief straight out of my lungs.

"Your mom's in the hospital."

"The hospital?" I ask. Cameron calls out to me, "What's

going on?" but I can hardly hear him above the pounding in my ears.

"New York-Presbyterian," Marcia says. "They're running tests. I should know more in a few hours. I just thought you should know."

"Wait! What happened—" I start saying.

"I gotta go." Marcia quickly hangs up. I stare at my phone.

"Babe, get back here!" Cameron calls for me. But I speed-dial Mom, pulling up Twitter as I wait. If Mom fell so badly she needed to go to the hospital, it would be all over social media. It rings and rings but she doesn't answer.

I scroll through Twitter, looking for posts from the award dinner. And then I see it.

Lily Lee, looking emaciated, falls down red carpet stairs at InStyle Fashion Awards Dinner.

My jaw drops. Mom fell down the stairs? I stare at the picture of her kneeling on the stairs in her dress, trying to steady herself, surrounded by her team. She looks thin, but *not* emaciated. How dare they?

"Hellooooo?" Cameron complains.

"Sorry, my mom's having a problem!" I reply, continuing to scroll through Twitter as I try Julien. Maybe he's with her.

American Designer Lily Lee taken to the hospital at New York Fashion Week, fighting for her life.

Fuck! I pace the kitchen. *Pick up, pick up, pick up!* It goes straight to voice mail. Where is that tight-jeaned fucker when you actually need him?

Cameron walks in. Thankfully, his fly is zipped as he crosses his arms. "What's the big emergency?"

"My mom's in the hospital," I tell him. I pick up my phone and show him the picture of Mom on the floor.

"She probably just got drunk. You should see my mom after a couple of martinis," Cameron says. He reaches for my arm and tries to lead me back. "Now c'mon, let's get back—"

I shake my arm free. "No," I tell him. I start googling the number for New York-Presbyterian. *I* should be the one the doctors talk to. Not Marcia or Julien. I instantly regret staying for my AP test. "You have to go."

Cameron throws his arms up in protest. "You always do this," he says, shaking his head at me as he glances down at his pants. "I'm gonna start calling you blue balls."

I glance down at his pants, imagining, feeling mildly bad but mostly relieved I don't have to look at *that*.

"I'm sorry," I tell him. "I just really need to deal with this right now. . . ."

I push Cameron out the door. As soon as he leaves, I dial the main number for New York-Presbyterian. As I listen to the hold music, I tell myself everything's fine. It's just social media making a big deal out of everything, as usual. When

Mom's back, we'll engage Sabrina the publicist to make it better, just like when I made the mistake of going to 1 Oak.

Mom is the toughest person I know. She'll be *fine*. She has to be.

4

Lian

ACCORDING TO THIS Medium article I read, in order to succeed in stand-up comedy, I have to first be the class clown. This guy swears that it's an unskippable step, because if you're not the class clown, you're not funny. Ergo, every day I go to school with one goal: to be the clown, dammit.

But it's hard to clown around when you're invisible.

Serene Li, with her long flowing black hair with purple highlights, walks right by me on our way to AP Calculus. I wave but she doesn't see me. She's checking her phone, like an atomic bomb is about to explode. Her friends, though, they see me. They give me the kind of eye roll usually reserved for toddlers who squat and take a shit in the middle of the street in China (yeah, that still happens, but we're working on it).

The girl rolling her eyes the most is Quinn, Serene's best friend. When I first got here Quinn went out of her way to make my life hard. She laughed at my shorts in PE, told a bunch of people I couldn't speak English, and insisted I couldn't park in the school parking lot because I didn't have a California driver's license yet. It took me six months to get a driver's license, and in the meantime I had to walk five blocks each way. Do you know how hard it is to find parking in a beach town?

Worst of all, Quinn was the one who renamed me. She just kept calling me Liam until it caught on. There was not a thing I could do to stop it. Even my own phone started autocorrecting my name. That's when I gave up. I can't compete with Siri. Now I don't even bother correcting people anymore.

While all this was happening, my friends in Beijing, Lei and Chris, wouldn't believe a word. It's like they could not reconcile the real America with the movies of American high schools they'd seen, where everyone hangs out together on the weekends, and even Jonah Hill managed to get to the party. I keep telling them that's not real, none of that is real!

"What about the other Asians? There must be other Asians," Lei had asked.

There's only Serene, I had told him. And while she didn't join in the Liam renaming, she didn't exactly stop Quinn either. Her rule of thumb for me has been STAY AWAY.

Maybe it's because I live in the Dunes. The entire town of Sienna Beach is divided into three main communities.

There's the Cove, the most expensive area, where ocean-front houses cost three million dollars. That's where Serene and all her friends live. Then there are the Highlands, which is slightly less expensive but still gives some serious *fuck off* vibes, mostly due to the fact that it's housed some "ex-celebrities." Finally, there's the Dunes, where I live, which are not gated at all, and therefore the equivalent of charcoaled turd in my classmates' minds.

I've never seen a group of teenagers more obsessed with real estate than a broker. I tell myself that's why they don't like me, because of my sad, gateless neighborhood. Because the other reason is a lot harder to swallow. Which is that I'm different. And even though Serene is too, she's assimilated and I haven't.

I bend down to tie my shoelaces, sneaking peeks at Serene, when I hear a voice call out, "Hey, Liam!"

I look over to see Noah, Oliver, and Stu, three guys from my AP Calculus class, walking over. Even before they open their mouths, I know what they want.

"Cough it up, bro!" they call. "Where's your math homework?"

I hesitate for a second before handing over my problem sets. How Noah, Oliver, and Stu got into AP Calculus is a mystery to me. Their idea of a fundamental theorem is to dot their chin with a Sharpie, in an effort to add more stubble. As they copy my hard work, I gaze over at Cameron, Serene's boyfriend. He's in a category all his own. He doesn't even bother calling me Liam, he just calls me "Belt Bag"—for the record, I wore it *once*. I don't know what Serene sees in him. Just because he's the captain of the water polo team? Right now, he's got his wet, sweaty arm draped over her soft shoulder.

"Don't even think about it. Cameron will eat you for lunch," Stu says, following my gaze.

"What are you talking about? I'm not thinking anything," I mutter.

"Ever since he got tall, he thinks he's better than everyone. One time, he tried to flush my shoes down the toilet, just for bumping into him in the hallway," he says. "I had to walk around with shit-soaked Vans for a whole day."

I tear my eyes off Serene and look down at my own shoes. That would not be good.

Stu leans over. "I heard she went down on him this weekend while her mom was out of town."

"Fucking unfair," Oliver protests. "I had to help my grandma clean up her garage this weekend. I had to sort through her hairnets and wigs."

I turn to Stu. "Where did you hear that?"

"He bragged about it on the water polo group chat. I'm still on it," Stu says, practically glowing because his number hasn't been kicked off the chat.

He pulls out his phone. Noah and Oliver both turn to look. I want to chuck the phone halfway across the field. I can't believe Cameron would brag about that in a group chat. Then again, I can totally believe it. I try and distract the guys by offering up my AP Econ homework, instead. That gets their attention.

"Sweet! Econ!" They get right back to copying.

Stu points to my penmanship and starts giggling. "Shit, man, your handwriting is so neat."

"It's neater than my little sister's!" Noah agrees.

I try and grab my paper back from them, but they take off with it, running through the maze of people to the cafeteria. They stuff it behind the Coke machine and by the time I finally get it back, I'm ten minutes late for calc.

I slip into calc as quietly as I can, hoping the teacher doesn't notice me. But of course he does. I stick out like a neon filter on Instagram.

"Liam Chen!" my teacher, Mr. Dabrowski, exclaims. "Where were you?"

"I was just . . . getting something," I say.

"Yeah, getting off in the bathroom!" Cameron calls out.

There's a loud chortle of laughter from his water polo buddies in the back row. I look over at Serene, mortified. She meets my eye for a second, then quickly looks away before anyone sees.

I am most decidedly *not* the class clown.

I am the class . . . nobody.

Maybe getting out of here early wouldn't be so bad.

5

Serene

WHEN I FINALLY reach Mom on Monday, she acts like nothing happened. She's back at the show, putting last-minute touches on the models. She's more interested in talking about the models' hair.

"This hair spray is just not working. I'm trying to make it messy, but every time, it just looks sticky," Mom says, frowning into the FaceTime camera.

"Mom, you're not answering the question. What happened at the hospital?" I ask.

Mom puts the hair spray down. She waves to the makeup artist to take over. "It was nothing. They're running tests but it's total overkill. I feel *fine*."

Mom smiles into the camera and shows me the backstage area. I am temporarily distracted by the dizzying kaleidoscope of dresses and models and lights behind her. I relax and tell myself I probably would have fallen eight times just looking at all those people and lights!

"You know what tests?" I ask, leaning against the hallway. I have a couple more minutes before French.

"Oh, blood tests, they think my bilirubin is a bit high. But I keep telling them it's just the stress of everything. They have no idea what it takes to put on a high-profile fashion show!" Mom says. There's a tap on her shoulder as one of the models exchanges words with her. "I gotta go."

Mom hangs up before I can say bye. I type "bilirubin" on my phone, ignoring the texts from Quinn that keep popping up:

So what happened this weekend??

Tell me you guys FINALLY hooked up. 👋📱🤙🍑🤠

OMG stop, I text back.

Google spits out various different possibilities associated with high bilirubin:

1. Gallstones
2. Bile duct inflammation
3. Liver dysfunction
4. Hepatitis
5. Gilbert's syndrome

Hepatitis? Liver dysfunction? That *can't* be right. Mom doesn't even drink much.

Quinn and Emma walk over to me and I throw my phone into my purse.

"SOOO?" Quinn asks, peering at me. "How was your

candlelit dinner? I saw you cooking on Instagram in your apron . . . so hot!"

"Ugh," I tell her. "My mom had some kind of emergency in New York and Cameron had to leave."

"Oh no!" Emma says, looking up from her phone. "Is she OK?"

I put on a smile and assure them she's fine. My cardinal rule since fifth grade. Never show any weakness. Don't let people think anything about you is less than perfect. Because in Sienna Beach, the minute they start wondering, it might as well be true.

"Well, that's disappointing. So you guys didn't do *anything*?" Quinn asks. "That's not what he told Luke."

Luke is Quinn's boyfriend and Cameron's best friend. And even though it's massively annoying that Cameron tells Luke everything we do, it's also helped cement my status in our circle, from guest star to series regular. I remind myself of this as Quinn and Emma poke me for details.

"We . . . explored," I admit.

Quinn, always the budding reporter—her dad owns a bunch of magazines—keeps prodding. "And? Did you like the goods?"

I blush, trying to cover my face—this is so embarrassing. "I'm *not* going to answer that."

Quinn and Emma glance over at Cameron, on the other side of the courtyard, as if trying to decide for themselves. "At his level it doesn't even matter," Quinn concludes.

"Exactly. His pubes could be metal wires—"

"Shut up!" I scrunch my face, disturbed, but they're probably right.

"So when's round two?" Quinn smiles mischievously. The bell rings and we walk back to class. I can feel the eyeballs on us, girls watching as we parade down the hall. I used to be one of those girls, looking in. Now I can't believe I'm one of them. "C'mon, you guys have to catch up with us, so we can go on double dates!"

"We can still go on double dates," I remind her.

"Nah. Won't be as fun. You and Cameron still have that awkward two-people-who-haven't-had-sex energy," she shudders.

Her judgment is so strong, it almost makes me want to grab Cameron and consummate the relationship right there in the bathroom. Instead, I bring up the only thing that puts me back on even keel, my ace card.

"You know who's going to be at my mom's show at New York Fashion Week today? Ariana Grande!" I say.

"Oh my God! That's so amazing! So, do we get some free samples?" they ask, clamoring for my phone. "Hook us up!"

I hesitate for a second.

Quinn frowns at me. *You owe me.* And she's right, I do.

"Come to the office after school today. I'll see what I can do," I say. I feel bad, given Mom's out of town. But I tell myself she'd get it. It's a game she's had to play too. A different variation of it, with fancier people and company stock instead of clothes. But what about my dad? Would he get it, if he knew what I'd had to do to survive? Would he be proud? Or disappointed?

Later, Quinn, Emma, and I are cruising down PCH in my car to Mom's office in Santa Monica. It's across the street from the Snapchat campus and as I park, Quinn and Emma taunt the army of tech guys who lumber into work in their black hoodies and jeans.

"Come and snap this," Emma says, sticking her ass out as she exits my car.

I grab my friends and head inside.

Stepping off the elevator, I scan my employee card and open the doors to my mom's office. Inside, it looks more like a luxury boutique hotel than an office. The reception area is warm and inviting, with thick white carpet that all the designers' stiletto heels sink into. Today the junior designers are wearing flats and sweats. It's New York Fashion Week, baby! Which means we get to be totally unfashionable for once.

I stop by my desk and log on to my computer to check the updates.

"Did you see? Your mom's *Harper's Bazaar* profile just went live!" Carmella, one of the junior designers, says.

"What's it say?" I ask.

Ali, another junior designer, hands me a printout: "Lily

Lee Knows How to Turn Up the Heat—New Collection Shines at New York Fashion Week."

I beam as I read the piece. It's a beautiful profile of my mom's latest collection, concluding her show today was *masterful*.

"This is amazing!"

"And they haven't even seen the tulle!" Carmella adds with a wink.

The tulle is this jaw-dropping five-hundred-layer couture gown my mom's been working on for nearly a year. Her masterpiece. Each individual layer is so delicate, it feels like you're holding up a fragile flake of croissant. She was going to show it in New York, but she hadn't completely finished before she left. The buyers will have to wait until Paris. I turn around to show my friends the *Harper's* piece, but they've disappeared.

I find them in the sample closet. The sample closet is where we keep all the samples of our latest collections for model fittings. And inside, Quinn and Amber are grabbing shirts and dresses and pants faster than their hands can pry them off the coat hangers. Some of the pieces in their arms aren't even fully done—there's still loose string and fabric hanging off the side. I rush to try and save them from my friends' grabby hands.

"You guys, I think they still need some of this stuff," I say gently, closing the closet doors, worried what will happen if my coworkers walk in. I know it was my idea, and we've done it many times before, but it's always been when my mom was here. With her gone, it feels mildly like . . . we're stealing?

"Can't you guys just make another?" Quinn shrugs.

I bite my lip. It doesn't quite work that way. I look into Quinn's eyes, trying to reason with her.

"Relax. Your mom's not even here," Emma says. "She'll never know."

I hear a sound by the door and look over to see some of the junior designers standing there, gazing over at Emma and Quinn. I know what they must be thinking, but they're kind enough not to say it out loud.

"I just need one more shirt! To go with these pants!" Quinn says. She reaches for a silk charmeuse top.

"Careful with that!" Carmella calls out from the doorway. "I'm playing around with that material for our ready-to-wear collection."

Unfortunately, Quinn pulls a little too hard. And the delicate fabric rips.

There's a collective gasp as all the designers take in what happened. I want to shrink into a mothball, I'm so mortified.

Later, after my friends leave, I overhear the designers talking as I'm hunched in Jonathan's office, dealing with his chocolates.

"Can you believe she let her friends come in here and raid the closet like that?"

"Of course she did. It's Serene. The same girl who got drunk at One Oak and told a reporter she thought her mom's last season was '*bland*.'"

I shrink under Jonathan's desk. For the record, I didn't know he was a reporter. He told me he was a fashion student at UCLA. I hadn't meant it. I was just trying to seem cool.

"And to think she still has a job here."

"She's the boss's daughter. What do you expect?"

I hide my face under Jonathan's desk for hours, too ashamed to come out. Because they're right. I have no business being here. I messed up. I should be shown the door.

Sandwiched against Jonathan's trash can and his sneakers, I use my phone to repurchase the items my friends took. Quiet as a feather, I take out his design files from his filing drawer and study them. Because even though these people think I'm a joke, I'm not going to give up on my dreams just because I made a mistake.

6

Lian

MY MOM IS island walking when I get home, doing circles around our kitchen island like a hamster on speed. She says it's for exercise but I'm thinking *Oh shit*. She usually only island walks when she's lost at Bragathon.

Bragathon is what I call it when my mom meets up with her friends. They get together, usually over chrysanthemum tea and stale pastries, and brag about their kids. One of them will bring over the latest Korean face mask, which they'll all put on to try to smooth out their wrinkles but really it's to cover up the shock and horror of hearing about someone else's kids' accomplishments. Invariably it sends my mother on a nonstop kitchen island sprint.

"Hey, Mom," I say. "You want to go to the beach or something? Jog there? I can drive you."

My mom's eyes stab into me.

"This your problem. This why you not get eight hundred

yet on ECEP." She pokes her finger into my chest. "You thinking about the beach! You know Auntie Linda's son Edward got eight hundred on SAT when he was twelve?"

"Wow, twelve . . ." I shake my head at this tragic news. It means he had to study for it when he was ten or eleven, poor kid.

Mom wraps her hands around the glass vase of fresh peonies in the center of the island. I can smell the sweet scent drifting toward me. Even though our house feels terrifying at times, at least it always smells nice.

"You don't appreciate what you have here," she says to me. She points to me and my sister. "Neither of you appreciate."

"What do we have here?" I ask, crossing my arms.

"You have *chance* here," she says. "America is meritocracy. Doesn't matter who you are, or what your family owns."

She gazes regretfully down at the peonies, and I wonder if she's referring to her old shop in Beijing. Is that what this is about?

"I think it still matters here," I offer.

"No. In this country, you in charge your own destiny." Then she lifts her finger and digs it into my chest. "If you fail, that's on *you*. Nobody else to blame." She picks up her keys. "Come on. Let's go see Highway Robber."

"Now?" I ask, glancing to my room. I want to write a joke about island walking in my notebook before I forget it.

"Now!"

o o o

Highway Robber is the super-expensive college admissions consultant my mom hired when we moved here. He's the one who told us about ECEP and recommended the schools in Sienna Beach. We call him Highway Robber in our house because he's so expensive, it's basically highway robbery. He charges a whopping eight hundred dollars per session, which is what cancer doctors charge. I guess to Chinese parents, not getting into Harvard *is* a cancer.

Mom calls Dad in the car on the way over and tells him to meet us there.

"You want me to leave work now?" he asks. "I can't do that. What will Roger think?"

Dad's new boss, Roger, is the reason he stays up till three a.m., working. Even though it was his idea to have Dad come out, so far he's been impossible to satisfy. Something about Dad not exceeding all his KPIs. Sometimes at night, Dad is just sitting there, staring at the computer. He looks miserable, like the life has been sucked out of him with a vacuum cleaner.

"We're paying *eight hundred dollars a session*," Mom reminds him. "This is your son's future!"

"I'll see what I can do," Dad mutters.

Mom and I sit outside Highway Robber's office, my butt sinking into the brown leather chair that smells faintly of a decomposing animal, studying all his various degrees and certificates on his wall. *Columbia. Yale. Princeton. Cornell.*

University of Pennsylvania. That seems like an illegal number of degrees for one person.

The door opens and Highway greets us as another set of Asian parents and a nervous-looking boy scurry out. Highway's a fifty-year-old white guy. He's wearing a striped shirt with a bow tie and a tweed jacket with elbow patches. His preppiness is blinding me.

"Come on in, Lian! Mrs. Chen! Will your husband be joining us?" he asks.

Mom takes one last hopeful gaze toward the parking lot.

"I'll just leave the door open, in case he comes," Highway says. His unusually white teeth gleam at us as we take a seat on another set of leather chairs. He has an identical set of degrees on his wall. I wonder which are the originals—the ones inside, or outside? Definitely outside, I think.

"All right, well, let's get started," he says. "How are you liking junior year so far? Sienna High's the best, isn't it?"

I gaze down, then start to nod. "Yeah, it's OK. Not the most diverse place in the world."

"Oh, well, sure it is!" he insists. He starts listing all the different types of diversity with his fingers. "You have religious diversity, physical abilities diversity, behavior and ethno-diversity—"

"Never mind," I say.

"He's a straight-A student," my mom cuts in. Her face beams with pride. "Ten APs."

Highway jots this down in his notebook. "Very impressive. And your SATs?"

"I got a fifteen eighty."

"Just twenty points shy of perfect." My mom shakes her head. I picture an American mom saying it, "Just twenty points shy of perfect!" Mom says it like a baby died.

"I also took the ACTs—"

Highway cuts me off. "OK, so you have a good SAT and good ACT scores. But ECEP is a highly competitive program. I mean, this is MIT we're talking about. Home of the Whirlwind! The CSAIL! Every Asian kid in the country's gonna be applying. What else you got?"

Mom looks like she's about to start doing laps around his desk.

"Does Lian have activities? Hobbies? Things he likes to do after school? And *please* don't say piano!"

"What's wrong with piano?" Mom asks. Both me and my sister played until we passed all the exams, which meant hours and hours of practice every day until our fingers practically bled. When we passed the final exam, it was the proudest moment of my mother's life.

I quickly tell Highway all the various clubs and activities I'm a part of at school—there's the Summer Camp Club for underserved youth and the American Red Cross Club.

"Are you the president or co-president of any of them?" Highway inquires.

I shake my head. "Just a member. We distribute first-aid kits whenever there's an event. For the Summer Camp Club, I'm the volunteer coordinator. But since it's in the summer, we only start meeting up in the spring."

Highway frowns. "That's not good enough, you need to show leadership. That's one thing Asian applicants don't have enough of—leadership."

I flinch every time he says Asian. Like he knows everything about us. Like we're a monolith.

"But I just got to Sienna Beach. Last year," I remind him. "Most of the club presidents are seniors. And they've been at the school their whole lives. They know everybody."

"So start your own club!" Highway suggests.

Oh yeah, like that's gonna work. People barely sit next to me at lunch, they're really going to join my club after school? But then I start thinking. There isn't a stand-up comedy club in my school. . . .

When I point this out to Highway and my mom, they both burst out laughing.

"A stand-up comedy club?" Mom asks.

"Good one!" Highway says.

"What's the matter with that?"

"You not funny," Mom decides.

I frown. That's rich, considering she's never even heard me.

"You too serious. Not gonna work. Those stand-up

comedy people, they drink and do drugs, then write jokes," Mom says.

I roll my eyes. Like she knows what they do. And in what order.

"I'm going to have to agree with your mom," Highway says. "No offense, but you don't strike me as a stand-up comedy type of guy."

"Oh, and what kind of guy do I strike you as?" I mutter.

"An aeronautical engineering guy!" he announces. "A biochemist! A econophysicist!"

"Can you suggest something that maybe people can actually spell?"

Mom laughs. I look over, pleased. And who says I wasn't funny?

"What about a Chinese club?" he suggests. "Something to appreciate Chinese culture? Maybe teach other kids the language? Hell, we can even call it a club to help improve US/China relations!"

A high school club to improve US/China relations? Does this guy even listen to himself?

"Uh, I don't think—" I start to say. Then stop. I realize it doesn't *actually* have to be a Chinese club. How will Highway Robber ever know? If no one shows up—which they're not *gonna* if I call it Chinese Club—then I can do anything I want. I can finally practice my stand-up without the threat of Mom barging in. "That's a great idea!"

"Wonderful!" Highway says.

Mom beams at me, like for the first time ever, she might consider skipping the army office. And just like that, it's settled. I'm starting a fake Chinese club so I can become the real Ronny Chieng.

7

Serene

MOM'S SUITCASES ARE by the door when I come home from school on Wednesday, her strappy sandals lying on the marble floor.

"Mom?" I ask, putting my laptop and keys down. I kick off my boots and hurry inside. What's she doing home so early? Did something happen with the show? She's not supposed to get back until Friday.

"In here," she calls from the formal living room.

I walk inside and see her lying on the couch with a blanket over her stomach.

"What's wrong? Are you sick?" I ask.

She gets up and pats the spot next to her on the couch. I take a seat.

"I have something to tell you," she says. I stare at her, mind going to the million and one dark places I've been terrified of ever since I was young. Her business is folding. We're losing our house.

I tell myself to stop it. It's gotta be the test results. Mom probably has gallstones. I stayed up late last night looking it up and while it's a pain in the butt, gallstones are common, actually.

I open my mouth to tell Mom, *It's going to be OK. They'll just take them out. You'll be in and out in one day,* at the same time she blurts out, "I have cancer."

"WHAT?"

Mom presses her lips together, eyes welling. I feel the room spinning as I shake my head. *No.* She's so young—just thirty-nine years old. And she takes care of herself—she has a Peloton bike, for crying out loud!

"I couldn't believe it either. But the doctors, they ran the tests twice," Mom says. She reaches for my hand. "It turns out there's a tumor the size of a walnut in my pancreas. That's what was causing the bilirubin levels to go up. And that's why I haven't been eating."

Mom keeps explaining but all I can hear is "cancer." Pancreatic cancer is the deadliest form of cancer. Not even Steve Jobs made it.

"Are they sure it's pancreatic?" I ask, my throat so dry I'm barely able to push out the words.

As Mom nods, my eyes start to moisten. Pancreatic cancer is *not* in our collection of things that can happen to us! It just can't!

"I know it's shocking," Mom says. With a shaky voice, Mom starts telling me more about the cancer, how it can go undetected for years, how it's one of those diseases with virtually no symptoms until the late stages.

The whole time, I'm waiting for her to say GOTCHA!

But she doesn't say GOTCHA. Instead, she whispers three words that knot my own stomach. "It's stage three."

The next few hours disappear. I go down an endless loop of internet searches. Forget homework. Forget texting Cameron back. All I can do is stare at WebMD. And even though each page is scarier than the next, I can't stop clicking.

Pancreatic cancer is a silent killer.

Median 5-year survival rate of patients with pancreatic cancer—9%.

Stage 3 prognosis—many only survive months after diagnosis.

MONTHS?! My eyeballs burn as I stare and scroll. Finally, there's a glimmer of hope.

Survival rates increase with surgery.

I put the iPad down and burst out of my room, looking for Mom. I find her in her office, looking over designs. She's got the tulle dress specs pulled up on her computer. *Forget the tulle,* I want to scream. *Forget the collection!* I can't believe she's still working.

"Mom! We've got to get you to a surgeon," I tell her.

"It's why I flew back. The doctors in New York said they

can't operate in my condition, but I want to get a second opinion," Mom says.

"Well, let's go!"

"Later this week. I have an appointment with Dr. Herman at UCLA."

"Can't you get something earlier?" I ask.

Mom shakes her head.

"Later" seems like an eternity. Later is a luxury we don't have. I grab at my hair. Why did this have to happen to her?

"Hey, I know you're scared," she says. "But it's going to be OK. . . ."

It takes every ounce of willpower not to lose it and start bawling when she says that. Because we don't know that. And the question that's been growing uncontrollably like a mass inside me is—what am I going to do without her? She's all I've got.

My phone dings with a text. It's Quinn with another nosy Cameron text. Mom glances at my phone.

"Don't tell your friends," she says. "Until we figure out what to do with the company, we have to keep on the d/l."

I scrunch my eyebrows. "What do you mean, do with the company?"

Mom takes a breath. "Well . . . the reality is, there's only a five percent chance I survive this thing," she says grimly. "And now with Trish gone . . ."

Trish Blair was her second-in-command up until last year, when she jumped ship to Stella McCartney. The official story was that Trish wanted to focus more on foot-wear, but really it was because she was tired of waiting for the reins.

"Does Julien know?" I ask.

Mom tenses. I'm guessing that's a *yes*.

"He wants me to sell," she says.

I roll my eyes—of course he does. That's what he's been saying to her for the last three years. "Dream on . . . ," I start to say.

"Well, this time, maybe I don't get to wake up," Mom replies. She lifts her eyes slowly to mine, and whispers, "Five percent, Serene . . ."

In that moment, I see how terrified she is. "It's a nine percent chance," I correct her. "Which is really like ten percent. . . ."

It's a game my mom and I used to play, whenever I'd get a bad grade in school. It's a B- which really is a B, which really is a B+, which really is an A.

Today, Mom gives me the saddest of smiles.

Later, I'm making pumpkin soup for Mom, even though she says she doesn't feel like eating, trying not to oversalt the soup with my tears as I dice up the ginger. I add lots and lots of ginger, hoping the spice will cover up my emotions.

Cameron texts me. **Hey! We gonna finish what we started?** 🌱

I wipe my fingers on a paper towel. **No. I'm sorry.** I

hesitate, wanting to tell him, but I promised Mom. **I'm going through something.**

You're always going through something, Cameron replies.

Soup splatters in the pot and I want to scream, *Yeah, well, this time it's fucking cancer!*

Instead, I switch my phone to silent and turn it upside down.

I turn off the heat and ladle out the soup into bowls. I place them on a glass tray. Carefully, I carry the tray upstairs. When I was little, Mom would bring me meals in bed when I was sick. I used to love eating on my bed together—it felt like camping. Tonight, though, I find Mom asleep on her bed. I tell myself it's not the cancer. She's just exhausted from her trip.

I put the soup down and curl up next to her, eyes gazing over at the picture of Mom by her bedstand. It's the only picture of Beijing we have. In it, she's pregnant with me. She's standing in front of a lake and there are cherry blossoms blooming behind her. She has the look of a terrified young woman, mustering a brave smile.

I've always assumed my dad took the photo. At the thought of him, the tears that I've been hanging on to come gushing out. I reach for the photo and hug it in my arms. I have to tell my dad somehow. He needs to know. Then a far more terrifying thought occurs—if something happens to Mom, what if I can't find him?

I suck in a breath as I imagine my fate. I'll be an orphan.

They'll take our house and all our stuff.

I'll be nothing.

I have to find him before it's too late.

8

Lian

IT TURNS OUT all you have to do to start a club at Sienna High is get two faculty signatures and a half-baked statement of intent. On mine, I wrote "to learn about China and practice Chinese" under club purposes and goals. And Mrs. Tanner, the counselor, approved it right away, no questions asked.

"You know what would be fun? If you guys had a potluck! Like every month. You could bring in spring rolls, chow mein, tempura!" She closes her eyes, smelling some imaginary takeout aroma. "I *love* tempura!"

"Yeah, maybe." I nod politely, not wanting to break it to her that tempura is not really Chinese.

"Or instant noodles!" she suggests.

She assigns me room 318, Mr. Sheldon the math teacher's room, and tells me to make some flyers—a minimum of fifty—and pass them out around school.

I smile and thank her as she hands me back the form. I stare at my new title.

Chinese Club

President: Lian Chen

It's not class clown, but it looks pretty sweet.

I walk around school handing out flyers the next day. I give them to the skaters, the artists, the vapers who hang around by the bathroom, and the football team. When it's clear no one has any intention of coming, I broaden my circle.

Most people take a flyer and toss it straight into the recycling. Person, recycling, person, recycling, it goes. Some people ask if there's going to be food. I say no. They shove it even harder into the recycling bin. But that's OK. I get a temporary high by their rejection, excited by the prospect of having my very own private stage to practice every Monday.

Then I see Serene. She's by herself for a change, leaning against the vending machine, lost in thought. I quickly walk over and hand her a flyer.

"Hey," I say. "I'm Lian. I'm in your calculus class?"

Serene glances at me for a second, mumbles, "Thanks," as she takes my flyer and puts it in her purse.

She looks like her pet gerbil just died. I study her sad eyes. Before I can ask her what's wrong, Cameron walks over. He bumps into me hard, like knocking all the flyers out of my hand *hard*. He grabs one off the floor.

"Chinese Club?" he asks. He grins and starts shouting to his buddies. "Look! Belt Bag's starting a club to teach us to be more like him!"

As Cameron's water polo friends chortle with laugher, I sneak a glance at Serene, who looks equally mortified.

I grab the flyer back from Cameron and push by him. I dump the rest of my flyers in the trash can, fighting the urge to march to my counselor's office and call the whole thing off.

But I remind myself the club's for me. So I can finally do what *I* want to do.

I just gotta block out my shitty classmates and get through the year.

A Volvo SUV races by me as I drive my sister down Wilshire after school to SAT class. For a second, I think it's Serene, but it's some older woman speeding like a maniac.

"Watch where you're going!" I call after her.

Amy looks up from reading my one last flyer for Chinese Club. "So did lots of people want to join?" she asks, bouncing up and down next to me. "Are you going to have to do roll call each time? Oh! You should get one of those bells to call the meeting to order!"

I glance over at my little sister and chuckle. I don't have the heart to break it to her that there will be no need for bells. "Yeah, maybe."

Amy's bright smile turns into a frown as I turn into Avalon Plaza.

I park the car, staring at the candy apple red of the 888 Education sign. Out of all the SAT tutoring companies, our mom picked 888 over Kaplan and Princeton Review because it was started by two Chinese roommates out of MIT. Every day after school, it's crammed full of Asian kids.

"Asians know tests," she had explained. "Plus eight means get rich in Chinese."

I didn't have it in me to break it to her we know a lot more than tests. So I had to sit through *hours* of SAT instruction every week when I first got here last year. And now my poor sister has to do it too, at just twelve years old!

"How's Kevin?" I ask her. Kevin's the managing director of 888, a guy who has a tendency to sigh for a full eight seconds before telling you your score. No matter how good it was, it always warranted a sigh.

My sister picks at her fingers. The skin around her pinkie is practically chewed raw. I can tell how stressed she is.

"Hey, it's OK. You're only twelve," I tell her. "You're not supposed to ace the SATs."

"But I only got a four hundred on the last math practice test. But Kevin says the other twelve-year-olds, they're all way ahead of me. I don't know what's wrong with me."

She bangs her head with her chewed-raw hands.

"Nothing's wrong with you," I assure her. "Kevin doesn't

know what he's talking about. You're *fine.*"

Amy looks hesitantly at me. Her eyes slide over to the dance studio next to 888 Education. A trio of girls are coming out wearing tap shoes, laughing and chatting. They look so much happier than the poor kids in 888. See, this is what twelve-year-olds should be doing, not beating themselves up over reading comp. Judging from the way Amy stares enviously at them, she thinks so too.

"Hey, you wanna go to dance instead today?" I ask.

Amy nods eagerly.

"C'mon." I grin, getting out of the car. She deserves it.

Amy hangs back while I step into 888 Education and tell them she's not feeling well. Then I take my sister's hand and sign her up for dance class. As Amy runs onto the dance floor, squealing with joy, I laugh. I'm pretty sure Mom will kill me. But seeing Amy's face as she tap-dances across the room, I decide it's worth it. I'm proud to have liberated my little sister.

If only for one day.

9

Serene

I REACH FOR Lian's flyer and read it as I wait for my mom. I'm taking her to the doctor today.

> *Chinese Club – Want to learn Chinese and communicate with more than a billion people?*

Lian Chen. Sweet guy. Could even be cute if he did something with that mop of black hair. But this is Sienna Beach. He should know the only people they want to communicate with here are rich white people who live in the Cove.

My mom walks down the stairs in a sleek black jumpsuit, like she's going to a cocktail party, not the oncologist's, and I stuff the flyer back into my bag. I smile. You wouldn't think there was any problem just by looking at her. She looks great.

"You ready?" she asks.

I nod, throwing my keys, phone, notepad, and a pen into my purse. I reach for a packet of tissues, just in case. I tell myself I'm not going to cry. I'm going there for Mom and I'm going to be strong.

"Ready," I tell her.

Mom taps her heels on the waiting room floor so loud, the other patients give her a look.

Sorry, she mouths.

A couple of people point at us, recognizing Mom. I tell myself they're not looking at me. Sabrina had done a great job burying what happened. Of course Quinn's folks helped too. There are just a few pieces still up online—*Lily Lee's daughter, Serene, caught underaged and drunk at LA club, wearing rival brand Alexis.* Of all the things that happened that night, the fact that I was wearing Alexis bothered my mom the most.

"Ms. Li?" the nurse calls. "Dr. Herman will see you now."

Mom takes a second to compose herself then stands. She turns to me, hesitating. "You sure you really want to go in there with me? You don't have to."

I give her a look. *Mom, you're not getting rid of me.* "I'm sure."

We walk inside Dr. Herman's office. I open a notebook to take notes.

Dr. Herman is an older white man in his sixties. He sits behind a mahogany desk with a YOU CAN BEAT THIS poster hanging behind him. It's a poster of a woman in a hospital gown wearing boxing gloves. I never used to understand these inspirational posters. Now I cling to them. He puts his reading glasses down as we walk inside.

"I'm Dr. Herman. Please, have a seat," he says, extending a hand as we sit down.

"Thanks for seeing us," Mom says. "I'm Lily Li and this is my daughter, Serene."

"I know who you are. I've been reviewing your case. The doctors at New York–Presbyterian forwarded me everything. How are you feeling?" he asks.

Mom glances at me. "A little tired," she says. "Stressed. I haven't been eating very much."

"That's typical of pancreatic cancer. The PET scan shows the cancer has already spread to the lymph nodes outside the pancreas as well as the nearby arteries and veins. In other words . . ." He looks solemnly at us. "It's metastasized."

"But what about surgery?" I interject. "Can you cut it out?"

"I'm afraid they can't operate once it's gone to the nearby arteries and veins. The risk of damaging these other structures is too great."

The news slams against my own artery walls. Without surgery, Mom's chances of survival plummet to 2 percent.

"What if the scan was wrong?" Mom asks.

"They did the biopsy, the endoscopic ultrasound, the CT, blood tests . . . everything corresponds—"

I shake my head vigorously. Not everything corresponds. *I* don't correspond.

"But they *could* all be wrong, couldn't they?" Mom continues. It breaks my heart, hearing the vulnerability in her voice, my strong, fearless mother. It makes me want to dig into her body and claw out her cancer myself.

The doctor takes his time finding the right word. "It's . . . unlikely," he says gently.

Mom reaches for my hand. Her hand is freezing cold and I sandwich it between my two warm ones.

"What about chemo?" I ask.

"Yes, certainly an option, especially considering your general health and young age," he says.

Mom lets go of my hand. "I don't want to do chemo," she says.

I'm startled by the outburst.

"It'd just be a lot of unnecessary suffering," she says. Her fingers reach up and she coils her long, voluminous hair around them. I can tell what her real concern is. I want to shake her—her hair will be fine! And what a frivolous concern at a time like this! But for my mom, who's spent her entire career cultivating a certain look, hair is not frivolous.

"Chemotherapy, in my experience, prolongs survival in many, many patients," Dr. Herman says.

She looks unconvinced.

"Mom!" I give her a look so urgent, she gulps down a breath. My eyes plead with her, *You need to do this. I need you to do this. PLEASE. You'll be the most fashionable chemo patient in the world!*

She takes a second to collect her thoughts and then finally says, "I'm sorry. OK, fine. If you think it'll help."

I turn to Dr. Herman.

"We'll start you on a course," Dr. Herman says. "I'm not going to lie, it won't be easy. There will be nausea and vomiting, loss of appetite, hair loss, extreme fatigue. You'll need lots of rest. My nurse will schedule you to get fitted for a chemo port. In the meantime, I'm going to give you some pills. It's important you do not skip a dose—understood?"

Mom nods.

"Great," Dr. Herman says, folding his hands. He gestures toward the door. My mom starts getting up. *Is that it? The visit's over?* But I still have so many questions, not the least of which is what exactly is my mom's prognosis?

"So if she does the chemo, how long do you think?" I swallow hard. "Like if you had to guess, how long does my mom have to live?"

Dr. Herman looks down at Mom's chart. He then peers at my mom, their eyes talking. He doesn't answer the question.

"Every single person is different."

"But in your experience," I press. "Someone with my mom's circumstances. On average."

"Serene, he just said, everyone's different," Mom says.

I shake my head. Mom might want to live in a state of forged ignorance, but I'm a planner. And I need answers.

"Six to eleven months," the doctor finally replies.

Walking out of the doctor's office, I keep my gaze glued to the ground, the tears heavy in my eyes. My feet are just floating above the ground. I don't know how I'm moving, how the world is still spinning. I look everywhere, except at Mom. I know if I look at her, I won't be able to stop crying. I tell myself to be strong, for her. For us.

But once we're inside the car, the tears sneak out from under both our sunglasses. I reach over for her and we cling to each other, sobbing. She assures me as she holds me, "Don't you believe that fucker for a second. Your mama is strong. I'm not going anywhere."

I nod and wipe my tears madly as I recite to her the stories I got off the internet.

"There's this guy in Florida. He's still alive," I tell her. "And this lady in Baltimore. I think she was stage three too."

"Exactly," Mom says. "Dr. Herman can take his six months and shove them up his ass. In six months, I'll be showing in Milan."

A laugh escapes, and I smile through my tear-soaked lashes.

"You'll beat it, Mom, I know you will." I hug her tight.

Mom gives me one more squeeze and starts the car. Instead of a left, though, she makes a right when we get out of the parking lot.

"Where are you going?" I ask.

"To the office," she says.

"No, Mom, you heard the doctor, you need rest. Let's go home." I try to reach for the wheel.

But she won't turn back. A look of determination crosses her face. "I refuse to let this thing steal from me what I've worked so hard to build."

Mom power walks into her office, like nothing's wrong. Marcia rushes over and fills her in on all the press coverage, the trades, and buyer feedback from the show.

The whole time I'm trying to hold my tongue. *Slow down, Marcia, she's just had major news dropped on her.* But Mom responds to every single one of Marcia's inquiries, setting meetings and approving dates, like the boss she is.

"Thanks. Oh, and some of the investors are here," Marcia says. "I put them in the conference room."

Mom stops walking. She gazes over at the glass conference room at the end of the office, at Julien and the others. It always stresses Mom out when there's an investor meeting, especially one not on the books. Julien and the other guys gaze right back at her. They look . . . concerned. I walk over to my desk and sit down as Mom enters the conference room.

"What's going on? Why are they all here?" I ask Carmella, who sits by me. I hope Carmella has forgiven me for letting my friends mess up her concept sample the other day. "By the way, I'm sorry about my friends, Quinn and—"

"Forget about it!" She waves away my concern. "How's your mom doing?"

I furrow my eyebrows. Does she know?

"She's . . . good," I respond, not knowing how much to say.

Carmella puts a hand to her chest. "Oh, that's great," she says. "Those pics on Twitter, so inappropriate people took them. Your mom may be a total icon, but she's human. She's allowed to fall once in a while. I'm so relieved."

Me too. I let out a sigh that she and the others don't know more. Let's hope it stays that way.

Ali leans over and asks if I can help her get back to all the internship requests. We get about twenty requests per day from new grads of the nation's most prestigious design schools.

"Sure!"

As I type polite rejections to people ten times more qualified than me, feeling incredibly lucky and incredibly shitty—none of *them* went to a club and lost control because some reporter was making heart eyes at her—I hear my mom's voice rising. "No! I'm not going along with that!"

I jump up from my desk and start walking over. I know

I'm not supposed to barge in, but today's special. I push into the conference room.

"Mom, are you OK?" I ask. "You need anything? Water?"

"Yeah, a new board of directors," Mom mutters.

I glance at the suits, who shake their heads at her. "Lily, we're just being pragmatic here. You're the face of the company. What's going to happen if the news gets out you have cancer?"

Fuck. They know. I close the glass door behind me, but it's too late. Judging from the shocked looks on the faces outside, they all heard the C-word.

"I'll be fine," Mom insists.

"That is statistically impossible and fiscally irresponsible to say." One of the investors, Chris, lays into her.

Mom responds tartly, "How extremely kind of you."

Julien, Mom's chairman and the biggest investor in the room, puts his hands up. "Gentlemen," he says. "Lily obviously needs time to digest the sale."

"I've digested it and I've shat it out. It's not happening."

He turns to her. "Lily, we've talked about this. You knew that was always the goal."

"It was *your* goal. It wasn't my goal," Mom corrected.

"Nothing lasts forever, Lily. That seat you're sitting in, that's never forever. All this cash that you need to run your business, it's not forever. It was only to get us to the next chapter, which is to sell the company so—"

"So you guys can all cash out," Mom finishes for him. "That's what this is about, I get it. But guess what, it's different for me. I'm trying to build something here. I'm trying to create a legacy—"

"Which is exactly why you should sell, so your name and brand can stay timeless. Classic. Forever preserved by the vanguards of fashion," Julien urges her.

"Oh, don't give me the vanguards of fashion," Mom says, rolling her eyes.

"OK then, think of the designers working for you!" Chris points to the workers outside, every single one of whom was staring inside. "Who's going to protect all of them? Who's going to run the day while you're getting chemo? And lead the company when you can no longer come in? We don't have Trish anymore. She's gone!"

Mom stares at Julien. "You think I drove her away, don't you?"

"I didn't say that."

Mom shakes her head.

"C'mon, Lily, you know how this works. She had offers from Tom Ford, Marc Jacobs, Tory Burch. Why do you think she picked us? She wanted a chance at the wheel. And you just wouldn't give it to her."

"She wanted us to stop carrying anything above size eight!" Mom protests.

Julien rolls his eyes. Sizes are like napkins to him— doesn't matter how many we have. But to my mom, they're everything. She gets up, blocking the neon-lit sign of her name on the wall.

"Thank you, gentlemen," she says. "But I think it's best to resume this conversation with the wider board, at the next meeting. Until then, if you'll excuse me . . ."

Mom starts getting up and I'm relieved. As Mom walks to the door and holds it open, Julien tells her in clear terms, "Get your house in order. Find a second-in-command, and let's get this company into position for sale."

"Please," I urge. I wish they'd have some empathy. She's sick. Give her a beat.

As I'm pleading, Mom drops a bomb so powerful, it ricochets through the office.

"I've already found a second-in-command."

"Who?" Julien turns, surprised.

"My daughter."

My eyes jerk up at my mom. *WHAT?*

"Are you joking? She's seventeen years old! And after the stunt she pulled at that club?" Chris explodes. He says it so loud, the whole office gawks. I peek at the appalled looks on the senior designers' faces and want to shrink into the floor.

"She can and she will," Mom decides. And just like that, my mom puts a fear in the investors' minds even more terrifying than cancer: me.

10

Lian

"THAT WAS *SO* fun!" Amy says, getting into the car.

I grin at my sister as I back out.

"You're really good," I tell her. I mean it too—I watched her entire class. She hit every single beat perfectly. I know it's been a long time since she danced—my sister used to take ballet when she was little, until Mom made her quit to focus on school.

"Thanks!" she says. "I'm thinking of starting a TikTok account—you think Mom and Dad will care?" I give her a look. "I mean, do you think they'll find out?"

I shake my head. The only app they ever use is WeChat—if something's not on WeChat, it doesn't exist.

"Nah," I tell her. "Just don't use your real name. They'll never find it."

Amy grins and puts her hands behind her head and her feet up on the dash.

"Maybe we can do this every Thursday," she says. "Instead of SATs?"

Every Thursday? I don't know . . . I think of Mom and the many *many* slippers she's going to whoop my ass with when she finds out. *You let your sister do WHAT?*

"Please, I promise I'll study on my own!" Amy says, reading my mind. "I'll do two hours of Khan Academy, every day!"

As my sister promises hours and hours of studying in exchange for the opportunity to pursue her passion, I feel my willpower softening. I finally relent.

"OK, but no one can know about this," I tell her.

She zips her mouth and throws out the key. Then turns to me. "What about you, Lian? Is there something you wish you could do?"

I press on the gas. Back in Beijing, Lei and Chris knew. We'd talk about going to Sanlitun and doing open mic one day. We never did it, but we still planned sets, mostly about our parents, and wrote jokes we only said out loud to each other. I smile at the memory and shrug.

"Some stuff." I leave it at that.

"Like what?" she asks, studying the tips of her hair. I notice the tips are all sticky and clumped together.

"What's with your hair?" I ask, pointing to it. "Did you get gum in it?"

"No, it's toothpaste!" Amy says brightly.

"You put toothpaste in your hair? *Why?*"

"The other girls in my class all have blond hair," Amy says, looking down. She holds the gummy tips to the window so they shine in the light. "Do you like it?"

"No!"

"But blond's prettier! Michelle says if I put toothpaste in my hair, it might turn blond too! Then maybe they'll invite me to be part of their dance group for the talent show." The talent show is the big school-wide event at the end of the year. I grip the steering wheel, listening to this horseshit.

"Michelle has as much brains as a glow stick!"

"But look, it's working! It's getting lighter!" she says, thrusting a fistful of sticky hair at me.

I pull the car over and look into my sister's eyes. "Listen to me, forget those other girls. If you want to join the talent show, you should just go for it. You don't need to have golden hair. You're great just the way you are."

Amy looks like she isn't so sure.

"I know what it's like to not fit in. But you know what? One day you're going to look around and you're going to realize, it's not so bad to be different," I tell her.

"Really. Why?"

I rack my brain for a reason. "So you can start a club." My sister smiles. I realize then that my Chinese club is important, even if it only has myself in it. Even if all the other flyers are in the recycling and not one word of Chinese ever gets uttered.

"Thanks," she says as I start up the car again and drive the rest of the way home.

"Hey, Lian?"

"What?"

"You should go after your dream too," she says. "Whatever it is."

I smile as I pull up to our yellow cheese house.

Dad's home early for a change. He sits at the dining room table doodling a highly stylized picture of a mountain on his iPad while Mom makes dinner.

"How was SAT?" Mom asks Amy, moving a fresh vase of roses to the dining room table.

"Good!" She glances at me. "Best class ever!"

"That's good to hear. You usually come home so grumpy," she says as she stir-fries eggplants in garlic sauce.

"Lian makes it fun," Amy says. "He always tells me stories in the car."

"Then you taking your sister every week," Mom says to me, returning to the kitchen and handing me a bunch of chopsticks. "How's school? Anyone want to join your club?"

I nod awkwardly. "Hey, you think I can get some money—" I start saying in Chinese.

Mom interrupts me. "We in America now. Speak English."

I try again.

"You think I can get some money for my new club? To buy some notebooks and stuff," I ask in English. I calculate in my head how much Amy's new dance class will cost. The first class was free today, but I gotta figure it's going to be twenty-five dollars a pop from here on out.

Mom walks over and pulls out a hundred dollars from her wallet. Hands it to me. "Notebooks," she says. "Just notebooks."

I nod, and stuff the cash in my pocket. As I set the table, I ask Dad about the mountain he's drawing.

"This is Yosemite," Dad says proudly, showing me his colorful re-creation. "Maybe this summer, we can all go. I'd love to see the light so I can get this right."

Amy sits down at the table and peers at Dad's stylized art. For as long as I can remember, Dad's been playing around with stylizing pictures with wild neons and futuristic glows on the iPad. He calls it "coloring," but what he does is so much more. He really should have been an artist.

"Wow, Dad! You should send that to Apple!" Amy suggests. "They could make it one of the backgrounds on the new iMac! You could be famous!"

Dad laughs. "I don't think so. I'm just an old man fooling around. . . ." Dad points the iPad stylus at Amy. "When I was *young* though, there was a time I thought about it."

"Don't put ideas in their head!" Mom calls from the kitchen.

"Oh, c'mon, Mom, like you didn't have any dreams

when you were little," I tease her. "I bet you were thinking of how to tie-dye orchids."

"I was," she admits. "And you know what? I now wish I'd listened to my parents and learned something more marketable. Like data analysis."

I roll my eyes.

"How can you say that? You're such a talented florist!" I tell her.

"Talent doesn't always cut it. Especially in China," Mom says. "That's why we move here. Still, better to prepare *safe* plan for success, not crazy plan."

"Pursuing your dreams is *not* a crazy plan!"

Sick of arguing with Mom, I turn my attention back to Dad.

"Anyway, so what happened?" I ask, putting down the last of the chopsticks and sitting down next to him.

"Well, I submitted my art to this contest and I didn't win. Back in those days, art in China was mostly Chinese watercolors. Still, the rejection was *so* painful." Dad shakes his head. "And it was a different kind of pain, not like at work when Roger yells at me for not coming up with the best sales strategy. This cut deep. I'll never forget it."

Hearing Dad talk about his passion is both inspiring and heartbreaking.

"So then what happened?" I ask.

"That was it. I decided from then on to keep my art for myself."

Oh. I look down.

"If you truly love something, nobody can ever take it away from you," he says, patting his trusty iPad. "You can always do it when you're old."

"*After* you succeed," Mom adds from the stove.

As Dad puts away his iPad and gets ready for dinner, the questions linger in my mind: What if I don't want to wait until I'm old? If Dad had given his art a real shot, would he still be sitting here wondering, doodling on his iPad for all of twenty minutes a day?

That night, I walk into Amy's room. I'd printed out pictures of famous Asian musicians and dancers who do not have toothpaste-tipped hair.

"Look at these girls," I tell Amy. "They have black hair." I show her various K-pop stars, including my personal favorite, Blackpink. Out of four band members, three of them have all-black hair.

"Yeah, but they're in *Asia*," Amy points out.

"So?"

"So everyone has black hair there. We're normal there."

"We're normal here too," I tell her.

My sister shakes her head.

"No, we're not. Do you know the definition of 'normal'? I looked it up." She whips out her phone and reads, "It means 'the usual, average, or typical state or condition.'

We're not the usual or typical condition. We're *so far away* from typical."

It depresses me, listening to Amy. To think that my parents thought moving here would be great for us. We might have gained access to Highway Robber and a million AP classes, but there's a lot we lost too.

"It's not always going to be like that, Amy. That's just Sienna Beach." I try to think of a way to explain it to her. "It's like being stuck in Jell-O. When you're in it, you can't see past it. But one day, you're going to get out of here and you'll see, the world is *so much* bigger."

"But I like the Jell-O," she says. "I have way less homework here and Lao Lao's not on my case every day to practice my Chinese."

I let out a small smile. "That's true," I tell her. "You can like the Jell-O. Just don't let it change who you are inside."

She takes the K-pop pictures from me and puts them up on her wall.

11

Serene

"YOU CAN'T BE serious, me lead the company?" I whisper to Mom, following her into her office and closing the door. Julien and the other investors have left, thank God, but there's a whole floor full of people who overheard and are staring at me like the *They Wore What?!* back page of *Us Weekly*. "There's no way!"

"Well, you're going to have to. I'm not going to let those investors bulldoze me into selling." Mom's thin, frail body shakes in her white leather chair. "For them it's just money. But for us . . . They don't know how hard it was for someone like me to get here. If we just sell, then my name, my brand, my *legacy* . . ." Mom shakes her head. "It'll all be forgotten. Erased."

At that moment, I suddenly understand why this means so much to Mom. I breathe in the honor, the responsibility, the *pressure* of carrying on her dreams. "What about one of the senior designers?" I ask. "Jonathan?"

"Jonathan jumps from house to house faster than he can update his LinkedIn," Mom says. "He's like Trish, always looking for a better opportunity elsewhere."

"Then what about Carmella? Or Ali?" I ask.

"Julien will make them bend to his will, you know that. I need someone I can trust," Mom says.

Mom reaches for my hand and I gaze at the dozen designers outside.

"They're not gonna want to listen to a seventeen-year-old," I say. "Especially considering . . ."

"Forget about that. No one even remembers. It's over."

Uhh . . . the room outside? They definitely still remember.

"Please. It's gotta be you, bao-bier," Mom says.

Our eyes meet. Bao-bier means "baby" in Chinese. I know when my mom calls me that, it's serious.

In a moment of weakness, Mom's voice hitches. "I should have never taken Julien's money. Or Chris's. But I was young and desperate. And I thought I needed *them* to succeed. I didn't believe in myself enough."

"Oh, Mom." I walk over and put my arms around her.

"But I can fix this. I just need you to help me hang on a little bit longer, so I can replace some of the board and hopefully take back control. Will you help me?"

I look into Mom's steady eyes. A woman who, on top

77

of being handed a six-to-eleven-months sentence, has to worry that her life's work might be wiped out by a single decision from men in suits. And I promise her I'll try.

Carmella, Ali, and the other junior designers crowd around me when I walk out of Mom's office.

"Tell me it's not true," Carmella asks, eyes welling.

"What kind of cancer?" Ali asks.

They burst into tears when I mutter, "Pancreatic." Everyone knows PC is the LV of cancers—untouchable, in a league of its own. Half a dozen senior designers surround me, suffocating me with their questions.

"Is it true she's stepping down?" Jonathan asks. "And who's taking over?"

I look away.

"Are we going to be sold?" Monica, another one of the senior designers, inquires. "To who—do you know?"

I try to quell the rumors. "Nothing's being sold!" But no matter what I say, the speculation runs rampant.

"I hope it's to Michael Kors. I hear they let all their employees work from home," Jonathan says.

"No way, we're a much better fit for Tory Burch!" another senior designer chimes in. "And the employee discounts are unreal."

My jaw drops. My mother's still in the building and they're already thinking about getting discounts at their new employers!

"Guys! We just had our best fashion show ever in New York!" I remind them. "What are the trades saying?"

Nobody answers my questions. The senior designers carry on gossiping while Carmella and Ali dab their eyes like Mom's already gone.

I blow at my bangs in frustration. How am I supposed to take charge if no one takes me seriously?

I take my phone out and text Quinn:

Help! How do you get more experienced people to listen to you?

How much more experienced? Like college boys? ♀

Very helpful. I put my phone away and gaze over at Mom, sitting inside her glass office. She's hunched over her desk, probably going over design sketches, but from where we're sitting, it looks like she's dropped her forehead on her desk. This visual does not help.

I get up to go and talk to Marcia, but before I can get to her desk, Mom walks out. The whispers and gossip freeze. Slowly, Mom makes her way through the sprawling open space to us. All eyes are on her.

"You may have heard that I had a health scare," she says to her team. "It's true. I'm getting treatment. In the meantime, everything is going to proceed exactly as usual. We're here to do a job, and that is to make every customer look and feel good, no matter what they might be going through."

A few designers look down guiltily. I smile at her. Yes!

Michael Kors and Tory Burch can shove it—my mom's not going anywhere!

"Now if you'll excuse me, I'm going to head home. I'm kind of tired," she says. "I'll be reachable on email and text. Make sure to cc Serene, she'll be helping man the fort."

Oh shit. All eyes turn to me.

"Wait, what do you mean helping man the fort?" Jonathan asks.

"Exactly what I just said. She'll be my second-in-command, my eyes and ears while I'm getting treatment," Mom says as she makes her way out of the office.

The senior designers size me up, their new spy. I wish they knew I'm not. I'm here to learn, to support. Sure, one day I want to have my own company, but it's going to be totally different, a complete reimagining of what a fashion company does. I'm not here to take this one over. I want to step out from my mom's shadow.

But today, I turn to everyone.

"Thanks, Mom, and you guys, I just want to say I'm so proud of—"

But before I can even finish my sentence, everyone's already back at their desks, jumping on LinkedIn.

"Save it for One Oak," someone mutters.

Great.

After Mom leaves, I move my stuff into her office. It's too awkward sitting out there, watching the senior designers count how many unused vacation days they still have to take before they leave and listening to Marcia field calls from various papers about Mom's fall in New York.

I wish I had the guts to get up and say, *C'mon guys, get back to work.* But who am I to say that? I'm the idiot who got drunk and publicly dissed Mom's line. Who's only still here because of who my mom is. And without her, there is no brand, and there is no work. The inspiration, the luxury, the *story*, all of that is gone.

So I get it.

I sit at Mom's desk, gazing at the pictures. There's one of me and her at the Design Museum in London when I was about ten. Mom had just quit her job at the Gap. We strolled through London all week, giggling and popping into candy shops, as Mom told me she was thinking about starting her own line. She had some money saved up and she wanted to invest it in her own designs for once. She had met a guy, Julien, whose family had made a fortune in high fashion and wanted to back her.

Over salted caramel sundaes, she leaned in, took my hand, and told me that the next few years were going to be a lot of work.

And yet. She still made time for school plays and potlucks. When I told her the teacher never called on me, she quietly gifted the teacher a silk scarf. Or when I was the only girl not invited to Quinn's birthday party back in seventh grade, she organized a party for me that included a runway and fashion show—complete with supermodels. *That* got Quinn's attention.

And now . . . the thought of her not being there after six to eleven months, it makes me want to scream at my coworkers outside, *All you fuckers are thinking about your next job—I can't LinkedIn a new mother!*

My eyes water. I quickly turn my chair around, grab a tissue, and start dabbing. The last thing I want all my coworkers to see is me crying.

As I'm throwing away my tissue, I notice a black-and-white picture of my parents on the floor. One I've never seen before. I pick it up. In the picture, my father is leaning against a tree in a suit and my mother's got her hands on her swollen belly, smiling. They look happy.

Why does Mom keep this picture in her office? I always thought she wanted nothing to do with my dad, nothing to remind her of their relationship. That's why there are virtually no pictures of him in our house.

I turn the picture around. On the back are some Chinese words scribbled in pen, words I don't understand. I close my eyes and imagine all sorts of statements—*I will always love you and Serene. I miss you guys so much.*

My mind races. What if he still loves Mom? Oh God, what if she still loves him? Is that why she was looking at his picture after getting back from the doctor? What if they never have a chance to say goodbye to each other?

Desperately, I tap open Mom's computer and pull up

Google Translate. I type in random English words, trying to see if any of the characters match—"love," "miss," "daughter." None of the strokes match. I stare at the mysterious symbols, trying to make sense of them.

I wish I knew Chinese.

Then I remember and bolt from the desk to grab my purse—the flyer!

Want to learn Chinese and communicate with more than a billion people?

12
Lian

ON THE DAY of my first meeting of Chinese Club the next week, I drum my fingers on Mr. Sheldon's desk, waiting until it's safe to assume no one's coming. I gaze at my Chinese dictionary and some blank notebooks for Chinese characters that I picked up at a stationery store in the San Gabriel Valley. I'd brought them along just in case.

By half past three, the door still hasn't budged. I stand up, hope pumping in my heart. This is it—my private stage, for one hour a week!

I walk the length of the empty classroom, picturing a sold-out crowd at Madison Square Garden. The lights, the laughter. The pressure and excitement of an arena full of people all waiting to hear what I have to say.

And I grab the whiteboard eraser and speak into the mic.

"The thing about being invisible at school is I can kind of do whatever I want. Like the other day, I just walked out of PE class. Just walked out. Went and grabbed a bag of Flamin' Hot Cheetos from the cafeteria.

"Ever noticed there are thirty-eight kinds of Flamin' Hot Cheetos? There's Xxtra Flamin' Hot, there's Baked Flamin' Hot—that's for people who want to be healthy while stuffing artificial seasoning and sodium with no nutritional value into their mouths. But hey, it's baked!

"We have good snacks in China. A lot of good snacks. But we don't have thirty-eight different ways to burn your gastrointestinal tract.

"But you know, it tastes good. And that's what America is all about, am I right?"

"Um," a voice says.

Oh shit. I was so in the moment, I didn't even hear the door. There's someone here. I spin around and there's Serene Li staring back at me.

"Serene! What are you doing here?" I ask, chucking the whiteboard marker behind my back.

"Is this Chinese Club?" she asks. "Am I in the right place?"

"Uhhh . . . yeah!" I nod, gesturing for her to take a seat. I hadn't actually planned on anyone showing up. I hand her one of the blank Chinese notebooks to buy time.

Cautiously she opens the notebook, taking off her backpack and wrapping her long, flowing dress around her legs.

I sneak peeks at her.

"What were you just doing?" she asks.

My face turns Flamin' Cheetos red. "Oh, that? That was . . . nothing."

I hold my breath, hoping she doesn't judge me for going on and on about snacks. She probably thinks I'm such a weirdo.

"Just this project I'm doing," I lie. "It's really stupid."

A long, awkward minute goes by. "It was kinda funny," Serene says.

I stare at her. Really? It's the first affirmation from an actual person outside myself that I'm funny. And even though she's probably just saying it to be nice, my heart is bursting—Serene Li thinks I'm alive! And funny!

"So . . . can you teach me Chinese?" she asks.

"Absolutely!"

13

Serene

I'LL ADMIT WHEN I first walked in, I thought I was in the wrong place. Nobody else was in the room, and there was Lian Chen having a monologue about Flamin' Hot Cheetos.

It felt like a private moment, like I had caught him masturbating to the *Rocky* theme song.

But then he said the thing about how in China they don't have thirty-eight ways to burn your GI tract and I nearly burst out laughing.

And now I'm in a room with him.

And he's asking me what I already know in Chinese, and I don't want to seem like one of those ABC who don't know any, so I say the only phrase I know—wo zhi dao, which means "I understand."

Lian's eyes light up whenever I say wo zhi dao. He starts talking in Chinese, firing phrases at a rapid pace, and I say wo zhi dao over and over again. And it seems like we're having a conversation. Except I don't understand any of it.

"That was amazing! OK, we'll move on to something harder," he says.

"No, no," I say. Then I bite my lips and confess. "Actually, I was just saying wo zhi dao. I didn't actually get that."

"Oh," he says. "That's OK! You'll pick it up in no time."

I give him a small smile.

"Actually, can you teach me to read?" I ask.

"Sure!" he says. "We can do that later, after you learn speaking. . . ."

"Can't we do both at the same time?" I ask him.

Lian tells me reading Chinese is hard. "It's not like English—there's no alphabet, so every word is different. Back in Beijing, my friends and I would slog through hours and hours of dictation, trying to master all the characters."

My eyes dart up. "You're from Beijing?"

Lian nods.

I resist the urge to thrust the picture of my dad to him— *Do you know him?* But that would be way too presumptuous. So I sit, as patiently as I can, trying to contain all my Beijing thoughts to myself.

"Anyway, there are eight thousand characters," he says. "Technically there are fifty thousand, but you only need eight thousand to read books and stuff."

I glance down at the Post-it Note in my purse. I don't

need to read a book. I just need to read a note. There are only seven characters. I copied them down.

"Don't worry, you'll get there. It just takes time."

Something in the back of my throat tickles at the mention of time. I dig into my purse to get a Kleenex, trying desperately not to lose it in front of Lian.

"Are you OK?" he asks.

"Sorry, it's just allergies," I say, finding a tissue and pretending to blow into it.

Lian waits for me to finish pretend-blowing my nose, then asks gently, "Is there something in particular you want to read?"

I hesitate for a second, then reach for my purse. Oh, what the hell. I show him the Post-it.

He studies my awkward, boxy Chinese writing. "Does it make sense?" I ask.

I chew my lips as I wait, feeling nervous and exposed. I still remember when Lian first joined our school. Was this how he felt too? I remember once he raised his hand and asked the teacher, "May I go to the toilet?" Everyone had laughed at him. I wish I could go back in time and not chuckle, too. It's hard learning a foreign language.

"'Wo nao hai li dou shi ni,'" he reads. "It means you're always on my mind, or I can't stop thinking about you."

I gasp at the confirmation. They *did* love each other.

I point to one of the only characters I successfully

googled: 海. "But this one, it means 'ocean.'"

"Yes, hai means 'ocean,'" he says. He takes his finger and points to the character next to it. Our two fingers touch slightly. "Nao hai means 'mind.'"

I glance at him, not fully understanding.

"In Chinese, the mind is an ocean," he explains.

Wow. That's so beautiful and makes perfect sense. How many waves have crashed onto my shore, drifting me further away from Dad, and yet, my mind still pulls me toward him?

"Where did you get this?" Lian asks with a smile.

I struggle to answer. Should I make something up? Finally, I blurt out, "My boyfriend wrote it to me."

Lian's eyebrows jump. "Cameron?"

"He . . . uh . . . used Google Translate." I blush.

He doesn't respond.

"What?" I ask.

He leans back in his seat. "Nothing," he says. "He just doesn't strike me as the type of guy who looks up Chinese phrases on Google. But hey—"

"You don't know anything about him!" I jump to Cameron's defense.

"I'm just surprised," Lian says.

I gaze into Lian's eyes, at the judgment on his face that he's trying to hide. It embarrasses me that he thinks he knows something about my relationship with Cameron. And what does that say about his opinion of *me*?

I get up. I've got enough else to deal with.

"Serene, wait, I'm sorry—" he calls to me.

I thank Lian for his time and head out.

If this is the price of learning Chinese, I'll take an online course.

14
Lian

WELL, *FUCK*. THAT went well.

The girl of my dreams joins my Chinese club, tells me I'm funny, asks me to translate a note, and what do I do? I give her a hard time about her boyfriend.

I stay behind in the classroom, banging my head against the wall for a full twenty minutes.

Why. Do. I. Have. To. Be. Such. A. Moron.

Ugh.

I can't even run through my set after she leaves. I'm too distracted by my own stupidity. So I pack up all the empty notebooks and my dictionary and head home.

Mom's in the kitchen, folding plastic bags from the grocery store into little squares and stuffing them inside tissue boxes. She's always saving plastic bags and keeping them everywhere—in boxes in the garage, scrunched inside random shelves, and even taped under tables. I don't know what apocalypse she's preparing for. One with mini trash cans the size of blenders.

"How'd it go? Your first club meeting?" she asks as she folds.

"Pretty good," I say.

"Did lot of people show up?" Mom asks.

"Just one . . . ," I tell her.

She makes a disappointed noise through her teeth. "Who?"

I catch myself from saying Serene just in time. If I tell my parents, I'll never hear the end of it. They'll think I impregnated her just by talking to her. I don't think my parents ever had sex ed in school. They warned me in sixth grade that if I look at a girl for too long, I'll get her pregnant. I spent a whole year avoiding female eye contact. To this day, I keep my eyes glued to the PIN pad at Ralphs when the cashier asks me cash or credit.

So I don't tell my parents about Serene. Besides, after that first meeting, she'll never come back.

"Just this guy in my economics class. He's trying to learn Mandarin so he can get into NYU Stern."

"What Stern?"

"NYU Stern," I repeat. "You know, NYU? One of the greatest schools in New York City. Right in Greenwich Village." *Where lots of stand-up comedy clubs are,* I want to add. "As good as Harvard."

Mom stops folding plastic bags. She takes a tissue box

and, out of nowhere, throws it at me.

"What the hell, Mom!" I cry, rubbing the spot where the sharp corner hit my arm.

"NYU NOT GOOD AS HARVARD!"

"I think it's just as good," I say.

Mom takes a plastic bag and looks like she's about to suffocate herself—or me—with it.

"OK, OK, it's not as good!" I flee up the stairs to my room.

I try and find a way to talk to Serene all week, but the popular kids guard her like Fort Knox. On Sunday, I pull out my computer to look up Serene in the school directory. I have to find a way to apologize to her.

I find her email and her mom's email. No address (not that I would dream of going over there). Should I just email her? Stu texts me as I'm debating.

Hey man, can I count on u for US history homework? he texts. **I just got invited to this party tonight.**

What party? I text back.

Luke Styler's house.

Damn. How'd that happen? Luke is Cameron's best friend and is like eight gated communities away from Stu, social-status-wise.

He liked my answers for econ.

I frown. **You mean MY answers,** I text back.

You should come, Stu offers.

An invitation? This is a first. Stu's usually so nervous about sucking up to Cameron and Luke, in the hopes of getting back on the water polo team. Why would he want me anywhere near that?

Meet us at the front of his house at 11 and bring the answers.

Ahhh, that explains it. He wants to offer me up to his crab lice friends.

No thanks, I text back. **I don't want Luke copying off me.**

OK OK, you don't have to give em to Luke. But you should come. I'm gonna be too wasted when I get home, and if I fail history, my old man's gonna make me retake it over the summer, and there goes my chance to be a beach concierge to hot babes!

Beach concierge is Stu's plan to meet girls this summer. In Sienna Beach, rich people pay you to be their beach servant for a day. You haul their beach chairs, set up their umbrellas, give them fresh coconuts, which you gotta lug all the way to the beach, along with a bag full of ice. Stu's convinced it'll help him get laid.

I dunno, I text back.

Serene's probably gonna be there, he adds.

I sit up. I can hear my mother downstairs, washing dishes and pots and placing them inside the dishwasher to dry.

She'd make hotpot out of my head if she knew I was con-
templating sneaking out, but how cool would it be if Serene
saw me casually hanging out at the same party? I could
apologize, we could talk . . . take a midnight stroll on the
beach and maybe finally get to know each other.

I'll see you there, I text back.

15

Serene

I'M STIRRING UP chicken noodle soup, still thinking about Dad's words about Mom being in his mind ocean (is there seriously anything more romantic in the world?) when I get the text from Quinn—**party tonight @ Luke's!!!**

Mom hears the ding too and looks at me from the kitchen island where she's sitting, watching me cook. She had her first IV chemo session on Friday while I was in school. I know they put a chemo port into her chest, which she refuses to show me. She has it covered under her shirt, plus a variety of scarves and blankets on top. "What's up?" Mom asks.

"Nothing. Just some stupid party," I say. "How is it, the chemo?"

I hadn't had a chance to ask her because Quinn dragged me to yoga and then the salon yesterday. Mom groans.

"Tell me everything—what'd they put in you?"

I tap Notes in my phone to write down the names, so I can keep track of her side effects.

"I can't remember all the names of the drips, but they're all done. I just have to take these guys now." She shows me her bottle of tiny pills from her bag. CAPECITABINE, I read on the label.

I put the bottle down. It couldn't have been easy. I take the ladle and serve up the chicken soup into two bowls. Mom pushes it aside.

"C'mon, Mom, you have to eat," I say.

"Later, I promise. I'm just going to rest for a little while. It's been a long day."

I glance down at the soup that I just spent an hour making. She's been like this for days now, hardly eating, living on protein shakes and the occasional Luna bar. How's she going to get through chemo?

"How about some roasted potatoes?" I ask her. "We still have some from yesterday. . . ."

"No." Mom pushes down on her heavy eyelids with her fingers. "I'm sorry. I'm just tired. . . ."

Reluctantly, I reach for her bowl. But Mom hangs on to it for a sec, lifting her spoon and taking a bite of chicken. I give her a small smile.

My phone dings again.

"You can go if you want," Mom says, pointing to it. "I trust you."

I start shaking my head.

"I'm serious. Go," Mom insists. Gazing out of the window, she adds, "Sometimes I think about last year . . . if I'd just let you go with Quinn, you wouldn't have had to sneak out."

"Mom . . . is that why you think I said what I said?" I ask, instantly filled with regret. And guilt.

"Why else would you have worn Alexis that night?" she asks.

A small smile escapes. Can't believe that's still bothering my mom, after all this time. Not the fact that her daughter was caught in a club, photographed drunk and sprawled across some guy's lap, shit-talking her collection.

"Do you remember what we were talking about before Quinn asked me to go out?" I ask Mom.

She shakes her head.

Earlier that night, I'd been reading *Far from the Tree* for English class, about an adopted girl, Grace, who goes looking for her biological siblings, and how the three teenagers connect. Mom vaguely recalls.

"And do you remember what you said about the book?" I ask.

Again, Mom shakes her head.

"You said that could never happen in real life. They'd never just welcome her into their lives. That only happens in Hollywood."

That's why I'd snuck out that night. That's why I'd said those ugly words to the reporter about my mom. My hand still twitches at the memory.

"Real life . . . has a tendency to be a lot more messy," Mom says by way of explanation. "You know that."

I walk over to the portrait of me and her, sitting on the dining room console table. I trace my finger along the white background, the empty spot where Dad could have stood— *should* be standing. "Do you think about him sometimes?"

"Never," she replies.

I turn to Mom, so sure in her answer, even as I have concrete evidence in my purse that she's lying.

Mom hugs her blanket as she walks out of the kitchen to her room. "It's useless looking at the past, Serene. Always keep moving forward. That's my motto."

I nod tenderly. It's a motto that's served my mom well. At the same time, I'm scared to ask, what happens if there's no more forward to move? What then?

After the dishes are done and Mom's sound asleep, I stand in front of my full-length mirror trying to decide if I should go to the party or not. It might be good for me to get out of the house. It's been a week. But what do I wear? Mom brought back plenty of dresses from New York, but they're all couture. I reach into the back of my closet for one of the few pieces I've been playing around with, altering the backs and the straps, just to see.

I'm nowhere near as talented as her, but I like to experiment. It's fun adding a strap here, a cut there, and being able to make the clothes my own. If I had my own fashion company one day, I'd make it so the designers are just everyday people, messing around and having fun, with none of the top-down hierarchy and investor politics. A Reddit for fashion, if you will.

I settle on a black jumpsuit with a plunge neckline and a gold chain strap I sewed. It's maybe a little too sexy, but seeing as how my mom's asleep and Cameron's gonna be there, I decide what the hell.

"*Nice* side boob," Luke greets me when he answers the door. I hit him lightly on the stomach and walk inside. He points in the direction of his enormous living room, which opens up onto the beach. "Cameron's out back. Booze on the terrace. Jet Skis on the beach."

I spot Quinn on the couch. She's in a sequined red mini dress, a gift from my mom's summer collection, and she's doing shots with Cameron.

"You made it!" she says, throwing back the Icelandic vodka they're drinking.

Cameron greets me with a smile and a kiss. "Hey, babe," he says, pulling me in close. "Wow. You look . . ." I follow his eyes down my neckline. "Stunning."

I blush. He immediately ditches the shots and leads me out to the beach.

"Where've you been?" he asks when we're alone. He puts his hand on the small of my back and kisses me. "You haven't returned my texts."

"Sorry . . . ," I say. "I've just had a lot on my mind."

He looks into my eyes. I want so badly to tell him. To tell *someone*. Yet, to utter the words would be to make them more true.

"What's going on?" Cameron asks.

I blink furiously, leaning back and trying to save my mascara. A tear rolls down my neck anyway and into my plunge line. A few classmates' heads turn. The salt of my pain sits on top of my breasts.

"What are you looking at, jerkoff?" Cameron barks at them. He takes my hand and leads me farther down the beach where it's more private. We sit down on the wet sand.

"My mom has cancer," I whisper.

"Shit," Cameron says. "I'm sorry."

He puts his arm around me, and we look out at the waves. I lean into his muscles. It feels good telling someone. I hug him, a raw hungry hug, not like my mother whom I'm afraid to break when I hug her now. We start kissing in the ocean breeze. It feels nice to be able to do something with my body, other than wait and cry. Nice to know that my body still wants and needs. But it also feels wrong at the same time. I think of my mom in bed, too weak to eat soup, while I'm here making out on the beach.

I stop. We sit quietly for a while, the loud waves drowning out our thoughts. I rest my head on his shoulder.

"Why didn't you tell me earlier?" he asks.

I shrug.

"I don't know . . . ," I say.

"Does she need to have chemo?" Cameron asks. "She gonna lose all her hair?"

I nod and shrug.

Cameron reaches up a hand to my hair.

"What are you doing?" I ask.

"Trying to imagine you bald," he says. The expression on my face cracks him up and I realize he's teasing me. Still.

"She might not. It just depends on the person."

He puts a hand through his own sun-kissed surfer hair. "I don't know if I can deal with that." He shudders. "Hey, if you need somewhere to crash, when the shit gets too hard, you can always stay with me. My parents are cool. Ever since they botched my mom's plastic surgery, they have a lot more sympathy for medical stuff."

I stare at him, almost at a loss for words. It's the nicest thing he's ever said to me.

"Thanks," I say.

Cameron kisses me again, his hands traveling down my neck. He might not be the most eloquent speaker, but he's an eloquent kisser. I reach for his hand as his mouth caresses mine in ways his words can't. And it feels good, even as it feels empty. But I don't care. I just want something to do for five minutes that doesn't involve cancer.

16

Lian

I WAIT UNTIL my parents are both sound asleep before sneaking out the kitchen door with the trash. I jump on my bike and I'm at Luke's in twenty-five minutes (tailgating a Tesla SUV to get in, and nearly getting squashed by the gate). It's one of those completely over-the-top houses right on the beach, a glass-and-concrete mega box. Music thumps from the walls and I can see the faint flames of a bonfire on the beach.

I walk inside. Some classmates from school look at me, puzzled. "What's up?" I mutter.

Stu, who's hanging in the corner like a petrified turtle, walks over to me.

"Oh good, you're here," he says.

He sticks out like a Goodyear Blimp in a sea of organic beach towels and spray-tanned beach bodies.

"How's the party?" I ask.

"Good!" He nods to the sound of the music, not entirely on beat. "I haven't talked to anyone yet, but you know, I think it's pretty dope." He turns to me and asks, "What's that line that Sandra Oh said? It's an honor just to be here?"

"No, I'm pretty sure she said it's an honor just to be Asian."

"Same difference." He shrugs. He points toward the drinks table. "Want a beer?"

I shake my head *no thanks*.

"Good, because I don't know if they're all reserved or something."

He glances over at Luke, who's with a bunch of his water polo buddies. They're all throwing back beers and laughing. Luke looks in our direction and waves. Stu waves back, his face blooming.

"Did you see that?" Stu asks excitedly.

He ditches me and starts walking over, only to realize half a second later, Luke was looking *through* him and waving at someone else.

Stu crawls back toward me.

"It's cool, we'll catch up later," he says of him and Luke. He points to me. "So, you bring the goods?"

I hand him my US History answers. I look around and see Serene's best friend, Quinn, in the corner, doing shots and Storying the party. As Stu copies down my answers, I squeeze by the sweaty bodies and walk onto the beach. Then I see her.

Serene's by the bonfire, with her boyfriend. They're kissing passionately, like two people starved for each other. I immediately look down.

My heart punches in my chest as I peek at Serene. Cameron's got his hand up her shirt. I can see their wet tongues moving in the moonlight. The two of them are so into it, they don't even care who's looking at them. I turn and start walking back.

I shouldn't have come.

I find Stu inside.

"I need to take off," I say to him, trying to yank my paper back.

"Five more minutes," he says, frantically scribbling on a piece of paper. That he actually brought a notebook with him to Luke's party gives me some hope that he won't entirely turn out like the rest of these butt-chugging lunatics. I glance over at his progress. He's on question fifteen.

"You're not copying my words verbatim, are you? You're changing up the language?" I ask.

"Relax, bro. I know what I'm doing."

I study the pictures on Luke's walls as I wait for Stu to finish copying. There's a picture of the barren cliff in Sienna Beach, before all the luxury houses in the Cove went up. Luke's parents must have been among the original owners. I study the framed picture of his grandparents dining with Ronald Reagan. Next to it is a picture of young Luke and his smiling cousins vacationing on a yacht near Catalina

Island. Old-money-meets-California-sun.

I spot Serene walking outside. *Is she leaving?* I quickly scramble up.

"Hey," I call out to her when we get outside.

She looks over at me standing in the dark, temporarily confused. Then responds. "Oh hey!" she says. "What are you doing here?"

I glance back at the house and shrug. "I'm just here with my friend Stu . . . ," I tell her. "Leaving already?"

Serene gazes down the street, debating. "Yeah, my mom's . . . not feeling well," she says. "So I thought I should maybe . . ."

"I'll walk you home," I offer.

"No, it's OK," she insists. "It's only two blocks from here."

But I tell her it's totally fine. We start walking east, toward her house. I hope the distant sound of the waves crashing drowns out my heartbeat. I hope the blocks in the Cove are as long as the Great Wall. The ocean breeze moves between us, sending little goose bumps onto my arms. Still, I hold my jacket in my arms, in case Serene gets cold and wants it.

"Hey, I'm sorry about what I said on Monday," I apologize. "I was way out of line."

"It's OK," she says finally. We turn to a quiet street. With every step away from Luke's house, I feel myself relaxing and becoming more me.

She peers at me as we walk. "So why'd you move here?"

I shake my head. It's such a depressing story.

"You really want to know?" I ask.

She nods.

"Because of a guy named Highway Robber."

Serene chuckles. I beam. Second time I've made her laugh—SCORE!

"What'd he do? Rob you and make you guys move to the whitest city in SoCal?"

My turn to laugh.

"Something like that. He's a college admissions consultant—Derek Baldwin."

"Oh yeah, I've heard of him!" Serene says.

"You go to Highway too?"

She chuckles. "No, but a few of my friends do. I'm . . . not into the whole college admissions race thing. I'm more interested in what happens after college."

"You mean like when they lobotomize us and all we want to do on the weekends is go to Home Depot?" I think of my mom's *many* trips to the garden section.

She laughs again. I'm on a roll!

"That too." She smiles. "So where else were you guys looking at? Besides Sienna Beach?"

"My parents were thinking about Irvine. But Highway said too many Asians live in Irvine." I give her a look. "The Asian to Ivy ratio was all fucked up."

Serene claps her hands and throws her head back, letting

out a full, hearty laugh. "Asian to Ivy ratio. Wow."

"His words! Not mine," I clarify, throwing my hands up. "Did you know according to Google, Sienna Beach has the least Asian population in Southern California?"

"Oh, I don't have to google it—I've lived it," Serene says.

I glance at her, hoping she'll say more. I wonder what it's been like being the only Asian kid here all these years? Couldn't have been easy. Though, judging by how popular she is, maybe not.

She doesn't say anything. I take a chance and throw out, "Anyway, now I'm here, in a town where the local religion is farmer's market and everyone mispronounces my name, but tells their therapist they're not racist because they eat hummus."

"*So* true," Serene marvels.

I smile. "So what about you? Why'd you move here?" I ask.

She thinks for a long while. "My mom and I like the beach," she answers at the same time that we get to her house. I look up. It is a palatial pad that sits next to the beach, about ten times grander than our fake cheese house.

"Holy shit! Look at this place."

Serene blushes. "Yeah, my mom . . . she kind of has a stressful job, so she really wanted to have a chill home."

"Well, it's beautiful," I compliment Serene.

She lingers in the moonlight. For a second, I wonder if she might show me the beach behind her house, but then she quickly says, "Thanks for walking me home," and hurries inside.

I tread back to the party, feeling like I'm on cloud nine. I got to talk to Serene. I smoothed things over. And she actually laughed at my jokes—multiple times!

I could still hear her laugh in my head, a melodious sound that fills me with hope. Hope that I'm actually funny. Hope that I'm not invisible. Hope that if I just work on my sets and perfect my deliveries, maybe, just maybe, I can actually do this comedy thing.

Back at the party, I find Stu passed out on the couch. He must have finally siphoned off one of the beers.

Carefully, I pull my US History homework out from underneath his hand, trying not to wake him.

As I'm stuffing my paper into my backpack, I see Cameron in the kitchen. He's playing beer pong with some blond girl in a crop top and shorts that look like they were made for a squirrel. I'm outraged on behalf of Serene. They're laughing and flirting. Cameron puts his hands on her hips, trying to teach her to play beer pong from behind. The girl moves her hips closer to Cameron's. I'm shocked—how can he do that to Serene? She was just here!

Then Cameron jerks his head up and registers me. "Belt Bag?" A disgusted look crosses his face. He turns to Luke. "Who invited Belt Bag?"

The whole room goes silent.

Stu wakes up from his slumber. I gaze at him, hoping he'll vouch for my existence. But he pretends to pass out again, too petrified to tip the scales on his own precarious invite.

"Get the fuck out of here," Cameron says. "You don't belong here!"

"Yeah, get lost, loser," Luke says, walking to the door and holding it wide for me.

I hold my head high, letting the words wash over me as I walk out. I'm relieved Serene is not here to see this. For once, it reassures me that I'm not important enough to make the recap from her friends. Still, I wonder, was it really worth it coming here? Just to feel great for a minute, and then so incredibly shitty afterward? Am I that desperate for a laugh, for some sort of human interaction, that I'm willing to crash the parties of total assholes and endure their verbal abuse?

As I bike home, their words *you don't belong here* jab at me like a broken spoke. I climb through the kitchen window and tiptoe up the stairs, nearly tripping and cracking my head open on a karaoke microphone my sister left on the floor.

In spite of everything, I decide it was totally worth it.

17

Serene

I FALL ASLEEP with my phone in my hands, looking up Lian's Instagram. He doesn't have Snap, surprisingly, or TikTok. Unlike Cameron's profile, which is full of pics of him in various no-shirt or open-shirt situations, Lian doesn't have many pictures of himself on Instagram. Instead, he just has pictures of places, mostly in Asia—Taiwan, Japan, Seoul, Shanghai, Hong Kong, and Beijing. I don't know if he's one of those people who Story everything, and never posts. Or he's just not into social.

There is *one* picture of him—his profile pic, an artistic black-and-white photo of the back of his head. I wish he were facing the camera. He's actually kind of cute. He has a certain Seth Cohen vibe about him, tall and lanky. And adorable in that super nervous and talks-too-much kind of way. I think of when he apologized and smile. Even his hair's growing on me. It's this wild mop of curly black hair. I didn't know Chinese people could have curly hair like that. Then again, I've only met a sample size of two. I kinda want to run my fingers through his hair.

Stop, I tell myself. I'm with Cameron.

The sound of retching wakes me up at dawn. I jump out of bed and rush down the hall to my mom's room. I find her in her bathroom in her silk nightgown, sitting on the cold marble floor, her face in the toilet.

"Mom!" I cry, pulling her hair back.

"I'm fine," she says. "It's the pills. The doctor said this might happen."

I look around for a towel and wet it for her. She wipes her mouth with it. I reach out a hand to pull her up, but she shakes her head. "I'm gonna need to stay here for a while."

I run into her room and find a robe for her. Slowly, I lift her back up. We walk together to her bed, my arm around her. I can feel her fragile bones under my fingertips. They stick out like thin pretzels. It's frightening how much weight she's lost since her diagnosis.

"Do you want me to stay home from school today?" I ask. "We can watch *Project Runway* and eat waffles."

Mom lets out a weak smile.

"No, I want you to go to school," she says. "I'll be better in a little while, then I'll go into the office. It's just those stupid drugs Dr. Hurtme gave me."

I give her a look. "Mom, Dr. Herman is trying to save your life, not hurt you." I start telling her about some of the exceptional stories of people for whom chemo shrank their tumor so they could have surgery. But my mom doesn't want to hear about exceptional cases.

"I wouldn't count on it," she says. "I can barely keep soup down. I wish I were stage four so I can just get this over with already."

"Mom!" I cry.

I know she's venting but it makes me so angry that she's talking this way. She's not even started and she's thinking of giving up? It terrifies me.

"I'm sorry," she says, holding out a hand. "I'm just really stressed. My DNA results are coming back this afternoon."

"DNA results?" I ask.

"For the cancer," Mom says. "Dr. Herman ordered a test to see what kind of genetic mutations I have. To try and tailor my treatment."

"That's great!" I tell her.

She clings to the neck of her robe. "What if they come back with more bad news? I don't think I can take any more. . . ."

I put an arm around her and hug her tight. "If they do, we'll deal with it," I say. "What time's the appointment?"

"It's at four thirty," she says.

My face falls a little. Four thirty is when I have Chinese Club. I'll have to skip this week. Lian will understand.

"I'll be there."

"No, you should be at the office, manning the fort!"

I shake my head. I don't know why it's so hard for her to understand. This is more important. I want to be there for her. I want to find out everything there is to know. About her. About her cancer. About our family. That's more important than the office right now.

"I'm coming." I stare into her eyes. "We're in this together."

"OK," she finally says. "I'll meet you at the office and we can go from there."

I'm googling genetic mutations when I get to school, tumbling down a rabbit hole of scary genetic information— Mom's not kidding, there are so many terrifying mutations—when Quinn runs up to me.

"What did Belt Bag want with you?" she asks.

"Huh?" I ask, putting my phone down.

"I saw you guys leave together. From the party." She flips her auburn hair over her shoulders and checks her phone.

"We didn't leave together," I lie.

"Uh. Yeah you did," she says, putting her phone down. "I saw you guys."

Shit. I scramble to come up with a reason.

"We're in this club together," I say casually.

Quinn looks up from her phone. "What club?" she asks. "You mean that thing he was passing out those flyers for?"

The face she makes, like we're talking about a club for urinary incontinence, not a club for language and cultural appreciation, it brings me straight back to fifth grade when my mom packed me prawn crackers in my lunch and I made the mistake of opening them in front of everyone in class.

"You joined it?" she shrieks. "WHY?"

I dodge her gaze.

"Mrs. Tanner said I needed more extracurriculars."

Now her face is bathed in pity.

"Ugh, that sucks. Just because you're Chinese, she's making you join it?" Quinn adds, "That's terrible. I mean, you're not *that* Chinese."

My cheeks burn. Any other day, I would have taken it as a joke. I would have laughed it off, been annoyed later. But not today.

"What do you mean I'm not that Chinese?" I ask Quinn.

She switches her purse to her left side, uncomfortably. "You know what I mean."

"No, I don't."

"C'mon, Serene." She gives me a look like we've been through some shit. And we have. And I know a part of me will always owe her for her getting her dad to help kill the story, by telling him that that reporter had been plastering me with drinks all night, which wasn't entirely true. But a part of me also wonders, am I always going to have to owe her, forever?

"I gotta go," I say, heading in the other direction. One thing my mom's cancer has taught me. Time's precious. I don't have time for this shit.

18
Lian

I SLIP A note inside Serene's locker at school: instructions on how to download and set up WeChat. I figured she might be into it, since she wants to learn Chinese. WeChat is, after all, the window into China. It's what all my buddies at home use to chat, post, order food from restaurants, Venmo each other, and shop.

But it's so much more than that.

It's where I am more *me*.

On WeChat, I am confident and witty. I post pictures of things I see in America and write captions, without worrying I'm gonna get comments from rude Americans asking, "What Asian are ya?"

I can relax and like all my friends' posts without worrying I'm over-liking or under-liking or whatever other latest ridiculous social media rule everyone here seems to subscribe to.

Most of all, I can make fun of myself. And know every one of my friends back home who likes my post is doing it out of appreciation for my self-deprecating humor. Not because they *agree* I am ridiculous.

And so I invite Serene to add me on WeChat on my way to US History class, pushing the piece of paper with my WeChat code into her locker. I hope she doesn't think it's weird I'm trying to talk to her by QR code, like a Walgreens reward app.

Walking into US History, I spot Stu. He looks wrecked, as does half my grade.

"When'd you finally get home last night?" I ask Stu.

"Around two," Stu says. "I kept thinking maybe Luke would talk to me if I helped clean up, but he just went to bed."

"Why do you want to hang out with those jerks?" I ask.

He thinks for a long while, and shrugs. "Because they're the water polo team?" he says. "They've got this thing about them, like they're invincible."

"Yeah, it's called being an asshole," I tell Stu.

"I'd rather be an asshole but have, like, an identity," he replies. "Right now, I'm just nothing."

It makes me feel a little bit better that it's not just me who feels I'm a nothing, but also terrible that my friend had to endure it too. *Is Stu my friend?* I wonder. I look down at my answers on Stu's paper as he turns in his homework.

I turn mine in too and we all take a seat.

"All right, class, while I take a peek at your homework, we'll be watching a movie today about the Reconstruction period," our teacher, Mrs. Brooks, says.

There's a collective cheer in the class as Mrs. Brooks turns off the lights and my classmates settle in for a much-needed nap.

As the PBS documentary starts to play, I get on the Notes app in my phone and start writing:

American teachers love showing movies because they know none of their students will ever complain. Doesn't matter what movie it is. Even a shitty movie.

Even the movie Barry Lyndon, which we had to watch in English last year. It was 3 hours and 7 minutes long. There was a Part I and a Part II. That's three whole periods we had to endure bad organ music. And yet, nobody complained. Why?

I think it's because in America, there's an unspoken rule among students—ANYTHING is better than real instruction. Literally anything. That's why there are so many fire drills, evacuation drills, lockdown drills. There's a drill for everything—except do your own work drill. That we don't have.

As I'm writing a joke, Mrs. Brooks calls my name.

"Liam, can I speak to you for a minute?"

I put my phone down and look up. She's holding my US History homework from last night.

I follow Mrs. Brooks out of our classroom.

"What's going on?" I ask her when it's just me and her in the empty hallway.

"I was just looking over your history homework," she says, pointing at my paper. "And the answers are very similar to Stuart Mitchell's."

I freeze, glancing back at Stu through the glass window in the door. *Shit.* Stu's so busted. Poor guy. And he's still watching PBS, completely oblivious. He has no idea what's about to happen. There goes beach concierge.

"I'm sorry, I should have told you. Stu's a friend of mine," I start to say to her. "It won't happen again."

"Well, I'm glad you're owning up to the cheating," Mrs. Brooks says. "Copying is a serious offense, one we take very seriously at Sienna High—"

"Wait, you think I copied him?" I interrupt, shaking my head. "No! It's the other way around!"

Mrs. Brooks looks skeptical. "You're saying Stu copied off of you?"

"Yes," I say.

She gives me a look like *C'mon.* "It's American history."

The insinuation—that I can't do well on American history—burns in my throat as Mrs. Brooks calls Stu over.

"What's this all about?" Stu asks, looking at Mrs. Brooks and me nervously.

Mrs. Brooks proceeds to explain. And the whole time, I am standing there with my eyes closed, my skin breaking out in hives, just waiting for Stu to cop out on me.

But to my surprise, Stu confesses. "I'm sorry, Mrs. Brooks. I just had so much going on last night. And my buddy here helped me out. It won't happen again."

I stare at Stu in shock. It's an extraordinary display of ethics and I resist the urge to throw my arms around him. Stu, the most honest cheater I know. Mrs. Brooks is shocked too. She mutters a few sharp words to Stu, but none to me, and quickly sends us both back to class.

"Thanks," I mutter as we walk.

"Can't believe this shit. That's it, we're sticking to math from now on," Stu mutters.

As I slide into my chair, I think of how narrowly I dodged that bullet. If there was even a whiff of cheating on my record, that would be *it* for ECEP. Highway would chop my head off and use it to stuff another one of his many leather chairs. My parents would disown me and sell me to a watermelon farm in Jiangshu. I'd be lucky if my dad drew a screen saver to remember me by. All because of an assumption. I glance over at Mrs. Brooks, the relief pooling next to my anger.

Is it *that* hard to believe that a Chinese person is capable of learning the history of this country?

19

Serene

I FIND LIAN'S note in my locker after school.

> *Hey—*
> *Thought you might want to join WeChat. It's China's social media app! Here's how to add me in case you want to join.*
> *Best,*
> *Lian*

I smile and get out my phone to scan the code as I walk over to my car. I know my mom uses WeChat to communicate with the factory she uses in China, but other than that, I don't know a lot about it. As I wait for the app to download, I pull up my calendar.

Mom's meeting with Dr. Herman for her genetic results at four thirty.

I jump inside the car and head over to the office.

She's nowhere near ready to go when I get to the office. Mom's leading a team meeting, reminding her designers that while the critical response to the New York couture show is nice, what the buyers want more than anything is ready-to-wear. I take a seat and pull out my notebook to take notes.

"We have to diffuse couture to the average customer on the street," Mom says. "Keep the essence of the one-of-a-kind look, but make it accessible for every woman. Where are we on that?"

I notice a pen on the floor and as I bend down to pick it up, I see Mom's got a bottle of pills concealed in her lap. I wonder if her nausea has gotten better.

Jonathan throws out an idea. "How about the hand-sewn silk couture piece from the show? I'm thinking a short summer dress, in a hemp-and-silk-charmeuse blend."

The mention of silk charmeuse makes me bump my head. I think of Quinn and Emma coming over and raiding our closet during New York Fashion Week. Didn't Carmella say she was working on a silk piece?

"Good!" Mom says excitedly.

"You like that? I just came up with it!" Jonathan says.

Carmella's eyes plunge to her notepad.

"Love it. I'll start talking to the buyers," Mom says.

"Actually, I can take the lead if you want," I offer. "I can work with Carmella."

Carmella nods eagerly. But Mom shakes her head.

"That's nice, sweetie, but I've got this."

I nod awkwardly, wishing Mom hadn't called me sweetie in front of everyone. That's not going to help anyone respect me more. But the senior designers smile at Mom, clearly relieved she's taking the reins again. And I'm happy for her, too, though it does make it confusing. I wish she'd set some clear parameters on what I'm supposed to do as "second-in-command."

Later, I overhear Carmella talking with Ali in the bathroom.

"I've been working on that idea for weeks! Can't believe Jonathan just took credit for it," she says. I glance through the crack from the stall and see them drying their hands.

"I can believe it. He's probably maneuvering for his next gig . . . ," Ali says, reapplying her lipstick. "You know him."

"I'm just worried Lily's not going to see right past it this time," Carmella says. "Should I say something?"

"*No*. She'll figure it out. Let's just hope she sticks around. Or this place will turn more depressing than Ugg's underwear section."

They both toss their paper towels away. After Carmella and Ali leave, I stay behind in the stall an extra minute. How long has this been going on, Jonathan taking credit for their work? This is exactly why we need to get rid of the rigid hierarchy structure. No more of this crap! We can't have our junior designers feeling this way!

I reemerge from the bathroom to find Mom waiting for me in the hallway.

"Ready for Dr. Herman?" she asks.

"Ready," I say to her.

In the car, I tell Mom about what I overheard as I drive.

"Really? Carmella's been working on it for weeks?" Mom asks.

I nod.

"And she says this isn't the first time Jonathan's taken credit for her work," I say.

"I'll speak to him about it. But it does happen. It's just the way the business works—junior designers support senior designers."

"This is going way beyond support," I say. "He should come off as project manager on this piece, and we should put Carmella on, since it's her design."

"I don't know about that," Mom says, frowning at her phone.

I press her. "Why not?"

Mom sighs. "I'm in a tough position. I've already got the investors breathing down my neck—God knows, they're talking to every ear that'll listen on the board. I need the senior designers to be happy. If they all jump ship, I'm going to have an even bigger mess on my hands."

"They're not going to jump ship! And even if they do,

we still have the junior designers—"

"Junior designers don't have the experience. You need deep and extensive relationships with the buyers. It's not just about coming up with a good design. It's about the ability to take that design through, from conception to store racks—that all comes from experience."

"Is that why you didn't want me meeting with buyers?" I ask her gently.

Mom is surprised by my question.

"No, I just thought . . . I'd do them because it's easier. And because it's my collection," Mom adds.

My face flushes. I didn't mean to upset her. I just really want to know where my place is. "Well, I'm here. Whatever you want me to do. You said that you needed me to take over. . . ."

"And you will," she says, reaching over and patting my hand. I look down and see the marking on her hand from where they put in a needle to draw blood. "But I'm not completely last season yet. I still have a few more days left, right?"

"Of course you do," I quickly assure Mom.

She smiles at me, and I squeeze her hand back as I turn onto Wilshire Boulevard.

She points to the clinic and swallows hard.

"Speaking of which," she says, "let's see exactly what my sentence is."

We sit nervously outside Dr. Herman's office, both staring into our phones, silently googling genetic mutations. I wish we'd talk about it, but some of this stuff is too scary to say out loud.

From my limited research, it seems there are two big genetic mutations Mom could have: BRCA 1 and BRCA 2. Either BRCA strain puts you at a significantly higher risk of getting cancer—not just breast and ovarian, but also other types such as pancreatic. It could be as high as a 70 percent chance in some cases, which was why Angelina Jolie famously decided to surgically remove both her breasts and her ovaries, in hopes of reducing her risk.

I hug my breasts as I sit in Dr. Herman's chair, hoping my mom doesn't have it. If she does, that would mean I might carry the mutation too.

"Listen, if he tells us something, I want you to know, it doesn't necessarily mean anything at all, OK?" Mom says.

I look up at Mom and nod. Lately, she's been saying vague nonsensical statements that leave me feeling more worried than assured. I know she's uncomfortable talking in concrete terms about her cancer, but I wish we'd talk about our fears instead of sitting next to each other googling separately.

Dr. Herman's door opens. His nurse nods at us.

"You may go inside now," she says.

We get up and walk inside Dr. Herman's office. Today

he's wearing a leather vest over jeans. I'm trying not to be too encouraged by his casual look. It might just be casual Monday for him; it doesn't mean it's casual cancer day for us.

Again, I stare at his YOU CAN BEAT THIS poster behind his desk. Today, it looks like it should be premised with a BUT. You can beat this, *but* if you have BRCA . . .

"How are you feeling?" he asks her. "Are you tolerating the capecitabine well?"

Mom makes a face at the chemo drugs that have been making her sick. I looked it up and the drug Dr. Herman gave her gets converted to 5-fluorouracil (5-FU) in her body. Even though my mom hates taking them, I'm encouraged that my mom is literally fighting cancer with a drug called FU!

"The nausea and vomiting . . . it's a lot," she says. "I could barely make it to the bathroom. Remember that, Serene?"

I nod.

Dr. Herman jots down notes. "Even with the anti-nausea medicine?" he asks.

"They help a little."

"Try taking them as soon as you wake up and before you go to bed. See if that helps," Dr. Herman says. "And how about your appetite?"

I shake my head. "She hasn't been eating much. She barely touches her meal, even though I try to make her all her favorites."

"What are you talking about? I had a few bites of chicken

the other day!" Mom protests.

"The *other day*," I repeat.

Dr. Herman writes out a prescription on his Rx pad for Creon, which he says will help with her digestion. He tells me to keep trying to feed her, even if it's small meals.

"You're doing a great job," he says. "Both of you."

He gives me a smile, and the recognition makes me almost burst into tears. The fact that someone sees how hard I've been trying.

"Now let's talk about your genetic results," Dr. Herman says, getting out three pieces of paper.

Mom peers anxiously at the test results in Dr. Herman's hands, while I close my eyes and whisper a prayer. I'm not very religious, but lately, I've been finding myself whispering the words *Please let my mom be all right*, praying to Jesus, Buddha, my dad (I hope to God he's not already up there), anyone who will listen. . . .

"So it looks like you do have some genetic mutations," Dr. Herman says.

My stomach drops.

"Your mother has BRCA 1, unfortunately," the doctor says.

The news lands like a bomb, denotating his YOU CAN BEAT THIS poster into pieces. My worst fears confirmed. I wrap my arms around my chest tightly, rocking my body and whispering the figure "70 percent" to myself. I think of the game Mom and I used to play: 70 percent is so close to 90 percent which is basically 100 percent. Now the game doesn't seem so fun.

"Don't be alarmed," Dr. Herman says quickly, reading our expressions. "There have been some chemo treatments that have shown to be quite effective against BRCA mutations. So this is helpful news for us. Now we can take a more tailored approach."

"But what about . . ." Mom looks over at me. "My daughter."

"It doesn't mean she automatically has it," Dr. Herman says. He looks straight at me. "Every person inherits the BRCA gene from their mother *and* father. There's a fifty/fifty chance you don't have the mutation. You still have your father."

I choke on the rock in my throat at this reminder that I *don't* still have my father. I'm made of two halves and I know nothing about my other half!

"Anyone with cancer on his side?" Dr. Herman asks.

"He left when I was pregnant with Serene," Mom says.

I reach for Mom's arm. "Maybe we can try to get ahold of him."

Mom stiffens.

"You could. Or we could just have Serene tested," Dr. Herman offers. "Serene, would you like to have genetic testing?"

I look to him, and then to my mom, who shakes her head vigorously.

"I think that's quite enough testing for us," Mom says, getting up and walking out.

20

Lian

THE REST OF the week drags by, an annoying cadence of reminders to sign up for the ECEP test in a couple of weeks, to do the mock ECEP test administered by Kevin from 888 Education, to pick up vitamin C and alum, which Mom crushes up to make her own homemade flower food, and to not use too much hot water when I take a shower.

"You know how expensive the water is in California?" she shouts. "You dip! You just dip! Next time I set a timer for you."

I shake my head to try to explain it wasn't me—it's my sister singing in the shower after her dance class. But I stop myself just in time.

All weekend, I sit on WeChat, hoping Serene will add me, but she doesn't. I'm so bummed she didn't show up to Chinese Club on Monday. I thought she'd at least send me a message or something. But there are only messages from Lei and Chris, asking me to send them pics of Serene to prove she's real, and texts from Stu asking me if I think the pimple on his back will pop if he slams his body against the wall.

I don't understand—did Serene not get my note?

Finally, Monday rolls around again and I run to Chinese Club after school. I settle in for an hour and a half of door staring.

I wait.

And wait.

By four p.m., I glance down at my notebook of jokes, mad at myself for squandering so much time waiting—I should just practice my set, which was the original point of my club anyway! I'm getting distracted! I kick the leg of the chair in front, thinking of all the crazy things I've done this week just to see Serene—sneaking out of my house, lying to my parents, blowing off ECEP, letting Stu copy my home-work word for word!

I'm deep in thought, going over my reckless actions, when the door swings open.

And there is Serene, in a stunning red silk dress, her wavy, purple-tinted hair glowing in the light as she smiles.

And I know I would do all of that, and more.

"You're here!" I exclaim. "Hey!"

"Hi!" she says, sliding into the chair next to mine.

"How was your weekend?" I ask.

The burst of sunshine on her face disappears. She looks down and doesn't answer. Instead, she pulls out my note.

"I tried to add you on WeChat, but I couldn't figure out where to scan the QR code in the app."

"Oh, I can help you." I reach for her phone. With a few quick swipes, I add myself to her WeChat and add her new WeChat to mine. "There. Now you have Chinese Instagram, Uber, UberEats, Orbitz, all in one app."

"Really?" she asks. "What's the Instagram part?"

I show her where she can create posts and share them with people. "They're called Moments."

"Moments. I like that," she says.

"You can make them private, if you want."

She thinks about it for a second, then says, "Actually I think I might leave them public. Just in case I have a long-lost relative in China or something."

I can't tell if she's kidding or not. I show her a cool trick called Translate, which automatically translates Chinese into English in WeChat. If her relatives are anything like mine, they're constantly posting in Chinese.

"Oh, so I don't even need to learn Chinese?" Serene asks excitedly.

I bristle when she says this. It's the kind of thing my little sister says all the time. *Now that we live in America, why do I still need to learn Chinese?* And every time, I have to explain to her we don't just learn a language to communicate. We learn it to remember.

"I think you should still learn the language, you know, as a Chinese person," I say to Serene.

Serene's cheeks heat and I immediately worry I might have offended her.

"I'm sorry. I just meant—"

Serene looks down. "It's OK. Let's just get on with the reading . . . ," she mutters.

"OK."

I get up and walk to the whiteboard. I write down a few of the most common Chinese characters, like ren (person), ri (sun), rue (moon), zi (child), xin (heart), ko (mouth), shan (mountain), nu (girl), ma (Mom), ba (Dad), and mu (wood).

I start drawing the characters on the board, so she'll remember. For ren, I draw out a person walking, and show Serene how the two Chinese strokes depict the legs.

Serene's eyes widen.

"Oh my God, that's so cool! Like Egyptian hieroglyphs!"

"Kinda." I smile. I continue drawing out shan for mountain and rue for moon. "See, it's not just language . . . you're learning history. Our ancestors used this to draw the world as they saw it. And they put little pieces and clues into all the characters."

"Like what?" Serene asks.

I think for a minute, then write down another character.

"Like the character hao, or 'good.' It's a combination of two characters—nu for 'woman,' and zi for 'child.'"

Serene studies the two characters within hao.

"Our ancestors were trying to tell us that for something

to be good, it's not all up to the mom. The child, and what they want, is a part of the equation too." I add with a low mutter, "My mom seems to have forgotten that. . . ."

I can't believe what I just said. But she shares something equally revealing.

"Mine too," she says.

I study her face, trying to figure out what she means. But she doesn't elaborate.

Instead, she picks up her pen and scribbles down all my characters into her notebook. "Teach me more."

I'm all smiles later that day when I get home. Mom looks up from watering her plants. "How was Chinese Club?" she asks.

"Excellent!" I slide my backpack down and reach for one of the Pocky stick boxes Mom always buys from the San Gabriel Valley. You can't get them around here. I peer at the delicious chocolate-coated sticks, wondering if Serene's ever had them.

"Did that NYU guy show up again?" Mom asks, taking a seat next to me and reaching over for a Pocky stick too.

"Yup!" I say, trying not to smile too wide. The thing with Asian parents is you have to monitor your happiness around them. Too happy, and they'll know something's up. They're pros like that.

"That's great! Maybe I'll come and watch, one of these days. Check out your club, and the other clubs."

I suddenly panic. "Why, Mom? You don't need to do that—"

Mom jabs me with her Pocky stick. "What, are you ashamed of me?"

"No!" I start sweating. "I just . . . Don't you have something else you'd rather do than check out high school clubs?"

Mom looks down. "Well, I don't have a job anymore. And there aren't exactly clubs for adults . . . not easy if you want to improve yourself."

I furrow my eyebrows, surprised by the admission. How long has Mom been thinking about this? Does she want to get a job? Go back to school? I want to ask, but am scared to get more jabs with the Pocky stick.

"What about a book club?" I suggest.

"A book club?" She starts shaking her head. "I not that good at reading English."

"You haven't even tried. I bet if you found the right book, you'd have lots to say on it." I'm thinking something on gardening, or how to legally murder your children—and receive a government rebate.

"It would be nice to get together with other adults and talk about something else other than our kids," Mom admits.

"Exactly!" I exclaim.

"I'll look into it," Mom says as I wipe the Pocky crumbs off my shirt and pick up my backpack. "In the meantime, go get ready for Zoom with Highway Robber. He wants to know who you plan on asking for recommendation letters."

"Definitely not my history teacher," I mutter.

Mom looks at me, worried. "What happened? She not pronounce your name right again? Who cares? Just a name!"

"I care, Mom!"

"Well, we can't afford to care. Not until we successful. That's how it works in this country."

"No, that's not how it works!" I protest. "And what am I supposed to do if I never get there? Just live with people calling me Liam, or Ian, or Bugs Bunny!"

The last part gets a laugh out of Mom.

"No, you show them. You get into MIT. You surprise them by going to college early. That's best revenge."

"*Or* maybe the best revenge is to follow my dreams," I tell Mom. "What about that?"

She does not look amused.

21

Serene

WATCHING LIAN DRAW the Chinese characters on the board, I felt a sense of lightness. Like maybe there's a way to make some sense of this world. I stared and stared at the character for "dad," trying to memorize it in my head. I can't wait to learn all the codes and clues my ancestors put into every character to guide us and help us deal.

In the car on the way home from the doctor's office, Mom had asked me what I meant when I said maybe we can reach out to my dad.

"I dunno . . . I just thought, maybe he'd . . ." I struggled to finish the rest of the sentence. What *did* I want from my dad?

"He'd what? Come over and cure me of cancer?" Mom asked.

I snuck a glance at her as I drove. Her face was upset and I felt guilty for bringing him up.

"He can't solve our problems, Serene. Only *we* can solve our problems."

I nodded, even though that wasn't the point. I knew he couldn't solve our problems. Still.

"Is it the genetic testing?" Mom asked, her voice softening. "I knew I shouldn't have taken you." She sighed. "If you really want, I'll authorize it with Dr. Herman. But I think it's ridiculous to have it done at your age."

I looked at her. "Why?"

"Why know something that you can't do anything about? It'll just nag at you for twenty-five years. Are you really going to chop off your breasts at seventeen?" Mom asked. I nearly swerved into the next lane when she said that. I peeked down at my breasts, which I'd waited so long for. And which according to Quinn were my best assets.

I think of Mom's words as I walk to my car—was not knowing *really* better? It would just lead to a different type of nagging. And I know what that feels like.

I pull out my phone and tap on WeChat. I tell myself I don't even need Mom's blessing to find my dad. I can find him with modern technology.

There's a message waiting for me in the app.

I smile. It's Lian, texting me to say **Great job in class today!**

Thanks, I text back, and tap on emojis. I'm thrilled to discover that WeChat comes with a whole set of new emojis! **You're a great teacher!**

Thanks! 🦉

I climb into my car and start the engine, fingers tapping on the app to tell Lian **brb, gotta drive to my mom's office,** when our texting is interrupted by another text.

It's Cameron.

Hey babe, u free tonight? he texts. **Usual place by the beach?** 🌊 🔥 🍆 😈

Cameron's referring to a deserted cove by the beach near his house. A place with total privacy. It was where he first put his hand up my shirt. And I'd let him push against me through his jeans. Today, though, the idea of a sandy make-out session with some heavy petting just sounds . . . sandy.

I can't. My mom needs me. She's been going through chemo, I tell Siri to type while I drive.

That blows.

I frown as I turn onto the highway toward Santa Monica. Chemo blows? Or that I have to take care of her blows?

Hey does she have any medical marijuana?

NO! I yell at Siri.

Siri must have conveyed my annoyance to Cameron because his next text back to me is, **are you mad at me?**

And I feel bad. I sigh to the wheel of my car.

No.

Why don't you come over? I'll help u relax . . . he texts.

I reach to click off my phone. I don't need Cameron's horny pity.

Then, feeling bad, I dictate to Siri, **Maybe.**

Mom's not in the office when I arrive the next day. According to Carmella, she went to a buyer's meeting in downtown LA, along with the senior designers.

"Are they pitching your design? The hemp-and-silk-charmeuse-blend piece?" I ask Carmella, putting my stuff down at my desk.

"I think so. And thanks! For calling it my design."

I smile at her before turning back to WeChat. Lian was right. The app has so many features, including the ability to shop and transfer money.

"Hey, do we have a company WeChat?" I ask Carmella.

She pauses for a minute then shakes her head.

"Don't think so," she says as she continues sketching on Illustrator.

I gaze over at Eddie, our tech specialist whom Mom poached from Snap across the street. I walk over to talk to him.

"Oh, hey, Serene," he says, busy clicking on a million ad boxes on Facebook. "What's up?"

"I was just wondering . . . why don't we create a company WeChat account?" I ask. "I've just started playing around with it and did you know, you can start a shop on it? It's so easy!"

"WeChat's really not our thing," he says as he filters for age, location, and interests. I'm temporarily distracted by Eddie's ad buying. "We're more of an American brand."

I watch as he adds a bunch of random interests that have nothing to do with our brand—like aroma oil room diffusers, mindful running, rosé, dandelion greens, and labradoodles.

"What are you doing?" I ask him, pointing to his screen.

"Finding our buyers!" he explains. "People who will get us the most CTR." He explains to me that CTR means click through rate. "The number of people who actually click on the product from the ad and go to our website."

"What do labradoodles have to do with silk blouses?" I ask.

"A lot, actually." Eddie takes his time answering. I watch as he works, fascinated.

"Marketing says our brand is most popular with blond women ages twenty-five to thirty-eight who live in key markets where we have shops: LA, NYC, SF, Chicago, and Miami. So my job is to try to find them."

My jaw drops.

"Did you say blond? You're finding our customers based on *race*?"

"Well, not explicitly!" he says, throwing up his hands. "But it's a waste of ad dollars to target people who either can't afford or don't want Lily Lee. Hey, I'm just trying to get clicks. Gotta find the well-heeled!"

"By well-heeled, you mean white." I can't believe what I'm hearing. Does Mom know?

Eddie ignores me, happily adding interests and wielding

his considerable advertising powers.

I walk back to my desk, shaking my head.

While Eddie continues targeting blond customers, I get to work starting our first company e-shop on WeChat. I don't believe for a second that only white people want to buy our brand. And I'm going to prove it.

It takes me a little over forty-five minutes to set up shop on WeChat. The app is surprisingly intuitive and simple to use. I add staples from Mom's classic ready-to-wear line—wool cardigan, silk pussy-bow blouse with quill pens (a nod to the late-nineteenth-century female writers Mom adores), and gabardine slim-leg pants. I use WeChat Translate to add descriptions to each item and the price. Since I don't have our bank information, I can't officially accept money yet. Still, I figure it's better to start a presence on WeChat.

I click Live and do a little squeal. "Carmella!" I exclaim. "I did it!"

"What?" she asks.

I turn my phone so she can see.

"You did all this in forty-five minutes?" she asks. "It's brilliant!"

She waves Ali over. "I love it too!" Ali gushes. "And the clothes you picked are all our hottest pieces. Nice job!"

Pride gushes through me. It's the first time I've done something where I didn't need Mom's approval. I just went for it! As I scroll through the new virtual shop for Carmella and Ali to see, it feels so good to show my coworkers I can do something to help the business. I'm not just some teenager who gets drunk and spills the beans to reporters. That I add value.

Later, I'm still on WeChat at home, waiting for our first customer, but it's only ten a.m. in China right now, when I get an email from Dr. Herman.

From: Dr. Herman
To: Serene Li
Subject: Genetic Testing
Dear Serene,
Are you still interested in genetic testing? I do think that it is useful to have the test done, given your mom's BRCA mutation. Let me know if you're still interested. Your mother called our office over the weekend and gave permission, so if you want to have it done, you can.
Yours,
Dr. Herman

Wow. That was big of Mom.

I walk over to her room to thank her. When I knock twice and she doesn't answer, I walk inside. She's lying on the floor, by her fireplace.

"Mom!" I exclaim, rushing over to her. For a second I

think she's unconscious but I see her chest rising and falling. She's just sleeping.

She stirs when I push her gently, then falls back asleep. I put my arms underneath her as the fireplace flames curl, trying to lift her to her bed. She's mostly skin and bones, but she's still too heavy for me to carry all by myself, so I lay her down on the carpet and move her blankets to the floor.

As I tuck her in, I see little pink bumps along her lips in the flickering light. All the mouth sores she's been covering up with concealer and lipstick. *Oh, Mom.*

In the light, I peek down at the port. I've never seen her chemo port before. She's been covering up the patches of plastic with loose, fluffy blouses. Now I see the plastic tube sticking out of my mom's naked flesh up close. I stare at all the wrinkles sagging on her skin. Ever since she's started chemo, it's like she's been aging faster, her skin protesting the poison being injected into her. In two weeks, she looks like she's aged about seven years. And there's nothing she can do about it.

Because she didn't know in time.

I'm not gonna let that happen to me.

I leave Mom to sleep and go back to my room, where I stand in front of the mirror naked, staring at my breasts.

My lavender-vanilla candles flicker around me as I trace my fingers up and down my body. I wonder whether it's worth it, giving them up.

I want to be brave and say it is. To spare myself the pain of what Mom's going through. Still . . . the thought of never looking like me again. To be robbed of my body, before I've even had a chance to use it. It terrifies me beyond words.

My phone dings. I glance at it, for a hopeful second thinking it's Lian. But it's Cameron.

You coming? I'm freezing my ass off here waiting for you, he writes.

Shit! I completely forgot—our date on the cove.

Sorry, I text back. **I can't make it tonight.**

YOU ALWAYS DO THIS.

He's pissed. And for good reason. I blew him off.

I'm sorry, I apologize again.

You owe me, he says. **C'mon babe, at least send me some pics. I miss ur body.**

I stare at his words, desire and depression mixing in me in a dangerous tonic. I put my hand to my breast, wondering when's the next time I'll even be able to entertain such a request, if I get the surgery. And against the soft glow of my scented candles and my better judgment, I send him pictures of my naked, curvy body.

Mostly for me. Because I still can.

22
Lian

I SCROLL THROUGH Serene's new WeChat store. Not only has she set up shop in less than twenty-four hours, she's added some great descriptions in Chinese, too! I'm impressed!

I keep thinking back to the way her eyes light up during the club meetings whenever I teach her the origins of a new character. I remember when I was a kid, my dad would draw the characters, showing me the history and the clues. It felt special. I'm so glad I can give that to Serene. It makes me feel like maybe I'm at our school for a reason.

The sizzle of homemade dumplings hitting the frying pan zaps me from my Serene daydreaming. Mom's making dinner.

"I went to market in San Gabriel Valley today while you guys were in school," she says. "You ready for your ECEP mock?"

"That's today?" I ask her, opening my laptop on the kitchen table.

"Aiya! You don't remember? I pay Kevin so much money for it! He waiting for you online now!" she says. I get up with my computer to dash to my room, but not before stuffing another pot sticker in my mouth.

Mom pretends to protest, even though I know she's secretly thrilled. Dumplings are my mom's way of saying she loves us. She labors over them for hours, making the dough and the stuffing.

"*Go,*" she says.

I start moving, then pause on the stairwell. "You know, there are other programs at MIT. I don't have to go to college early."

Mom makes a face, like she just ate a dumpling stuffed with horsehair. "What you say?" she demands.

"Nothing!" I dash up the stairs.

I'm twenty-five questions into the mock test when my phone dings with a text. It's from Serene!

I peek over at it as I attempt the questions.

Hey I know it's not our Club meeting yet, but can you help me? People are starting to send me messages through my WeChat shop and I don't know if my replies are right . . .

I grab my phone and text back.

Sure! ~~Can you copy and paste them over?~~ I delete the words. Instead, I text, **You wanna meet up?** I press Send.

I race through the mock ECEP, guessing through the rest of the questions, as I wait for Serene's reply.

My phone dings again.

Yes!

Holy shit!

Never in my entire life have I ever finished a standardized test so quickly. I clicked on the answers like I was picking cafeteria lunch choices. Kevin, the drill sergeant of 888, would be horrified, but who cares—I have a date!

I jump down the stairs, two at a time, nearly knocking over the new giant pot of orchids Mom picked up.

"Where you going?" she asks. "You finish your mock?"

"Uh-huh!" I yell.

"You not gonna eat my dumplings?" Mom inquires, hurt.

I hesitate. Mom lives to feed us.

"I'll have some when I get back," I finally say before flying out the door.

We're meeting at the Sienna Steps, which are these steps that go all the way up to Sienna Summit, at the very top of the mountains. I've only been up there once, when my dad dragged me as punishment last year for messing up one question on SAT reading, only to realize halfway through that it was more punishment for him than it was for me. So we abandoned the mission halfway and went to get In-N-Out instead.

As I wait at the bottom of the Steps, I can feel the adrenaline racing in me.

Be cool. Be cool. Be cool.

"Hey!" Serene calls out to me as she walks over from her Volvo SUV in the parking lot. She's wearing sweats and a "Strong Female Protagonist" tank. I smile. She looks amazing even in sweats. "Thanks for coming out!"

"No, are you kidding? Thank YOU!" I say. "You saved me from this horrible test that rhymes with I WEPT." *Stop rambling.* I toss her an extra water bottle instead as we start heading up the Steps. "I saw your WeChat store—looks amazing! You've been getting lots of messages?"

"Yeah! They started coming in this morning! I wrote a couple of replies but I'm not sure if they sound right."

She hands me her phone and I tap on the app. We sit on the Steps. She leans in closer as I read the words. Her face is so close to mine, I can smell her. Her hair. Her lotion. For a second, I'm so distracted by her beauty, I forget what we're even doing. All I can think about is her soft violet hair as it catches in the light.

Then I remember, the messages. Right.

"This person says the shirt is beautiful, but asks if it is soft and comfortable," I read. "Because she wants to buy it for her mom who is sick."

Serene leans in even closer. "Where does it say sick?" she asks. I point to the character.

"Bing," I teach her. "It means sick."

"But isn't that the character for 'person'?" she asks, pointing to one of the smaller characters within the character bing.

"Right. That's in there because whenever someone's sick, there's always a person taking care of them."

Serene stares at me. Then she asks me what other clues are in bing. And I show her.

"This one represents 'bed.' And this one represents 'fireplace,'" I say, pointing to the various radicals and strokes.

"A bed by the fireplace, with a person taking care of them," she says, blinking furiously like she just got sand in her eye. "Wow."

She falls quiet for a second, looking out into the distance. Then she turns to me and asks, "Hey, can I ask you a question?"

"Anything."

"Would you want to find out something about yourself . . . even if it could be really bad?"

"You mean like a bad mock test score?" I joke, but the seriousness of her face makes me stop. I think hard about the question. And answer honestly.

"Yes, I think so," I tell her. "Because information is power."

There's a wave of emotions on her face. She gazes quietly out toward the ocean, looking so sad, I want to hug her. Whatever it is, I hope she knows she can tell me.

"What's going on?" I ask.

She quickly shakes her head. "Nothing." Then she points back at her phone. "Is my response OK?" she asks.

"Oh yes," I say, making a few quick edits. I hand her phone back with all the drafts in her Composed folder, telling her the rest of her Chinese writing is perfect. Then, I bump against her shoulder lightly, telling her I'm proud of her. She returns the smile. As we get up from the Steps, she turns to me.

"Hey, Lian, I'm sorry about when you first came here," she says timidly.

I freeze. I look down, like I've been caught without my pants. We don't have to pull that ugly memory out, right when everything's going so well. But then Serene puts a hand on my arm.

"My friends. They weren't very nice to you . . . ," she says. "I wasn't very nice to you."

The earnestness of her apology is so unexpected, I have to hang on to the stair railing. I lift my eyes to meet Serene's. Never in a million years did I ever expect to hear such words. I would have accepted our friendship without.

Forever. But hearing them, it makes it that much sweeter.

"It's OK," I tell her.

That day, we climb the rest of the Steps. And I finally get to see the view at the top of the Summit. It was worth coming all the way to this country for.

23

Serene

DRIVING HOME FROM the Steps, I switch open the sun-roof in my car, feeling the salty mist on my skin as I play back the conversation with Lian. My mind drifts with the waves, teasing my curiosity and pulling me closer. Lian's possibly the most genuine boy I know.

His posts on WeChat, they're all these little insights about living in America, like:

Only in America do people trip each other to grab stuff a day after expressing their gratitude on Thanksgiving for what they have.

Why are there so many prescription drug ads in this country? I just wanna go one day without hearing about erectile dysfunction and bowel movements!

I laughed my head off reading them. But it was his posts about his sister that warmed my heart.

Proud of this squirt for getting down a double black

diamond—without stopping once! 🌀 in Niseko, Japan.

My sis, guys. The kid can't clear the table. But look at her dance!

That one was posted last week from his room, which by the way is totally not what I expected. It's orderly and neat, and filled with surprisingly beautiful flowers.

Clearly he loves his family very much. Scrolling through the many pics of him and his friends hanging out in Beijing, it floods me with envy. He's so comfortable with his roots, when I've worked so hard over the years to erase my own.

And to think that he held on to it, even when Quinn and everybody else at school last year made fun of him, it makes me admire him. And regret not doing more at the time to make him feel welcomed.

He was kind to have accepted my apology, but I should have done better. *Been* better.

I think about the wonder in his eyes when we got up to the Summit and I showed him the view. I'm glad I'm the first person to take him up there. To be able to show him something beautiful, just as he's done these last few weeks for me with the characters.

Against the glow of the rich sunset, our eyes had locked. I'd be lying if I said a part of me hadn't hoped we'd kiss. It was such a perfect moment. The breathtaking view. The convo we had. The crash of the waves below.

But then my phone rang. I glanced down to see

CAMERON ARDEN flashing. Lian saw it too.

I should never have sent him those pics yesterday. He's been hounding me ever since.

"If you have to get that," Lian had said.

"No, I don't have to." Then I silenced my phone.

But when I looked back up, the moment was over. And we both fumbled awkwardly, reaching for water bottles and bending down to tie our shoes, before starting the descent.

The whole way down, my heart pounded. All I could think about was what would have happened if Cameron hadn't interrupted our moment.

I arrive at Mom's office excited to show everyone the messages from our new WeChat store. But before I can, Julien and some of the other investors summon me into the conference room. Mom's already in there.

"Was this you?" Julien asks, pointing to his phone. He has my WeChat store open on his phone.

I'm glad he's seen it. "Yes! And you should see the messages that came in," I say excitedly, getting out my own phone to read them. "We got a lot of questions about the pussy-bow blouse—"

"But *why* is my question. Why did you do this without asking?" Julien asks.

I look from him to my mom.

"I . . . I just thought, since we're not on WeChat—"

"Don't think," he interrupts. "Don't ever do anything like that again."

My eyes plunge to the table. Here I thought I actually had some autonomy.

"Julien, she didn't know. She was just trying it out," Mom says. I flash my eyes at her, betrayed. Why is she always so deferential toward them?

"We can't be making any big moves right now. I thought I was crystal clear—we're trying to get the company into position for a sale," Julien barks. "Everyone's looking at us, especially after what happened in New York."

"What *happened* in New York," I remind them, "is we launched our best collection yet. One people want to buy *all over the world*. And that's what we're here to do. Expand our brand. Not just stand around, looking pretty, hoping some other company will come along and solve all our problems."

Julien's nostrils flare at me.

"I've been expanding brands since you were in diapers," Julien says. "And guess what? You don't just do it with some half-baked WeChat shop. It takes *years* to build up. With cash. *Our* cash. Every decision is carefully calibrated. Every marketing plan, every ad."

"You mean, like ads to white people?" I press.

Julien jerks backward. The other investors look down.

He clears his throat. "If you're talking about our social media ad strategy," he says, "according to marketing, blond women identify most with Lily Lee. This is a fact. It's supported by data."

"Because you *only* advertise to them! How will our clothes ever reach other consumers if they never see them? It's a self-fulfilling prophecy!" I argue.

My mom motions with her hands for me to tone it down. "Whoa, Serene!" she says, but I'm fired up.

"It has taken us a long time to fine-tune our marketing strategy," Julien insists. "We tried cross-the-board advertising in the beginning, it didn't work. This is a strategy that stands the test of time."

"Yeah, well, times have changed. The world's changed! And the fact that people are messaging me shows that my strategy is working!" I argue.

I hold out my phone to show them the messages, but Julien grabs it out of my hand and tosses it aside.

"You think half a dozen messages on an account that's not even a verified account shows anything? What will people think?"

"People will think we're being fast and nimble. China's a huge market—"

"Yeah, China is a huge market. Which is why you have to go in with a plan. It takes a full marketing firm, not just some high school kid with a phone."

I look away before he can see the sting in my eyes.

Tense seconds pass by. Mom's face clouds with worry.

Finally, another one of the investors, Bill, speaks. "Look,

we appreciate you trying. But let's leave the digital marketing to professionals. We've been doing it a long time. We know what we're doing."

"Otherwise your mother wouldn't be where she is," one of the other investors adds.

I turn to my mom, who nods at me. "Serene, just delete it."

Fine. I pick up my phone from where Julien tossed it and pull up the WeChat page. As the investors watch, I press Delete on my beautiful new shop. I shake my head as I walk out of the glass conference room.

Carmella turns to me when I get back to my desk.

"For what it's worth, I thought it was a great idea."

I gaze over at the gray old men sitting with my mom. I know she knows. They didn't make her. *She* made her.

24
Lian

ALL WEEKEND, I can't get Serene out of my head. I'm in my private nirvana, replaying our date on the Steps. Not even my mom making me get on the phone with Verizon and protest them overcharging her cell phone bill (I am the official caller and bill disputer in our house) dampens my mood. I think about Serene's face as I listen to the hold music. I imagine her telling me whatever it was that was eating her up inside. I imagine me making her feel better.

On Monday, when she comes into Chinese Club, I surprise her with an idea.

"Let's go on a field trip," I say. "A cultural learning trip."

"Where to?"

I put a finger to my chin. "San Gabriel Valley," I decide. It's where my parents always go to stock up on Asian groceries and dim sum. It's about as Chinese as you can get without going to China.

We take my car. Serene kicks back and closes her eyes in the passenger side as I drive.

"You won't believe how much I need this," she says.

I glance at her. "Why? What's going on?"

"Nothing. Just work."

I look at her, intrigued. I wish I could get a job. I'd love to work at a comedy club. Or even at a gas station. I don't mind. At least I'd get some real-world experience, not just sit in my room in a never-ending testing bubble.

Serene explains that the stuffy old investors at her mom's office didn't like the idea of her starting a WeChat shop.

"So that's why it disappeared," I say to her. "I looked for it this morning."

"Yeah. That would be Julien." She rolls her eyes. "I don't know why my mom's so afraid of him!"

"Who's Julien?" I ask.

"One of the investors in my mom's company. And a complete hemorrhoid of a person." She tells me that he drives around in his Porsche convertible handing out fashion show tickets to pretty girls he sees on the street.

I imagine some old dude lingering by the trees at the park, ready to jump out at girls just trying to do yoga. Gross. "Why'd your mom get involved with him?" I ask.

"He was the first person who wanted to back her," Serene says. "Plus, he came from a prominent fashion family, had connections. My mom thought that was important."

"My mom says America's a meritocracy."

Serene chuckles. "Well, it's not."

"It's not?"

"*I* think it should be. Which is why whenever I start my own fashion company, I'm going to let the people decide. Whatever designs they like on the app, that's what we're going to make. It's going to be fully transparent, not decided by a bunch of suits."

I grin at her. "I like that!"

"Really?"

"I can see people getting totally into it—Tinder for clothes! And you can launch it in China too!" I say, turning off the 5 Freeway to get to San Gabriel Valley. "It's the biggest market for fashion outside the US!"

"Tell that to the suits," Serene sighs. "I'm pretty sure some of them still think China is synonymous with factories."

I'm so taken aback by that statement, I nearly drive off the ramp.

"Seriously?" I ask.

She nods.

"China's like the most futuristic place in the world," I say. My mind explodes with adjectives, trying to describe my country, because there's *so much* to describe. "Did you know you could take a bullet train from Shanghai to Beijing that goes two hundred miles an hour?"

Serene smiles, leaning against the headrest as she faces me, her eyes eagerly drinking up the details.

"Do you know that during rush hour, there are these traffic jam scooters? People will actually come to your car, give you a scooter, and then drive your car back to your house for you?"

"OK, we need that pronto in LA!"

I laugh and describe my hometown as I drive. The cashless restaurants, trekking along the Great Wall, feasting on roast duck with relatives, exploring the Forbidden City, getting coffee with friends at Central Perk, where they made a replica of the famed coffee shop from the TV show.

"They made a replica of Central Perk?" Serene asks. This is clearly blowing her mind.

"The guy who owns it even constructed an exact replica of Joey's apartment."

She grabs for my arm and I nearly swerve into another car.

"That's it, we have to go," I laugh. "I'm taking you."

"Deal! Tell me about the people. What are they like? My parents are from Beijing."

I start to tell her about the ladies who like to dance in the park, and the old men playing Chinese chess, xiangqi, in the park, as I exit into Alhambra. Then Serene's eyes turn to saucers. As she takes in the sprawling metropolis full of Asian supermarkets and restaurants, streets lined with

Chinese people and signs, the look on her face is priceless.

"Where *are* we?"

I grin as I turn off the car and grab her hand. "C'mon, let's go!"

25

Serene

STEPPING OUT OF the car, I spin around 360 degrees, taking in all the signs, the smells, the lights, the people! I've never seen so many people who look like me before! How could this China outside of China be here in Los Angeles all this time?

"Is it always like this?" I ask.

"Pretty much!"

He says his parents come here all the time. Like every weekend, if they're not at Home Depot. Every time he's been here, he's had the same *Wait, am I in Beijing? Pinch me!* feeling.

We walk into a Chinese grocery store and Lian buys Asian snacks like cuttlefish chips and Baby Star Dried Noodles, which are these tiny little crispy noodles. I take a handful and pop them into my mouth. *Oh my God, so good.*

As I munch, I think back to that dreaded day in fifth grade when I was too ashamed to enjoy my prawn crackers in front of Quinn and everyone. I wish I had the courage then to eat what my heart wanted. Now, surrounded by people who look like me, I grab fistfuls and devour them.

There's a small brown poodle tied up by the entrance of the store and Lian kneels down to pet it.

The poodle pokes his rubber eraser nose at our snacks. "Awww, you want some too?" Lian turns to me and says, "I used to have a Saint Bernard. His name was Lucky. He was like a hundred and forty pounds, but he was scared of tiny dogs." Lian shakes his head, laughing. "That's because when he was little, he got bit by a French bulldog. And he never forgot it."

"Why didn't you guys bring him?" I ask. I'm sure he would have loved to run around on the beach.

"My mom made me give him away," Lian says, his face falling. "Said I was spending too much time playing with him instead of doing my homework."

"Wow, that's intense," I let slip out.

"She made my sister give up ballet too."

Lian orders boba teas for both of us from the stand outside the store and as I sip the milky drink, an elderly woman walks over with her grocery shopping to get the poodle. She unties the poodle, and Lian offers to help her with her groceries. "Here, let me get that, auntie," he says.

She smiles and lets Lian carry the groceries to her car. The two chat in Mandarin as they walk, and I envy their immediate bond over a shared language.

When Lian finishes putting all the lady's groceries in her truck, he waves at her as she drives off.

"What were you guys talking about?" I ask.

"She told me she lives with her dog alone. She and her husband came to the States in the eighties. They never had any kids, even though they always wanted kids. He passed away a few years ago, leaving her with just the dog. But he's a good dog. Every morning when she gets out of bed, he gets her slippers."

I'm stunned. "You got *all* that in fifty steps?" I ask. "You should be a journalist."

"Actually I want to do stand-up," Lian confesses.

"Comedy? That's great!" I could totally see it. His hilarious WeChat posts, razor-sharp observations. That time I walked in on him giving a monologue. "You would *kill*!"

"Yeah, more like *be* killed by my parents," he says. "They don't exactly approve."

"Why?" I ask.

"They don't think I can make it," he explains. "Being an engineer—they think that's a much saner path."

"Have you tried telling them what you really want to do?"

He thinks for a while. "Sorta. Not really," he says. "They wouldn't understand."

I can tell how much this has been cutting him up inside.

"Well, you can tell them that my mom made it. She broke into the fashion industry here when there were no other Chinese designers. Everyone told her it was impossible, but fashion was her passion and she never let anyone stop her. And look at her now!"

I think of how hard Mom's worked to get to this moment, working day and night to prove herself to Julien and the others.

"When you talk about your mom, your entire face lights up," Lian observes, beaming.

I blush.

"So, you gonna do it?" I ask. "Promise you won't give up on your dreams?"

"Only if you promise never to give up on yours," he says.

I think about my dad, and the dream of reuniting with him, bobbing like a bottle in the ocean. And I hold out a hand to shake on it. Lian has a better idea.

"Here, we'll put it into a contract," he says, chucking his boba tea in the trash. He grabs my hand and leads me across the street.

"Where are we going?" I laugh, scrambling to keep up.

We cross the busy street and walk into a small shop selling jade pendants on thin red strings. Lian studies the inventory of pendants, most of them green, then picks up one that's pale purple. A small circular jade pendant. He asks, "How much?"

"Thirty-nine ninety-nine," the woman says.

Lian fumbles for his wallet and pulls out two twenties.

"What are you doing?" I ask.

"You'll see," he says, taking the pendant. He asks the woman for a mechanical pencil.

The woman lends him one and we walk outside and sit down on the curb. Lian holds the pendant up to the light and very carefully engraves the date onto the back with the mechanical pencil. He blows off the jade dust when he's done and holds it up to the lilac tips of my hair. I smile. So that's why he picked the soft purple jade—it's so sweet.

"You ready?" he asks.

I nod and lift my hair, thinking he's going to put it on me, but to my surprise, he snaps the pendant into two halves with his hands.

"Why'd you break it?" I ask.

"In the old days in China, that's how they did contracts," he says.

My eyes widen.

"Haven't you ever seen *Over the Moon* on Netflix? Chang'e searching for the other jade half?"

"*That's* where they got it from?"

Lian smiles. He holds up my piece. "Promise we'll never

give up on our dreams. No matter how crazy, or scary, or where they might take us. . . ."

"I promise," I say.

As he hands me a half, my fingers wrap tightly around the pendant. I lean my head against Lian's shoulder, feeling so content sitting in the middle of this town with a guy who actually cares about me. I don't ever want to move.

26
Lian

IT'S LATE BY the time I get home from San Gabriel
Valley. I walk inside the house, engulfed in a cloud of happiness. I see my mom sitting on the couch, reading a book.
I glance over her shoulder at the title—*Little Fires Everywhere*
by Celeste Ng.

"You joined the book club?" I ask excitedly.

Mom nods. "There's a parent one at your school. I read
about it on Facebook."

"That's great!"

"This what they're reading." Mom shows me. "Maybe
good way to learn English."

I point to the book.

"She's Chinese American, you know," I tell her. "The
author."

Mom flips to the back. "Really?" She admires the
author's picture. "Wow, look at that."

I smile, glad she has concrete evidence in front of her face that we can be more than engineers.

She puts the book down, and suddenly remembers. "Hey, where were you today? I called the school and they said you not in Chinese Club. They say your Chinese Club empty."

Shit.

"I was in the San Gabriel Valley," I blurt out quickly.

"Doing what?" Mom asks. "I thought maybe you with a girl."

Why does she always have to go there? I frown. "There's no girl. . . ."

But Mom's razor-sharp antennas detect something. She puts her book down. "What her name?"

"No girl, you're getting it all wrong." To cover my tracks, I throw out the first plausible thing that comes into my mind. "I was tutoring young Chinese immigrants for community service."

Mom's face blooms like a rose when she hears that.

"That's nice," she says. "Did you get a certificate for your résumé?"

"No, I forgot."

She frowns. "Aiya." She makes a regretful noise through her teeth. "What's the name of the organization?"

I make something up off the top of my head. "Smart Immigrant Kids . . . er . . . Exchange."

Mom's eyes knit. "Smart Immigrant Kids Exchange? Never heard of it."

"They're new . . . ," I say, bolting for the stairs.

Mom hollers after me, "Don't forget to register for the real ECEP—coming up in exactly two weeks!"

Back in my room, I lean against the door and exhale. There's no way I'm going to college early after my epic trip with Serene to SGV. I take my phone out and smile when I see a message notification from her on WeChat.

Thanks for taking me today, she writes.

Of course! I write back. **It was fun!**

I put my phone down, thinking it might be a while till she responds, but it dings immediately.

I still can't get over it. It's been there all this time and I never knew! Serene types back. **It's like a mini Beijing.**

I wish I could take you to the real Beijing sometime. Show you it's not just factories.

To my delight, Serene texts back, **Can't wait. Xx**

I spend the next forty-five minutes grinning like a fool at my desk, while googling "stand-up comedy open mics near me."

Fueled by my pact with Serene, I sign up for every newsletter, event notification, and contest I can find. Time to get serious about my dream.

27

Serene

CLUTCHING MY HALF purple pendant, I walk into Dr. Herman's office.

"I'm here to do the BRCA test," I say.

"Wonderful," he says. "Have a seat. It'll only take a second. My nurse will collect your blood."

I repeat Lian's words in my head—knowledge is power. Yet, the fear pitter-patters inside me. This is it. Once they have my blood, I can't pretend to live in the world where I don't have the BRCA mutation. . . .

I think about my box for Dad. Do I put this inside if the result is a *yes*? Will he still look at the other wonderful achievements, or will this be all he sees?

Dr. Herman touches my shoulder. "Hey, listen, even if it's positive, you don't have to do anything. It's just good information to have, so we can keep an eye on it."

I nod, knowing rationally that even if I'm BRCA positive,

it's not like I'm going to cut off my breasts and ovaries tomorrow. I'm only seventeen. By the time I'm older, they'll have figured this out and I won't even need to cut myself up. And yet. I know I'll be thinking about the precancerous cells living inside me. Wondering if they've multiplied and turned. Wondering if I'll stop them in time. There's always a moment, a point in time when everything changes.

And there's no going back.

The nurse comes over with a syringe the size of a water bottle to collect my blood. I fight the urge to call it off. But then I look down at my pendant and think of the promise to Lian, and I hold out my arm.

The nurse dabs the alcohol wipe over my vein and inserts the needle, telling me to make a fist. I squeeze my jade pendant tighter.

A minute later, it's done.

Walking out of the clinic, I want to call Lian. I want to tell him, but I'm also afraid to tell him. As I'm staring at my phone, it dings with a bunch of texts from Quinn and Cameron.

Pizza Thurs night at La Rosti's?

OMG love their cauliflower crust. #ketolife

I can't think about cauliflower crust right now, so I turn off notifications for the group chat and call my mom instead.

"Serene, where are you?" she asks.

"On the Westside. What's wrong?" I ask, sensing the anxiety in her voice.

"Can you come back to the office right now? I need your help."

I arrive at Mom's office. She and Julien and the others are fretting over what to do.

"Anna Wintour's office called," Mom says. "They want to do a profile on me."

"Oh my God, Mom!" My hands fly to my mouth. This is it—the moment Mom's been working so hard to achieve her entire career. I reach over and grab Mom's hand and I jump up and down in the conference room. My euphoria is interrupted by Julien sucking air through his teeth. *What now?*

"It's great," Julien says. "But I'm thinking maybe no pictures. Your mother looks so . . . frail."

"I do *not* look frail," Mom says, offended. Still, her eyes travel to the reflection on the conference room glass and her hand to her thinning hair. I want to kill Julien for making my mom self-conscious.

"She looks amazing!" I insist. "And of course she's gonna be photographed. She's the star! They want to know her ideas. Her vision. Her contribution to fashion!"

Julien glances at Chris. "What if we just gave them an old headshot? A profile with a headshot could be just as powerful."

I scrunch my face at the absurd suggestion. "It's *Vogue*! They're not going to run an old headshot!"

"We have to think about what makes sense for the company right now. A high-profile piece in *Vogue* about a founder that looks sickly doesn't exactly give customers *or* potential buyers confidence. . . ."

"And I'm just supposed to sit here and hide in my office?" Mom tosses a pen onto the conference table in anger. "This is the opportunity of my career!"

"You told us when we invested that you'd always do what's best for the company," Chris reminds her.

"And I am. This opportunity *is* what's best for the company. You have any idea how long we've been waiting for this?" Mom grabs the latest copy of *Vogue* lying on the conference table, her sunken cheeks more pronounced as she pleads with them. "It may not come up again."

"That's it." I make an executive decision. "She's doing it. Full sit-down interview. Big splashy photo shoot, *with* music. The whole nine yards." I'm *not* going to let them take this from her.

A smile escapes from Mom.

As I jump up to go to confirm the interview, I catch a glimpse of Julien's face. He looks supremely irritated with me, but I couldn't care less. Mom's getting her *Vogue* interview!

Later in the car on the way home, Mom turns to me. "Thank you."

Giddily, I tell her the details. The interview's happening

the day after tomorrow. It'll be at our offices. "I'm thinking a portrait of you at your desk, one with you in the sample closet *of course*. And maybe one with you on the roof, overlooking the Santa Monica Pier?"

"No roof." Mom shakes her head, running her fingers through her hair. "I don't want all that wind. It'll make it even more obvious that I'm shedding."

I glance at her hair. "You're fine," I tell her. I wish those investors hadn't made her feel so insecure. She looks *beautiful*. And besides, she could literally get up there and wear a dishrag, and she'd still be an icon. "You're going to rock this."

"I don't know about that," Mom chuckles.

I take a deep breath. "So I did the test," I tell Mom as I drive.

Her hand stops fussing with her hair. "Wow." She reaches over and puts her hand over mine. "How do you feel?"

Scared. Anxious. Like a bomb's about to detonate in my stomach at any moment.

"I'm fine," I lie.

"When do you find out the result?" she asks.

"In a week, I think," I say.

Mom squeezes my hand. "It's going to be fine."

"You think if it's positive, I should warn Dad?" I ask her.

She looks at me, puzzled. "That's not how genetics work. It goes from parent to child, not the other way around."

Of course I understand that. That's not why I want to tell him.

"So that's a no?" I frown.

Mom doesn't reply. In frustration, I go over a speed bump—fast—and suddenly she's grabbing for the door handle, trying to open it, her other hand over her mouth, as she pleads with me, "Pull over! I'm going to be sick!"

I step on the brakes and Mom's door flies open. She throws up on the sidewalk in front of a random house in Sienna Beach. My eyes widen at the flood of sick; it's more than I've ever seen anyone throw up, even at Cameron's house parties where drunk kids puked their guts out.

"Are you OK?" I ask her, frantically grabbing tissues and feeling awful. I shouldn't have gotten so upset, shouldn't have gone so fast.

Another wave of nausea comes on and she hurls again. I reach to pull her hair back, and she snaps at me, "Don't touch it!"

But it's too late. A fistful of hair comes out.

Mom grabs it from my hand and throws it out of the car. And we sit in the car in silence.

Finally, Mom says in the quietest of voices, "I can't think about your dad right now. I can barely think about myself." I look down at my hands, feeling so bad for bringing him up. "Maybe the investors are right. Maybe it's just not my time."

"No, Mom, it's been your dream since forever," I say. "You *deserve* this."

"But what if I throw up at the shoot? What will people think? Is that really the legacy I want to leave?"

It hurts so bad to see my mom finally here, achieving her dream, only to have her body fail her. I'd give anything to trade places with her. Take me instead. I'm just a normal girl.

Instead, I reach over for Lian's jade pendant. "Someone once told me, we can't give up on our dreams. No matter how scary they are." I stare into her eyes. "You're living proof of that, Mom. And you can't stop now."

Mom clutches my hand and I cling to her as tight as I can, wishing she knew how much the world needs her. *I* need her.

28
Lian

MY MOM INSISTS on driving me and my sister to school, so she can take the car after to Barnes & Noble to buy the other Celeste Ng books. Now that she's done with *Little Fires Everywhere*, she can't stop talking about it.

"I like the way she writes, this Chinese woman," Mom says after dropping off my sister at the elementary school. "You know I look her up and she went to Harvard?"

"Which just goes to show, you can go to Harvard and *not* be an engineer," I point out.

"Yeah, but so hard." She tells me what she googled about Ng as she drives. How it took her four drafts and one revision to write her first book. That's six years slogging away, with no real sign of certainty she'll succeed.

"But is there ever any real certainty of success?" I ask.

"Yes," Mom says. "Eight hundred on ECEP."

I roll my eyes. She doesn't stop! Still, it's clear from how she keeps sneaking glances at Ng's author picture on the back of her book that Mom is intrigued by her. I feel a sprinkle of hope. Maybe one day my parents will accept me for who I am. I just gotta show them, like Celeste Ng did.

I scroll through my phone, checking emails for messages from the comic newsletters I signed up for. And then I see it.

Calling all comics! Compete for the title of Next Big Comic!

I sit up. It's a mass email for an open stand-up competition. I swipe up.

To enter, upload your video link of your latest stand-up performance (must be minimum 5 minutes long and MUST be in front of a live audience). Your performance will be judged by a 5-judge panel. Finalists will be invited to perform their best 5 minutes live on stage at the Los Angeles Comedy Festival, where the winner will be determined by the audience.

Los Angeles Comedy Festival! That's *huge*! I turn to my mom, excited to tell her, then remember, it's Mom. I spend the next five minutes stuck about the part that says "*MUST* be in front of a live audience."

Hmmmm. How am I going to pull that off?

Mom parks in front of my school. As I'm about to get out, she waves to another parent, Leigh Norton's mom, from English, I think. Mom holds up her book. They both roll down their windows.

"Hey, I've been meaning to email you! I see you got the book," Leigh's mom says.

"Yes! I just finish it," my mom says to her. "It's beautiful. Can't wait to talk about it on Thursday. The book club is at six, right?"

The woman makes a regretful face.

"I'm so sorry—that's what I wanted to email you about—actually our book club is full."

It takes my mom a minute to register the words.

"Yeah, the club voted and we really want to keep the club small and intimate, so we can have better discussions. You understand."

I've never seen Mom so sad, not even the time when all her orchids died after just one week.

I get out of the car. "But this club is for parents of the school, right?"

"Well, it's not affiliated with the school or anything, so technically it's a *private* club . . . ," the woman clarifies.

My mom holds up a hand to try to stop me. "It's OK," she says.

But I'm not done.

"And you can't let one more person in?" I continue.

"I'm afraid not. The club voted."

"Stop," she says to me. Her voice is firm and threatening. She turns to Leigh's mom, issues a tight smile, and says, "That's fine. I understand. I still reading the books by myself."

As Leigh's mom rolls up her window and pulls away in her Range Rover, Mom turns to me and says, "Promise me you zheng qi." Zheng qi means "make me proud" in Chinese. "So white people never talk to me like that again."

I nod quickly. As I walk across the parking lot, my mom's rejection—and my promise—sit heavy on my shoulders.

"Hey!" a voice calls out.

It's Serene. I turn immediately to check if Mom sees us, but she's already pulled away.

"What's wrong?" she asks.

"Nothing . . ." I shake my head. "It's just this lady. Another parent. She was being mean to my mom."

"They can be brutal here," she says. "I have stories."

"I'd love to hear them."

"At the beach, after I get off work?" she suggests.

I smile. "Meet you there."

Later, I meet up with Serene at Sienna Cove, the beach in front of Luke's house. As we walk along the warm sand, I try to push the memory of her making out with Cameron out of my head.

"How was work?" I ask her.

"My mom's stressed," she says. "She got this amazing opportunity, but everyone's worried." Her voice trails off.

"Why's everyone worried?" I ask.

"I dunno. It's complicated."

I try not to pry.

186

"Anyway, so what happened this morning?" she asks.

I tell her about the book club.

"Ugh, I'm sorry," she says. "That's typical Sienna Beach bullshit." Serene takes a seat on the warm sand. I sit down next to her. She tells me about all the instances over the years where she and her mom struggled with racism.

"I remember in sixth grade, we were reading a nonfiction book about white privilege. Some of the parents complained that it was making their kids feel bad. That it wasn't appropriate. They didn't want their kids coming home and talking about it."

"Oh my God!"

"And my mom wrote back saying, this is absurd. How are we supposed to advance things if we can't even talk about it?" Serene says, picking up a pebble and throwing it into the ocean. "But the parents persisted. The next thing I knew, a petition circulated—the book was to be removed from the curriculum. Not only that, they made a new rule: parents who haven't lived in Sienna Beach for at least five years are not allowed to join the PTA."

I grab a fistful of sand. "They didn't."

"Oh yes they did," Serene says. "That's the Karens of Sienna Beach for you—*you can buy our houses, you can send your kids to our school, but you'll never truly be 'one of us.'*"

I shake my head and curse in Chinese at the crashing waves. "Wow. That's awful. I'm so sorry. And you guys still stayed here?"

Serene turns to me. "Why should we be the ones to leave?" she asks.

It's an innocent question that knocks the socks off me. I never thought of it that way.

I gaze over in the direction of Luke's house, wondering at what point, then, did she become one of the popular kids. Because she's obviously no longer in the same category I am. "So then what happened? How'd they finally accept you?"

"That took a while . . . and a lot of . . ." She rubs her fingers together, signifying money. "My mom went all out for my twelfth birthday. Chartered a boat, DJ, the whole nine yards." Serene throws another rock. She hugs her knees as she looks out at the waves. "We also gave out *a lot* of new clothes."

"Was it worth it?"

Serene takes her time thinking it over before nodding. "Guess I was tired of sitting out," she says. "But every now and then, it still creeps in, the fact that I'm not 'in' in." She runs the fine sand through her fingers.

I stare down at our two sandy hands, inches away from each other. I'm so tempted to lean over and kiss her.

She holds up a finger. "That reminds me!" She reaches into her pocket and pulls out a flyer.

It's the high school talent show, happening right after the lower school's talent show. The one my sister's thinking of joining.

She hands it to me. I look down and read the rules.

Acts must be no more than 6 minutes in length.

Acts must adhere to School's Rules of Conduct.

Auditions will be held on Monday, October 26. Must audition in person. No late applications will be considered after this point.

"You should totally do it!" Serene encourages me.

I gaze down at the flyer and shake my head. Performing is one thing, but to do it in front of everyone at my school? They'd be laughing all right, but not in a good way.

"I actually found this other thing. The Next Big Comic. I just have to find a place to do open mic." I pull out my phone to show her. "Somewhere *far* away from here."

"But Sienna Beach needs to hear you!"

"Sienna Beach does *not* need to hear me," I correct.

Serene sticks out her lower lip, *boo.* Then she adds, "You know, that's what my mom was saying this morning too . . . that maybe she doesn't really need to do this interview thing. But *I* need her to do it. The next Asian girl in Sienna Beach needs her to do it. Every other Asian American designer that's going to follow in her footsteps needs her to do it."

I grin. "Hell yeah!" I say. "You and your dad must be so proud."

Serene wriggles in the sand. "Actually, I don't have a dad. Or at least, I don't know where he is."

I turn to her. "Oh. I'm sorry, I didn't know."

The vulnerability on her face takes my breath away.

"It was wrong of me to have assumed." I feel like such a jerk.

Serene shakes her head, *It's fine.* Then runs her fingers along the sand, drawing out the character ba, for "father" in Chinese.

"Actually . . . that's why I'm learning Chinese," Serene confesses to her perfectly drawn *ba.* "So I can find him."

My mind starts racing with possibilities. "I can help you! We can use WeChat, QQ, oh and Weibo! I haven't even told you about Weibo yet! It's like Chinese Twitter!"

Serene laughs at my enthusiasm, her eyes sparkling in the sunset.

"I'm not sure I'm quite ready to put it on Twitter yet," she says. "But . . . I appreciate the offer." She shields her eyes from the setting sun. "You really want to help me?"

"Of course." My finger traces her *ba* on the sand. "You don't have to do this by yourself."

"I don't know anything about him. Other than his name—Li Jin. That's gotta be so common. And I don't know if he's even still in Beijing!"

"We'll find out!" I tell her.

A wave sneaks up close to us and washes away Serene's *ba* character. She gasps at the wet sand, sad for a minute.

"It's carrying it to the other side," I tell her. "To your dad."

She smiles. Another wave comes up close, and this time, our shoes get soaked. I lift Serene in my arms and carry her along the sand. Serene shrieks and laughs. Her half of the purple pendant falls from her pocket, and we shriek and point as the ocean waves engulf it.

We take turns plunging our arms into the waves and trying to save it, our legs splashing in the water. When at last I grab it from the wet sand, our laughter is interrupted by Luke's angry voice.

"*Belt Bag?*" he shouts. "The hell are you doing on my beach?"

I place the wet pendant in Serene's hand. "It's a public beach."

He studies me and Serene.

"What are you doing with Serene?" he asks, staring at the pendant in her hand.

"Nothing," Serene replies quickly. "We were just talking."

"Well, find another beach to talk." He throws me a look. "Better yet, another guy."

29
Serene

I PUSH LUKE'S rude comment out of my mind as I get up on the day of the big *Vogue* interview. Mom's up at the crack of dawn. She wants to skip her chemo drug, the one that has been making her so nauseous.

"I'm just gonna skip one day," she says, taking the little pink pill and throwing it into the sink.

"But Mom! Dr. Herman specifically said not to skip a dose."

"Well, Dr. Herman isn't gonna be in *Vogue*," she replies.

She sits down at the kitchen counter and, for the first time in weeks, asks if there are any more cinnamon raisin bagels left.

"Yes!" I grab them from the fridge. I toast them up and ask if she wants a little butter on them. Mom used to love eating bagels with butter. Now she hardly touches the stuff.

To my surprise, she says, "Sure!" She pops one of her digestion pills in her mouth. Wow, they must really be working. "I wanna pretend like today's a normal day. Let's just pretend!"

I grin as I spread the butter on her bagel. "Being interviewed by *Vogue* is hardly normal," I say to Mom, handing her the plate.

Mom smiles as she takes it. We eat our breakfast together, side by side at the counter, just like the old days.

As I pour her some more orange juice, I run through possible interview questions with her. I'd stayed up late writing them on my phone.

"What do you love about fashion?" I ask her.

Mom takes a breath, closes her eyes for a sec.

"I love the way you can reinvent yourself with fashion," she says. Her eyes smile as she takes me back to when she was a young teenager in China. "You can be whoever you want to be. My mother was a seamstress in Beijing, when she was still alive. And women from all over town would come to her and she'd make them these beautiful dresses. Dresses made of the finest silks."

"Is that how you learned to sew?" I ask. My mom's stitching is renowned in the industry.

"I would watch my mom every day. My family was poor, so I never had anything nice to wear. I'd wear the same nylon shorts with patched-up holes, a hand-me-down from my brothers. They were practically in threads by the time they got to me, like you could hold them up with your hand and blow and all the little pieces of shorts would fly away like a dandelion. That was the kind of stuff I wore," she chuckles. "But one day." She holds up a finger.

I lean in.

"One day, when a customer rang to say she'd be late picking up her dress, I put the dress on. I went out and I remember walking through the streets of Beijing in it. And just . . . feeling like a different person. I was the same person inside, but everything was different about me. The way people looked at me. The *respect* I got. It was like my world had gone from black-and-white to color."

I've heard the story before, of course, but every time, I still get goose bumps on my skin. *Vogue* is going to *love* her.

"Then of course I had to take it off." She looks down.

"And how did that feel?" I ask.

"Excruciating. To experience all that color and go back to black-and-white?" She shakes her head. "I vowed to work the rest of my life to get that feeling back."

I smile.

"But it wasn't easy. As an immigrant from China, I faced a lot of discrimination in the fashion industry."

"Definitely talk about that in the interview," I suggest.

"I remember at one of my first buyer's meetings, I was presenting a blouse. It had a modest neckline, which the buyer thought was too high, he wanted it lower, and he made this really off-color remark. Something like, 'This might work in China, but here in America, our women like to show off their cleavage. Just FYI if you're going to keep designing for Americans.'"

My jaw drops. "He *said* that?" I ask.

Mom nods.

"And it always stuck with me, just how much harder I'd have to work to prove myself in this industry. As an immigrant and as a woman with no connections."

I think about what Lian said his mother believes, that America is a meritocracy. Did my mom fall for it too? Is that why she left everything behind and came here?

"It took a lot to work past all the comments to just focus on the goal, but I knew that if I focused on making the very best dress I could, people will eventually stop seeing me for the color of my skin, but for the quality of my work."

I clap for my mom, so pumped for the world to see her for the warrior she is!

"How was that?" she asks.

"That was *beyond*!" I shriek. "You're going to be amazing!"

Mom holds up her juice, and we clink glasses. Her fingers linger on mine as I add, "Wish Dad could see you."

"Why? So he'd regret leaving me?" She chuckles.

I bite my lip.

"I don't define my success by him or anyone else," she says, putting the last piece of bagel in her mouth. "And neither should you."

I wait until Mom leaves for the office before slipping into her study. I'm determined to search her computer top to bottom for my dad's address. There's *gotta* be a way to send him a copy of her *Vogue* piece when it comes out.

I know she's told me a million times she doesn't have his contact info anymore, but nobody deletes that clean. There's gotta be a backup copy somewhere.

So I move aside all her design sketches and prescriptions for anti-nausea medication and scroll through her in-box.

There are dozens and dozens of emails from Julien.

Your daughter is a liability. All your designers know it. They remember what we all had to do last year to clean up her mess at 1 Oak. And how much that cost the company. Only this time, it's gonna be even harder. I'm already getting calls from headhunters saying 70% of your senior designers are thinking of jumping.

Lil, you know I say this with all the love and respect in the world, but WTF. A pop-up WeChat shop? Are we some scarf-peddling street stall? Who came up with this harebrained idea? Oh wait, I know. A TEENAGER. She's Gen Z. It's not her fault she can't see or care beyond her next pedicure. But it's up to us—the grown-ups in charge—to make sure she doesn't set the whole building on fire.

Whoa. I knew he didn't like me, but I had no idea it was this toxic.

My skin burns as I scroll. The emails go all the way back to when the stupid thing at 1 Oak went down. Mom had gone to Julien, in a panic, about what to do. And Julien had helped her retain Sabrina for damage control.

But it's an email dated four years ago that makes me sit up.

$5,000 on the company credit card for Serene's birthday? What the hell, Lily! How's this a valid business expense? Julien wrote.

I'm sorry, it was an emergency! My daughter's starting 7th grade. You wouldn't believe the other kids at her school. She's had such a nightmare-ish year and I just wanted her to get off on the right foot. I would have charged it to my personal card, but you know I've given every penny I have to the company. I was desperate. It won't happen again, Mom had replied.

Julien replied back:

I'm only going to say this once. It's a misuse of company funds for personal reasons. But I'm going to let this slide. You owe me.

Fuck. That's probably why Mom's so afraid of him.

He caught her misusing company funds so I'd fit in. So people like Quinn's mom and everyone else at my school would tell their daughters that I'm cool. And let them into the club.

In exchange, she's had to live with Julien's abuse for years.

Walking out of my house, I double-check to make sure the curtains in Mom's study are drawn. She can't know that I've been in there snooping.

I reach for the piece of paper in my pocket.

In the end, I found an address in Beijing, buried under all the obnoxious Julien emails. It was listed on some wiring instructions. The email read:

Wiring instructions:
Account #: 2459507
Bank: Bank of China
Mrs. Lin Meilin
Recipient address: A8-601 Shuang Jing Qiao Fu Li Cheng, Beijing 10000

I'm not sure who Lin Meilin is. Maybe just a banker or someone we work with who helps with production, but my heart surges with hope that it's maybe my great-aunt, or a cousin?

When I get to school, I dash out of the car to find Lian. Maybe he knows where Shuang Jing Qiao is in Beijing!

Cameron holds out an arm as I jog across the courtyard to the library. He catches me as I'm heading up the steps.

"Whoa, where are you going?" he asks.

He pulls me in for a kiss, his lips parting. I tilt my head.

"What's wrong?" he asks.

"Nothing, I just have to return a library book," I say quickly.

"That can wait," he says, moving in again. His hand travels up an opening in the back of my shirt. I take a step back. The wind blows in my wrap top, and I tie the bottom tighter.

"Serene. What are you doing?" he asks. "C'mon, it's me."

He looks at me with whimpering, puppy-dog eyes. And I feel mildly bad for saying no. For being in a different place than him, all of a sudden. Mostly I feel bad for giving him a pic of me that makes him think that I'd do it again.

"I'm late for class," I tell him. "I gotta go."

"But—" he protests.

I hurry up the steps to the library, the only place I know Cameron will never set foot, no matter how horny he is.

Once inside, I feel my whole body relax. I scan the tables, looking for Lian, and sure enough, he's sitting by the stacks with Stuart Mitchell.

Stu used to be a part of the water polo team too, back in freshman year, until he got cut. The other boys' bodies all changed and poor Stu stayed the same height he always was. And he's been waiting ever since. It's like everyone else has gotten their luggage, and he's still sitting at the carousel, hoping for his suitcase.

"Hey!" Lian says to me.

Stu waves at me from the table. "Hey, Serene. You look really nice today. I mean, you always do. Will you and your friends be needing a beach concierge this summer?"

"You mind, Stu?" Lian asks, frowning. "Give us a moment?"

Stu packs up his stuff and tells Lian he'll be out by the picnic tables.

"Hi!" I smile. I pull out the paper with the address in Beijing. "I found something." I show him the address. "You know this place?"

He studies the address. "No, but this is out by the Silk Market. There are lots of tailors and fabric stores out there."

"Tailors!" My eyes widen. "My grandmother was a seamstress! Maybe this is her old house!"

"Is she still alive?"

My eyes fall. "She passed. But maybe some of my relatives are still living there?" I ask hopefully. "Maybe I can reach out to them?"

"I can help you with the letter!" Lian volunteers.

I reach out and hug him in my enthusiasm. I can smell the warm coconut scent of his shampoo and resist the urge to touch his hair. Out of the corner of my eyes, I see Quinn walk in.

I immediately take my arms off Lian before she sees us.

"Hey!" she says, walking over to us. She looks at me and Lian. "What's going on here?"

"Nothing. I'll text you after school!" I murmur quietly.

"Cool." Lian picks up his backpack and walks out.

Quinn waits until he's left, then turns to me. "Where've you been? You didn't respond to the group chat—are we on for tonight? You, Cameron, me, and Luke? Pizza?" she asks.

I bite my lower lip. "I can't."

"Why not?" she asks.

"I just have this thing. For Chinese Club—"

"Just tell Belt Bag you've got something else going on!" Quinn says with a roll of her eyes.

"Hey, don't call him that," I say to her sharply.

She looks at me, puzzled.

"His name is Lian," I tell her.

"Whatever."

"No, it's not whatever," I say. "How would you like it if people called you Quim?"

This disturbs Quinn on a level worse than wearing flip-flops with socks. She narrows her eyes at me.

"OK, I'm going to pretend you didn't just say that," she says. "I don't know what you're going through, whatever weird Stockholm syndrome you been catching at that club—"

"Stockholm syndrome!"

"But *we* are going to have pizza at La Rosti's tonight. And I suggest you show up."

She looks me firmly in the eye, a warning.

∘ ∘ ∘

After school, I run to my car, throwing my keys and purse inside as I hurry to Mom's interview. Have they already started? I hope they're styling her hair up—it'll look so great with the gown she's got picked out. It's a black-and-white tiered satin gown, which she's pairing with a black blazer. The whole thing is so boss. I hope Julien is not there. I wish I could take his emails and bobby pin them to his head.

I text Mom as I start the car.

On my way! How's it going?

Not well. I'm feeling sick, Mom texts back. **Must have been the butter I ate.**

Oh no. I start the Volvo and dictate to Siri.

Have you taken the anti-nausea pills? I ask her. **Is Vogue already there??**

Yes. Setting up now.

SHIT. I step on the gas.

I'll be right there!!

I weave in between lanes on the highway, speeding past cargo trucks. *C'mon, c'mon, c'mon.*

Thirty-eight minutes later, I arrive at the office. The *Vogue* crew is setting up in the conference room. There are lights and fans and cameras, and the photographer is fanning himself impatiently. The journalist sits at the desk, Face-Timing her editor instead of talking to my mom, who is nowhere to be found.

Carmella dashes over to me.

"Where is she?" I ask.

"In her office." Carmella points to the double doors of Mom's glass office, firmly closed and with the blinds drawn. She *never* closes the shades. It must be really bad. "She's not letting anyone in. We're trying to figure out if we can get her out through a back entrance somehow."

"She wants to *leave*?" I ask. I glance back at the *Vogue* journalist craning her neck, curious about what's going on.

I speed-walk to Mom's office, where Julien is standing, knocking, unable to get in. I glare at him. But today's not the day to get into his emails. I squeeze by him and knock gently on the door. "Mom?" I ask. "It's me."

I hear the faint click of the door unlocking and slip inside. Julien tries to follow me in, but I quickly close the door behind me.

Mom is on the floor next to her couch. There are stains on her gown where she got sick, her carefully styled hair is sticky with vomit, and she's manically trying to clean her thick carpet with tissue paper.

"Here, let me," I say, kneeling down next to her on the floor, grabbing the tissues out of her hand. "It's OK! We're going to get you cleaned up. It's going to be fine!"

Mom shakes her head as she says tearfully, "No. I can't. I'm a mess." Mascara runs down her cheeks. I hear the urgency in her voice, I really do, but I also know how hard she's worked to get here.

Julien knocks on the door again.

"The *Vogue* folks are leaving in ten, just FYI. You want us to make an excuse and do this by phone?" he asks through the door.

"No!" I call out immediately. I hold Mom's hand and try to pull her up. "We can still do this."

"No, we can't. My hair, my gown—"

She looks down at the sick on her clothes.

"Here, we'll swap!" I start taking off my own shirt. OK, so it's not couture, but she can rock anything. Besides, it's not about what she's wearing—it's about celebrating *her*. I strip down to my bra and underwear.

I help Mom out of her tight gown, taking the bobby pins out of her hair so her loose, flowing strands can better mask the sticky parts. She quickly puts on my shirt and pants. As I stand back to admire the new look—it's casual but chic!—I flash her a thumbs-up. She's got this! It's going to be OK!

But another wave of nausea comes on, and she runs to her trash can. Hugging the can, she shakes her head emphatically at me. *"I can't do this."*

And I know she's right. No amount of concealer can compete with the forces of the cancer. *Fuck*.

"OK. I'll let them know."

As I pick up her office phone to tell Marcia and the others outside, Mom lifts her head from the trash can for a second. "You should do it instead of me."

What? *Me* interviewed by *Vogue*? I look down at my bra and underwear. But the expression on Mom's face says she's dead serious.

"You'd be so great," Mom says. "A fresh face! A chance to change the narrative!"

Before I can even wrap my head around what's happening, Mom crawls up from the trash can. She grabs the phone, and presses for Marcia. My heart thuds as I think of how the hell I'm going to pull this off.

"Hey, Marcia . . . change of plans . . . ," Mom says. "How do they feel about interviewing Serene instead?"

Julien comes bursting in through the doors.

"Oh no no no," Julien says as I throw a cashmere shawl over my shoulders.

Marcia comes in with news. "They said they'd love to interview Serene! They've been curious about her ever since her comment last year."

"What? NO!" Julien says, shaking his head. "This isn't happening—"

"I'll do it!" I cry. Here's my chance to make it up to Mom and set the record straight. And in couture, no less.

As Julien sinks onto Mom's couch, grabbing his thinning hair with his hands, I turn to my mom and mouth, *I got this.*

30
Lian

I LOOK UP the address Serene gave me on Baidu. It's an old apartment building, built after the Cultural Revolution in the 1980s. That gives me hope that maybe Serene's right. This *is* her grandparents' house.

If only I could catapult myself over to Beijing *right now* and go knock on the door. That would be a lot faster than a letter. I start texting my friends in Beijing, Lei and Chris. I open WeChat. To my surprise, Chris is still online. Quickly, I explain the situation to him.

I can try to go next weekend, he writes back.

Next weekend? I ask.

Sorry, I've got this thing due.

What thing? I text.

Remember the sign thing we used to do?

Oh yeah. My friends and I, we'd go around town and take pictures of hilariously mistranslated signs in English, like road signs that say "Temporary Park Only, for Getting Off" or "Fresh Crap ¥12/kg" in a seafood restaurant.

I'm compiling them for this magazine. I wrote the editor an email and sent him some pics. They're paying me ¥300! I just need five more signs, he texts.

I feel a twinge of jealousy and missing out. That was *our* thing. But then I remind myself to be happy for my friend. He's going for his dream, just as I am.

That's great, I text back.

How are things with you and that girl?

Great!

You ever coming back? Are we going to get to meet her?

I hope so, I text. I smile at the idea of walking around Beijing with Serene, introducing her to my friends. I'd love nothing more than to introduce her to my city. Perhaps in the summer we'll go together. And she can be reunited with her dad properly.

If I can play even a small role in giving that to Serene, that would be amazing. And it's not just the reunion with her dad, it's the *many* reunions that will follow. I think of all my aunts and uncles and cousins back home, all the Chinese New Year dinners where my uncles would let me drink beer and my aunts would sing bad karaoke—I can't imagine not having that. And to grow up instead in Sienna Beach, having to justify why you deserve to take up more space than a tree. And yet she and her mom stayed.

I think of the character for "strong" in Chinese, tie.

On the left of the character is the radical for "gold," and on the right is the radical for "lose." I don't know why exactly "lose" is there, I guess it's a reminder to people that sometimes if you're too strong-willed, you might lose.

In Serene's case, I know she won't.

I get off WeChat and switch over to Weibo, where I type in "Li Jin." There are about five thousand people with that name—everyone from basketball players to binge-eating online stars who can stuff a hundred baozis in their stomach.

As I'm wading through the profiles, an ad pops up for a relative-finding agency.

I'm a private detective in Beijing. Reuniting families since 2005! Contact me to help you with your search!

A private detective! That's perfect! I try and call Serene but she doesn't pick up. While I wait for her to text me back, I write to the private detective in Chinese:

Hi! Yes, I'm searching for someone. Actually it's for my friend. She's searching for her dad. Her name is Serene Li. His name is Li Jin. She thinks he lives in Beijing. Can you help her?

He writes back in Chinese, That's what I do! I help reunite relatives—look at my testimonials page. I don't stop until I find the person. Can I have your friend's contact info?

I hesitate for a second, not feeling quite right about giving him Serene's info before asking her first. But when I click on his testimonial page, I'm so impressed by the many, many testimonials from satisfied clients. The guy clearly knows what he's doing. The reviews go on for pages.

So I copy and paste Serene's WeChat QR code into the chat.

Great! he texts back.

My phone rings. I think it's Serene calling me back and I get all excited.

But it's just Kevin calling me from 888 Education. I know I should get back to studying for the test—it's next Saturday! Instead, I go back to my list of "stand-up open mic nights" and start wading through all the various venues in Los Angeles, trying to figure out the one closest to me.

Most of them have eighteen-and-over requirements, but I'm not deterred. If Chris can get into a magazine, I can get on that stage. I pick up the phone to call the comedy clubs to explain my situation.

Stu texts me as I'm dialing.

Dude how do u tell if there's msg in ur food?

I chuckle. **I dunno, does it say msg in the ingredients?**

It's takeout, fool. I specifically told them No MSG! But now I'm worried. It tastes extra tasty.

Now I'm laughing my head off. **EXTRA TASTY? Maybe ur just hungry?**

A few secs pass.

That could be it.

I smile.

Hey so what did Serene want?

I hesitate. I want so badly to tell someone at school about us. **Nothing. I'm just helping her out with something.**

What??

Nothing. It's private.

OMG. You're not hooking up with her, are you?

My cheeks turn red. **No!**

Because that would be IT for you. Cameron's gonna whip your skinny Asian ass!

You can't say that, I text angrily. Whenever Stu spews shit like that, I want to chuck our friendship out the window.

Why can't I say that?

Because it's racist, I tell him.

No it's not. People say to me I'm gonna get my skinny white ass whipped all the time.

That's different.

Why's it different?

Ugh!

I turn my phone around. When it dings again, I prepare myself for another dim-witted statement. Instead, for the first time, there's an apology.

I'm sorry. You wanna come over?

31

Serene

MY PHONE'S TOO buried in the sample closet for me to reply to Lian's texts. Carmella and Ali help toss dress after dress at me—I have exactly forty-eight seconds to find something and put it on before *Vogue* and Julien come barging in.

Ali hands me a white stretch crepe dress. But I shake my head. To pull this off, I have to go BIG. I've got to wear something so out-of-this-world gorgeous, there's no denying the sheer talent in these halls.

"What about the tulle?" I ask.

Carmella's and Ali's eyes sparkle.

"The tulle! Yes!" They run to the back and hand me my mom's masterpiece. She just finished it last week. Carefully, they place it in my arms. The delicate black fabric feels as light as air as my fingertips drape the dress over me. It's like touching a cloud.

I look at Carmella, hesitating for a second—it almost looks too good to wear! "Should I really?"

"DO IT!" they cry back, quickly rummaging through the drawers and tossing me the perfect pair of black lace underwear to wear underneath. Because even though the dress has about five hundred layers of fabric, the part right in front of my underwear . . . is sheer. Oh yes. My mom did that.

"Holy mother of couture!" Ali puts her hands to her mouth when I put it on. Carmella adds extra pins in the back to fit it to me. I look down at the soft tulle, like waves spilling out in 360 degrees. I walk over to the mirror and suck in a breath when I see my reflection. I look like a royal princess out for revenge, with the strapless neckline, the fitted bodice, and the peek-a-boo panties. DAMN!

Julien walks in, along with the *Vogue* team. The looks on their faces when they see me in the tulle are *priceless*.

"Wow," the photographer says. "I'M DEAD."

"Hi." I extend a hand. "I'm Serene. I work at the company too, and I'm excited to answer your questions. Thanks for being so flexible, my mom's just tied up at the moment."

The reporter fires off the first one.

"So I take it you don't find your mother's collection bland anymore," she says, pointing to the see-through tulle.

"I do not." I smile. "And I'm proud to say that this collection isn't just gorgeous, it's about the radical detonation of old norms, ageist thinking, and smashing the patriarchy."

I glance over at Julien, who looks like he's about to stuff the tulle in my mouth.

But the *Vogue* reporter is impressed.

"I love it!" Vivian, the reporter, says. "Let's do it!"

That afternoon, draped in see-through ruffles, in front of the blinding lights and my mother's entire team, I experience my first ever *Vogue* photo shoot. As the photographer clicks, the reporter fires away questions—about how my mom first got into fashion and how she started the company. And of course, why I said that comment about her collection being bland last year.

I decide to answer honestly.

"I'd like to say that it was because I didn't think she was designing to her fullest potential. Or that her collection wasn't edgy enough. But to tell you the truth, it was much simpler. I was mad at my mom. We had an argument that night, I didn't like a comment she made. And I said the thing I thought could hurt her."

"What was the argument about?" Vivian asks.

I think for a beat. "I guess about the past. My mom lives for the future. She's incredible that way. She just has this never-ending ability to reinvent herself, to always be moving forward."

I glance toward her office as I say this, wishing she could reinvent her way out of this one. I tell Vivian how Mom always thought fashion was a way to catapult her life toward her dreams. And that's exactly what she did, hand-stitching each dress from our living room for years.

"And what was that like for you, growing up? Watching her build her empire?"

I think back to Mom sketching next to me while I did my homework. The other kids had cupcake baking time; my mom and I, we went to the fabric district to scour shops trying to find the perfect pattern for her signature bustier maxi dress.

"Exhilarating. Intense," I answer honestly. "A little scary."

"Scary?"

"It's a lot to be a single mom, an immigrant, and an entrepreneur."

"And what would you say was the point where everything changed? Where it went from small time to big time?"

"Probably when Diet Prada put Mom's dress on Instagram. And we got our first order from Neiman Marcus."

"That must have felt so validating," the reporter says.

"It was," I say.

"And how did you celebrate?"

"Truthfully?" I glance over at Julien craning his neck in the corner. It was right around the time he invested. He reached out to her after her dress was on Diet Prada—proof that she'd already *made it* before he came into the picture. Still, he convinced her if she wanted to become a household name, she needed him. "We celebrated by pigging out at a Chinese restaurant."

"Oh, I love that!" She beams, scribbling this down. Julien shakes his head at me, a sharp frown on his puckered face.

"And what's it like working here now? Rumor has it, you're being groomed to take over. . . ."

The question catches me off guard and I flush.

"Is it true?" she says coyly.

"I'd love to follow in Mom's footsteps," I say carefully. "Designing is my passion. I'd love to one day lead a company just like Lily Lee."

"And what would you do differently?" Vivian asks.

As the camera zooms into my face, I go with my gut. "As we get bigger, I think it's really important that we keep the fire of being a start-up. A company where everyone feels seen. We have an incredible team of junior designers here— they've been instrumental in designing our ready-to-wear this season." I introduce the reporter to Carmella and Ali.

As I pull up our new ready-to-wear collection on my phone and show the *Vogue* team, Jonathan exits the conference room. He's shaking his head in dismay as he complains to the other senior designers. Pout all he wants, it's my interview. And I'm giving credit where credit is due.

"How'd it go?" Mom asks, finally stirring from the passenger side of my car as I turn onto our street. That was one super-powerful anti-nausea drug she took, because she slept through most of my interview. Marcia and I had to carry her from the velvet couch in her office down to my car.

"It went well! I think," I tell her. "I wore the tulle for the shoot."

Mom's eyes go big. She snaps out of her nausea-chemo-coma. "Ooooh! How did it look?"

I point to my phone so she can see some of the pics Carmella snapped from the back. Mom puts a hand over her chest when she sees.

"Oh, WOW. You look *gorgeous*," she says. "They better put you on the cover!"

I laugh, still feeling a smidgen guilty for taking Mom's spotlight. It should have been her up there today, instead of me. But I was grateful for the opportunity to sing her praises. "You should call *Vogue* tomorrow and answer the rest of her questions over the phone," I suggest. "If you're feeling better. She had lots of great questions."

"Like what?" Mom asks.

I start telling her and Mom closes her eyes, tired. She pats my hand weakly. "I'm sure you answered them all well," she murmurs as she drifts back to sleep.

"Mom, we're almost home. Stay with me," I say as I turn hurriedly into the Cove, unlocking the gate with my remote.

But the gate takes forever to open and by the time I get home, she's passed out. I try and carry her inside, but I can't lift her by myself. As frail as her body is, she still weighs well over a hundred pounds.

I grab my phone and try Marcia, but it goes to voice mail. I try my neighbor, just in case she's home, but she doesn't answer either. I scroll through my contacts, stopping at Lian. I know he'd pick up and be over here in ten minutes. I just know he would. But then he'd know about my mom. . . . He wouldn't just know, he'd *see*.

I try Cameron instead.

Hey. Where r u? Need ur help with my mom, I text.

Sorry. At pizza, he texts back.

I frown.

I put away the phone and run into the house in search of a big blanket. I fall asleep curled up next to my mom in the car, which, in a weird way, is the perfect ending to this surreal day.

32
Lian

STU LOOKS UP from munching on a spring roll. We're in his kitchen eating possibly the most MSGed food on the planet. His parents aren't home and we're crowded around his kitchen island trying not to make a mess, because Stu's mom's a real neat freak who won't let anyone use the dining table unless it's a bank holiday.

"So let me get this straight. You and Serene been hanging out this whole time? You went to the beach with her?" he asks.

I don't know how or why I ended up telling him about my "date" with Serene. I blame the moo shu pork. It always gets me talking.

"Yeah."

"This is the best fucking thing I've ever heard!" Stu says, getting so excited he squirts soy sauce all over the marble island.

"But then Luke saw us."

Stu wipes up the soy sauce.

"You know what, fuck that fucker. If you want to go for Serene, you should go for her."

"I wish I could just tell her how I feel. But she's with Cameron. . . ."

"She's hanging out with *you*, dude," he says. "That's progress for us nerds."

I'm amused Stu has included himself in the general category for nerds, given how we became friends. But I go with it.

"But what if she's *actually* just trying to learn Chinese?"

"At the beach? There are only two reasons girls ever invite guys to the beach. To carry their shit. And look into their eyes when the sun is setting. Not to learn Chinese."

Maybe Stu's right.

"I'm telling you, she's into you, man. You just gotta give her a sign. It's like with my cousin last summer."

I nearly choke on my pork. "You dated your cousin?"

"Third cousin, eight times removed."

I furrow my eyebrows, trying to run the math on that.

"It's like my great-uncle's kid's kid. Basically like my gardener."

"OK . . ."

"Anyway, it took me forever to get out of the friend zone, but once you do . . . oh man . . ." He closes his eyes and envisions what I can only guess is cousin/gardener euphoria. It fills me with sadness that I've not yet experienced anything close to it.

"How'd you do it?" I ask him.

"I sent her an erotic picture of my unbelievable chest hair," he says, pulling down the neck of his T-shirt to show me. "FEEL THE FUR!"

I spit out my Diet Coke as he takes my hand and pats his chest with it.

"You sent that to your cousin?" I ask, yanking my hand back.

"Gardener!" he insists. "Look, Liam, if you're going to judge me."

I throw my hands up. "I'm not, I'm not," I tell him. Then hesitate and add, "By the way, it's Lian."

"What?"

"My name. It's Lian."

"Oh," he says, stuffing another deep-fried wonton into his mouth.

That's it, just "oh." Not exactly the response I was hoping for, but it's progress for us nerds.

Later, when I get home, I get a call from Laugh Club in Hollywood.

"Hey, is this Lian Chen?" the guy asks.

"Yup!" I reply, highly encouraged they actually called

me back. "Thanks for calling me back. I saw on your website that you have open mic?"

"That's right. You interested in being part of our Saturday-night showcase?"

"Yeah! Totally! I'm a junior in high school—is that OK?"

"Just a minute. I gotta talk to my boss." He puts me on hold, then returns a minute later. "You any good?"

I hesitate for a second, then blurt out, with the same enthusiasm as those people in the prescription bowel syndrome medication commercials, "Yes! I promise you're going to love it!"

"What's your set about?" he asks.

"Immigrant parents."

"Immigrant parents, huh. That's something we haven't heard," he says. "Tell you what. Come down to the club next Saturday to meet with the manager, and we'll see if we can squeeze you in."

"Next Saturday?"

"He's free at eleven a.m."

I hang up the phone, exhilarated as hell that I've got a meeting, and stressed stiff, because it's on the same day as the ECEP test.

Serene's not at school on Friday. I'm so bummed as I walk into the library. I was hoping to talk to her about the comedy club thing—should I just skip ECEP and go? But what if I go and the manager decides not to give me a shot? My parents will skewer me.

I text her a few times but she doesn't respond. Maybe she's sick. Maybe she got so excited talking to the private detective in Beijing that she stayed up all night. Maybe they've found her dad already! I hope that's it.

I wish I could go over and talk to her. Mom walks into my room after school as I'm googling how to get to Laugh Club.

"I just got off the phone with Kevin! And you know what he said? He said you got five eighty on mock! Five eighty!" She walks over and pushes her index finger into my temple. "Where your head at?"

"Ow!" I cry.

She reaches for the blue delphiniums on my desk and tosses them into the trash. Clearly I'm undeserving of them. "You know how much we sacrificed so you can come to America. We sold our flat in Beijing—in a *down* market!"

"Yeah, because of Dad's job!" I remind her.

"Not just because of Dad's job. I wanted you kids to have best chance at US university. That why I give up everything for you! You think I like living here where everybody read book about a Chinese immigrant but nobody wants to talk to actual Chinese immigrant?" Mom asks, sitting down in my chair and throwing my cushion on the floor.

The hurt leaks from her eyes and my mother grabs a tissue.

"We can't even go back to Highway Robber with this score—forget MIT. Forget Harvard. You lucky you get into UC."

"UC's not the worst thing that can happen," I mutter.

Mom turns to me. "*Not the worst thing that can happen?*" she repeats, as if I'd just said that about herpes.

I glance at the directions to Laugh Club on Google Maps, and reach to close my laptop. They'll never understand.

"You better be ready on the big day," she says.

"I will," I promise.

Mom drops five more preengineering books on my desk. They land with a thud, on top of my library book. Mom studies my book.

"What's this?" she asks, picking up my library copy of *Little Fires Everywhere.* "You check this out?"

"I thought . . ." I shake my head. So much for thinking that I might want to have a real conversation with my mom, not about ECEP. or MIT. For thinking maybe we could start our own book club at home. "Never mind."

Mom looks over at me, her face softening.

"It's good book," she says. "Maybe we talk about it after you read."

I gaze at her tentatively.

"After you score eight hundred on ECEP," she adds as she walks out of my room.

And there it is.

I lean back, close my eyes, and count the days to next

Saturday, when all this will be funny. When I'll get up on stage and bare my soul about my sad, sordid life. And tears will be dropping into vodka sodas, because it'll be so hysterical. Right now, it's just damn depressing.

33

Serene

THE DAY AFTER the *Vogue* shoot, Mom wakes up shivering. I put my hand to her forehead, even though she keeps flinching away, insisting she's fine. She's burning up.

"It was probably the car. It was so cold in there," I say. We only dozed for two hours, with a bunch of blankets, but still.

"You should have just woken me."

"I tried." I reach for the thermometer to put in her mouth, but Mom wriggles away.

"Just hand me the Tylenol," Mom says, putting her own hand to her forehead and gesturing to the nightstand by her bed, covered in pill bottles. "I don't need to know the temperature."

"Of course we need to know!"

Mom presses her lips stubbornly together. The sores on her mouth have multiplied.

"Mom, the sores!" I say. "How long have you had them? Does Dr. Herman know?"

Mom makes a face. "He's just going to give me more medicine, which will have more side effects. As it is, I can't sleep. I can't think. My whole head is a fucking chemo fog. I should just stop this whole thing."

I reach for the Tylenol, handing them to Mom with some water. She winces as she swallows, while I try to push the pain of her words away. I know she doesn't mean it. Still, it hurts. I leave her to go to the hallway to call Dr. Herman's nurse's after-hours line.

Thankfully, his nurse answers the call. As I quickly relay Mom's symptoms to her, she says she's gonna write Mom a prescription for more medication.

"Mom, Dr. Herman is writing you a prescription for the pharmacy—" I start to tell Mom as I walk back in. But she's already dozed off. I glance at the clock. The pharmacy doesn't open until nine thirty and I have school. I think about dialing Marcia to help. But I want to make sure Mom takes it. I dial my school instead and tell them I'm gonna be out.

For the next few hours, I sit at Mom's desk, waiting for the pharmacy to open as she sleeps off her fever, trying to compose a letter to my (maybe) relatives in Beijing.

~~Dear auntie/uncle,~~
~~To my Beijing family,~~

Hi,

My name is Serene Li. I'm Lily Li's daughter. I don't know if you still remember us, but my mom used to live in Beijing. She's an American fashion designer here now. I was born in the United States and I'm 17 years old. I'm also an aspiring fashion designer. I'm trying to find out more information about my dad. Do you know him? His name is Li Jin. As far as I know, he lives in Beijing. If you have any leads about him, please WeChat me at: sereneli310.

Looking forward to hearing from you!!

Best,

Serene

I cross my fingers when I'm done, and look around for stamps. I don't find any in Mom's drawer.

Instead, I find a genetic testing result from her primary care doctor. It's dated three years ago. And it shows my mom is BRCA positive.

"Mom, you knew you had BRCA and you didn't tell me?" I ask her later that morning, after I get back from the pharmacy.

She's in her bedroom watching *27 Dresses*, which is one of our favorite rom-coms. "I found the result in your desk."

She turns off the TV. "I didn't want to worry you. I didn't think it was a big deal at the time."

"Mom. It literally says on Google, people with BRCA

have a seventy percent chance of developing breast cancer."

"Yeah, but *breast* . . ." Mom dismisses it like it's not a big deal.

"It also increases your chances of getting pancreatic cancer, in case you haven't noticed."

She looks at me sharply.

"I've noticed."

I hand her the mouth sore pills and shake my head. "I just wish you had told me. . . ."

"Why? So you can make me cut out my breasts and my ovaries? It didn't even happen there," Mom says. "This is me. All of me. I'm sorry it's not perfect, but this is my body. Sores, tumors, and all."

Oh, Mom. I wish she hadn't misinterpreted my words—I don't mean it like that. I just wish she'd included me.

"I'm sorry your mother has such fucked-up genes." Mom sniffles.

"You don't have fucked-up genes." I hand her a tissue. "I just wish you'd told me. We're a *team*."

She puts her arms around me. "I know, bao-bier," she says. "But there are some things a mother needs to protect from her baby."

I don't have time to respond to Mom's comment because my phone dings with a text from Marcia.

Just heard from Vogue. They've decided to run the interview in Teen Vogue—it's going live tomorrow!

"Mom!" I turn the phone so she can see. Mom jumps out

of bed and we hold each other, savoring this moment. We did it! We refused to let the investors, the cancer, take this from us. And even though it's *Teen Vogue* instead of *Vogue* and it's me instead of her, still, we got here!

34
Lian

SERENE'S *TEEN VOGUE* profile blows up my phone over the weekend. The headline of the article reads "Designer Serene Li, Daughter of Lily Lee, Has Style and Taste—and a Few Ideas on What to Do Differently!"

SERENE!!! I text her. **CONGRATULATIONS!!!**

I stare at the stunning photographs of her, blushing at the revealing dress she's wearing. Whoa, the black lace underwear peeking through. Holy Buddha, did she design that piece? She looks smoking hot. Definitely my kind of ball gown. My mom would have a heart attack.

It just happened, lol, Serene writes back. **Did you read the piece?**

I inhaled the piece!

How'd I look? she asks.

This is it—my chance to get out of the friend zone! My fingers twitch as I tap. DO IT! 🔥 🔥 🔥 😍 😍

I hold my breath, waiting for Serene's reply. Is it too forward? Not forward enough? I put my hands together and pray to the American texting gods.

To my relief, she replies, 🦑 🦑

You wanna meet for lunch? I text.

Sure, she writes back. **Beach Club?**

Beach Club, whoa. The Beach Club is this super-exclusive country club right on the beach. You have to be able to name at least five Kardashians just to park. It goes without saying we're not members. But I assume Serene is. **12:30?** I ask. **I have something exciting to tell u too!**

Great, see u then.

Our first date. And somewhere really public, too!

I smile and turn back to my lines for my comedy set. I've been practicing in the shower, preparing for my meeting with Laugh Club. I've decided to go on Saturday. I walk back into my bathroom and prop up my phone against the medicine cabinet. This time, I'm going to record myself. I put a chair in front of my door and hit Record. Taking a deep breath, I start.

"Hi, I'm Lian and I'm from China. Which, in Sienna Beach, is basically like saying I'm from Best Buy. People come up to me like, 'Hey, can you fix my Roku TV?' No, dude, I can't fix your Roku!

"Either that or they go, 'You related to Jimmy Yang?' No. 'You sure? How about Andrew Yang? You gotta be related to a Yang!' I'm not. By the way, just to make matters clear, my name is Lian Chen. And for the last year and a half, I've been answering to *Liam* Chen.

"Now why would I do that, you ask? Why would I answer to a name that's not mine? Some people would say, Oh, that's beautiful. That's America, the need to assimilate. And it's like no, it's because there's too many of you and only one of me. I don't have enough time. That's why there's so many Asian people named Bob.

"Because we don't have time. We have to do twice the shit for half the attention. You know what that's like? That's like paying twice as much for shipping on Amazon and only getting half the stuff you bought—"

I'm interrupted by banging on my door.

"What you doing in there? Who you talking to?" Mom asks. She tries to open my door but the chair in front blocks her.

"No one," I say. I tap the button to stop recording on my phone.

She tries again to twist the doorknob. "Why you lock door?" she asks. "You watching porn on your computer?"

"No!"

"That stuff bad for you. Watch too much, you get addicted. You won't be able to have normal sex!"

Oh, what the fuck!

"It's true! I read an article!" Mom barks. "This poor man, he had this problem. Started when he was a kid. Watch too much R-rated movies!"

Before I know it, Mom starts giving me the whole story, about this guy's complete descent to poverty, starting with too much *Game of Thrones*, then soft-core porn, leading to hard-core porn, an erectile dysfunction, and finally, the complete inability to have sex without stuffing his pants full of peanut butter. I scream out, "I'm not watching porn!"

I scramble to remove the chair from my door—if this is the price, I'm never locking my door again. Mom walks into my room, surveying the scene like a detective.

I turn my computer monitor around. "See?"

"Then why you lock door?" Mom asks.

"I just want a tiny shred of privacy. Is that too much to ask?"

Mom places the back of her hand on my forehead, like I might be sick.

"Stop." I wriggle away. "What'd you come here to tell me?"

Mom tries to remember. "Oh yeah, I made congee. It's downstairs."

"That's it? That's why we had to have a screaming match about porn in the hallway?" I ask her. I glance at the clock. It's nearly eleven already. I'm meeting Serene for lunch soon. "I'm not hungry."

"But it's century egg and mushroom, your favorite!"

My stomach rumbles at the thought of century egg and mushroom. No doubt she spent hours at the stove, stirring it to perfection. I guess I could have one bite. I follow Mom down the stairs. As she lifts the lid off the pot, I'm in Beijing again. Walking around my favorite alleys, buying street food.

"I knew you'd like it." Mom smiles. "Do you want anything else?"

Yeah, a lock on my door so I can practice in peace. Instead, I shake my head and take five more bites. Because with Chinese mothers, it's always easier to eat more than to talk.

35

Serene

THE DAY THE *Teen Vogue* interview goes live, I sit on my bed stunned, staring at the first line—*Serene Li is anything but bland.* I never expected the piece to be all about me. I thought I was just filling in, playing the part, wearing the clothes. Instead, they devoted three whole paragraphs to my ideas and my vision for change.

My phone explodes with emails and messages from friends. Lian asks me to lunch, which I quickly agree to. Quinn and Amber text to say I slayed.

THAT DRESS, Quinn texts.

QUEEN, Amber adds.

I smile, savoring this moment. But it's the messages from the team, particularly Carmella and Ali, that mean the most. I'm so glad I got a chance to publicly apologize for what I said last year. And I'm so happy they finally got the recognition they deserve.

Mom walks into my room and I put down my phone, a little nervous. What'd she think of it, specifically the part about how I'd run things differently? Mom diffuses my worries with a smile.

"I'm proud of you," she says, sitting down on my bed.

"Really?" I ask.

"It was bold and courageous. You showed the world what you're about."

I bite my lip. "And Julien?" He's the one person from the company I hadn't heard from.

She rolls her eyes. "You know him. Always setting some higher goal. He thinks it should have been *Vogue* instead of *Teen Vogue* . . . ," she says.

"Is he mad I took your limelight?" I ask. Then I lift my eyes to meet hers and add, "Are you?"

Mom reaches out a hand. "Bao-bier, if I didn't want you to take the limelight, I wouldn't have asked you."

I smile.

"Anyway, don't worry about Julien. It's just his personality," Mom says. "He has to keep us all on our toes."

I want to tell Mom, I know. I know why she's put up with him all these years. She doesn't have to pretend. Instead, I ask, "Do you ever think about buying back his shares?"

Mom sighs. "I have a better chance in my condition scaling Everest than buying back his shares. . . . "

"Maybe if we hired a lawyer—"

"You just keep kicking ass in these interviews," Mom

says, getting up from my bed. "And let me handle the corporate affairs."

I feel the sting of disappointment that Mom still doesn't want me involved in the important decisions.

"Sure, Mom," I reply. I reach over to hug her, feeling her slender bones. She stumbles a bit, as though the weight of my hug is crushing her. "Are you OK?"

"I'm fine," she says, repositioning her shirt so I can't see her collarbone.

"Have you been taking the Creon?" I ask her, referring to the pills Dr. Herman prescribed her to help her absorb food.

"Yes, I've been taking the Creon!" she snaps back. She reaches into her cardigan pocket and pulls out a pill bottle with three red pills. As she gazes at them, she confesses, "Sometimes I think about the fact that I have to take these for the rest of my life . . . before every single meal. And I just think . . . is that even a life?"

I look up from the pills, alarmed. "What do you mean?"

"Nothing. I'm fine. It's just a lot." She stuffs the pills back in her pocket.

"You're doing great," I tell her.

Mom kisses the top of my head. "You're sweet. But I'd hardly call this doing great," she mutters. She searches for the right word. "I'm . . . passing time."

She falls silent, looking out at the crashing waves in front of my window.

I'm still thinking about my mom's words at the Beach Club later as I wait for Lian. I'm sitting outside in a long flowing yellow V-neck dress—this one my own design. I took a dress from last season's collection and made some changes to it. Now thin, soft strands of fringe flow in every direction when I move.

Lian arrives at twelve thirty on the dot. He's wearing slacks and a blue shirt, the sleeves folded above the elbow. I raise my eyebrows, impressed.

"Thought I'd make an effort, since I'm having lunch with the hottest fashion designer in town!" He smiles. He leans in and hugs me. "Congratulations!"

"Thanks!" I hug him back. I sit down and carefully unfold my letter to my relatives. I slip it to Lian as the waiter hands us menus.

"This is amazing," he says as he reads. "Really beautifully written."

"Are you sure? Not too overly sentimental or creepy? Or intrusive?"

He shakes his head.

"It's perfect. I'll translate it when I get home."

"Great!" I beam at the menu, starved. "Have you been here before?"

He shakes his head. "My parents only go to restaurants where they can bring their own stereo and blast it while we're eating."

The look on my face is priceless.

"Kidding! I think my mom's been here like once, with some ladies from her Bragathon club."

"Bragathon?"

He explains it's this club of Chinese mothers. "They get together every week for shopping and facials, and to brag about their kids."

"That actually sounds . . . kinda nice."

"You would definitely win this week," he says, smiling.

I blush.

I spot a few classmates looking over at us, but I couldn't care less. Lately, I've found myself on Instagram and Snap less and less, Sienna High's social gossip sliding further and further down my list of priorities.

"What was it like, doing the photo shoot?" Lian leans in and asks.

"Honestly, it all happened so quickly, there were so many lights and the photographer kept moving. He was just like shooting nonstop!"

"And your dress!"

I grin and lean closer. Our faces are almost touching at the table.

"You like it?" I ask.

"I, um . . . I like it a lot," he says. "I think you should wear it again, you know, like at the beach or something. Because I am like a really good photographer."

"Oh, you are?" I flirt.

He nods. "Like *the best*."

I laugh as a waiter comes by to take our orders. I order a Cobb salad and a lemonade while Lian gets the chicken tacos and a Shirley Temple. I tease him a little about his drink order, and he declares that Shirley Temples were literally the best part about moving to America.

"Well, until we started hanging out."

"Interesting." I smile inside.

"So was that why you were out yesterday?" he asks after the waiter leaves. "I was bummed when you weren't in school. I tried texting you."

"Yeah, kinda," I say, looking around. I don't want to tell him about my mom here. I pull out WeChat. I'd been so preoccupied with the shoot and taking care of Mom, I hadn't checked any of my messages.

"So I was thinking, maybe this PI I reached out to, he can give your letter to your relatives. Go over there and check it out."

"Wait, you reached out to a PI?" I blink in confusion. I suddenly start panicking, glancing over at the classmates sitting near us, wondering if they can hear us.

"Yeah! Well, first I tried to get my friend to go over to the address."

"You told your *friend*?" I ask.

"Just some buddies in Beijing." He studies me, not quite understanding the problem. "I figured mailing a letter takes so long . . . it'd be a lot faster if someone . . ."

His voice trails off.

The waiter arrives with our drinks, and I quickly grab mine. I can't believe he told people my most vulnerable secret. Why didn't Lian clear it with me first? And what if it gets out? The timing couldn't be worse—the article *just* came out!

I gulp down my lemonade, trying to keep my anxiety in check, while also trying to save our very nice lunch date.

"That was supposed to be private, what I told you," I mutter.

"It still is," he insists.

I shake my head at him. He still doesn't get it. That was *my* secret to tell, not his. This is *my* search for my dad.

Lian reaches for my hand as the waiter arrives with my food. I glance down at our fingers touching, then quickly move my hand. I hear Quinn's voice call out, "Serene!"

I jerk my head around and see Quinn walking over with Luke and Cameron. Oh great. Cameron's shooting daggers at Lian with his eyes.

"What are you guys doing?" Cameron asks, taking a seat.

The combination of Cameron and Lian sitting at the same table, and Lian spilling the beans on my dad, and Quinn looking at me like *Why are you dining with a puppet sock?* is too much and I jump up from the table.

"I have to go to the bathroom," I lie, and take off.

∘ ∘ ∘

In the bathroom, I splash cold water on my face.

Get it together, I tell myself as I stare at my reflection in the mirror.

He was just trying to help.

Still, the worry pokes me like sharp pins on the inside seam—what if Lian fundamentally doesn't get it. Doesn't get how private this is, how it *must* stay private.

I think about the people in Beijing googling my mother. Selling this info to the media. What if my mom finds out about this? Yet another scandal her wild daughter created! Another mess Julien can hold over me.

I take a deep breath and tell myself to chill. I dab my face with a paper towel and muster all my courage. I open the door and head back out.

Outside the bathroom door, I bump into Stu.

"Oh, hey, Serene," he says.

"Hey," I reply. I glance out toward Lian, Quinn, and Cameron. Cameron's staring at Lian like he's a commander in Guantanamo Bay.

"Lian told me about you guys at the beach. I just want to say, I think you're making a very wise decision."

I stare at Stu. *What? You've got to be joking. He knows too?*

36

Lian

"WE'RE JUST HAVING lunch," I tell Cameron as we wait for Serene to come back. Cameron helps himself to one of my tortilla chips without asking. Quinn's wearing this big furry thing, like she might have butchered a raccoon on the way over.

"With *my* girlfriend?" Cameron asks.

I look down at my Shirley Temple. They follow my gaze to the maraschino cherry. Now I'm deeply regretting my choice of beverage.

"Are you even a member?" Quinn asks. "I've never seen you here."

"You don't have to be a member to eat with a guest," I remind her.

"So she invited *you*," Cameron asks, digesting this supremely disturbing fact. "Why? D'you wash her car with your toothbrush or something?"

I fume at Cameron.

Serene walks back from the bathroom. I turn to her. "You OK?" I ask her.

"I'm fine," she mutters. I can tell from her face she's not. Is she still thinking about the PI? I know she's pissed at me. I shouldn't have talked to him without her.

Cameron turns to me. "I think you'd better leave."

I glance over at Serene, waiting for her to say *No, he's staying.* But she doesn't say anything. She keeps her gaze glued to the table. I take my cue.

Slowly, I get up from the table. "Thanks for lunch, Serene," I whisper.

I exit the club as calmly as I can, trying not to let my anger show. As I push on the double glass doors, it brings me straight back to when I first came to the school.

I'd worked so hard to move past those awful memories. That feeling of being unwanted, always on the outside. I thought I was done with all that. But apparently all it takes to get right back there is one wrong move.

I drop my keys on the kitchen table when I get home. Unfortunately, they land against Mom's glass vase, making a loud, jarring noise that sends Mom running over.

"Be *careful*!" she shrieks. "That's crystal vase! I got it for my wedding!"

"Sorry," I mutter.

Mom looks at me.

"What's matter? You sad because you bad grade?" she asks, suddenly looking even sadder than me.

"No."

"Then why you so sad?"

I take a seat and start playing with the petals of one of her hydrangeas, until Mom reminds me the flower is delicate. She reaches over for her scissors and starts cutting the stems of the wilted ones. I watch her work, debating whether to get it off my chest.

"I'm sad because I made a mistake. I wanted to do something good, but I ended up making things worse," I finally say.

Mom stops cutting. Her face softens. "You talking about the immigrant kids you helping?" she asks.

I stare at her for a second, not fully understanding. Then I remember. The community service project in San Gabriel Valley, that's what she thinks is up.

"Yeah," I lie.

"Everybody make mistake. Best way is to apologize," she tells me, putting her scissors down and sitting next to me.

"But you never apologize."

She frowns at me.

"Because I'm always right."

I try not to laugh. "Right."

She picks up the scissors and starts working again. As she

changes the water and adds sugar, and a drop of bleach, I look over at her by the sink.

"Mom . . . have you ever wanted something so badly to work out, because if it doesn't it could break you?" I ask quietly.

Mom stares down at the faucet.

"Yes," she finally says. "When I had to give up my flower shop. I was so upset, I almost took out second loan from bank to rent this place in new mall. Almost put you and your sister college money in jeopardy."

I inhale a sharp breath. *Mom* risking our college money? I just can't imagine it. She's so obsessed with good universities.

She shakes her head, hugging her vase of wilting hydrangeas to her chest, drenched with shame. "I just didn't want to lose. I wanted to save the shop."

"It's OK, Mom. I understand."

She looks over at me and sighs. "I ultimately realized I can't compete."

"Yes, you can! That situation was just rigged—"

"No, I can't. And that's OK. I'll find satisfaction in other ways." She hands me the vase.

I help her put it back in the center of the table, sprinkling some of her flower food on. I wish there was a human food to sprinkle on us, to make us bloom again.

Mom takes a seat next to me and sits back to admire her arrangement. Then she reaches over and squeezes my hand.

"I know you worried about your score. But everything will work out. You see."

I give Mom a half smile, glad she believes in me, even though what she thinks she believes . . . is an illusion.

37

Serene

I WATCHED AS Lian got up and left from the club. I could see the hurt in his eyes, and I knew I should have probably gone after him, but at that moment, all I could think about was Stu, and all those people in Beijing he told. My mind was a runway of worries. Headlines that the tabloids, the investors, my *friends* are dying to run:

Serene Li Searches for Long-Lost Dad.

Serene Li, Abandoned as a Baby, Desperate to Find True Origins.

I know Lian doesn't understand. But he's *supposed* to understand. Supposed to know the words that are so impossible to utter. That's what makes him different.

That's why I stay up late thinking of his lips on mine.

Instead, it's Cameron who lingers next to me after Quinn leaves lunch early for lacrosse practice.

"So whose idea was it that you wear the dress?" he asks.

"Mine," I tell him.

His eyebrows raise. I can tell he has opinions, but he keeps quiet.

"What?"

"I just thought it was . . . a lot, that's all," he says.

"A lot?"

He nods, eyes scanning the beach beneath us, enjoying the view of women much more scantily clad than I was in *Teen Vogue*.

"Funny you didn't say that when I sent you the pic," I fire back.

"That was for *me*," he says. "This is for everyone."

I snap a breadstick in half, at this insinuation of what I can and cannot wear. "It's a dress."

"It's lingerie. My *mother* saw it." He leans in and hisses, "Shit, I get enough of a hard time about you with her as it is, without adding this to the mix."

"What's that supposed to mean?"

He doesn't reply.

I fume. "I'm sorry the couture dress my mother designed is getting in the way of your mother-son relationship."

"Forget my mom. You know what? *I'm* not cool with it. Randy said the entire football team was looking at it in the locker room. What do you think they're doing with the copies?"

My face burns. "You're a jerk," I say as I reach into my purse and dump some cash on the table. I get up.

Cameron chases after me. He catches up to me when we're outside.

"Serene, wait!" he says.

"I won't be dress shamed!" I tell him.

"I'm not," he says, pulling me in for a hug. "I just . . . got a little crazy, that's all."

His hands wrap around me, and at first I resist, but it feels nice to be touched. And I give in to it, letting him kiss my neck, nibble on my ears, as I close my eyes. Trying to forget about his words. Trying to forget about Lian. It's easier than confronting all my feelings right now.

Cameron switches tones as he kisses me.

"So tell me about the interview . . . was it hot?"

I nod. I know what he wants, and I want to give it to him. I want to tell him about the sexy shoot, how the wind from the fan went right up my dress. How the photographer told me how beautiful I was and shot me in every angle. How my breasts were squeezed so tight in the dress at one point, it was hard to breathe.

But I don't. Instead, I tell him about afterward. How I tried to lift my mother out of the car, and I couldn't. How I texted him but he didn't come. How we had to sleep in the garage. How I'm scared shitless she's going to stop taking her cancer meds.

Cameron interrupts me with a finger to my mouth.

"Let's just kiss," he says, leaning in and quieting me with the brush of his lips.

I envy the fact that for him this is something he can just turn off with the heat of a kiss, but for me, this is my life. I wipe my lips, straighten out my bra, and walk to my car.

On my way home from the club, I stop by a post office.

I don't wait for Lian's translation of the letter to my relatives. I just use Google Translate to copy down the characters on one of the blank cards they sell at the post office. My characters are boxy and imperfect, and my grammar's probably all messed up. But Mom's right. I can't wait for a boy to solve my problems. I have to solve them myself.

I mail the letter.

Afterward, I look out at the waves crashing across from the post office, and smile. I hope my boxy Chinese characters make it across the ocean and carry me closer to my dad.

38
Lian

I PRACTICE MY set the rest of the weekend for my meeting with the Laugh Club manager. Mom makes me sign up for ECEP this Saturday, which I have no intention of actually going to. Then I pace my room, thinking of Serene. I've got my whole apology speech worked out.

I'm sorry. I shouldn't have talked to my friends or the private detective without your permission. But I was just trying to help, and I swear, I didn't tell my friends about your dad, just if they'd go to the address as a favor, to deliver a letter.

No, no, no, I decide. Scratch that last part. I have to *own* the apology. It can't be one of those "sorry, but" speeches. I hate those.

I overstepped. I realize this now. This is a personal search and decision and I fully respect that. I'm here to support you, to help in whatever way I can. I'm not here to get in the way or make things harder.

I pull out my laptop so I can continue writing my thoughts down. Sometimes it's easier to get it out on paper first, just like my sets.

I hope you know that I just wanted to get the letter there quicker because I don't want you to wait any longer. You've waited long enough. My actions stemmed from a place of ~~love~~ genuine care.

I don't want to scare her away with the *L* word. I continue typing.

These last few weeks have been amazing for me. I loved walking down the streets of San Gabriel Valley with you. Sharing our hopes and dreams. Hearing about your life growing up here and all the things you've had to go through. You inspire me, Serene. You make me feel like it's possible I belong here, even when all other signs point the other way. I guess I was so excited for your dad to get to know what he's been missing out on that I sort of jumped the gun. And for that I'm so sorry.
I hope you'll forgive me and give me another chance.
Yours,
Lian

I practice the speech over and over again, like I do my sets, until I've memorized it by heart.

On Monday, when Serene doesn't show up to Chinese Club, I email her my speech, along with her translated letter to her relatives.

Stu sees me as I'm leaving campus. He's crossing the courtyard from the guidance counselor's office.

"Hey, man, what are you doing this Saturday?" he asks.

"This Saturday, I'm pretending to take a test, while actually going to an audition," I tell him.

"Bummer, I thought maybe we could hang out again," he says. "What audition?"

I look down at my feet. What if he laughs in my face when he hears? Then again, we have gotten into the sharing-crushes-on-cousins part of our friendship.

"It's for stand-up comedy," I tell him.

The shock on his face is not quite as bad as his hairy chest, but it's up there.

"WOW," he says.

"Hey, you've never *seen* me onstage," I tell him. Then again, I haven't either.

He holds up his hands. "I'm not saying you can't do it. Where is this audition?" he asks.

"In Hollywood."

Stu studies me. "What are you planning on wearing?"

I look down at my Old Navy jeans and 30-percent-off Nike shirt, with a sloth hanging off the swoosh, that says: *Just Do it. Later . . .*

He shakes his head. "Oh no no no. You can't go to a night club in Hollywood dressed like that."

"Why not?"

"Why not? Oh, you're funny!" Stu chuckles, pointing to me.

"OK, so what should I wear? Tell me what to get!" I ask.

"How should I know?" Stu shrugs, looking down at his own joggers and flame T-shirt. I think he's going for combustible yet comfortable.

Cameron and Luke walk out of the locker room, along with the rest of the water polo team, as we're talking. Cameron's got on a hoodie under a tight jacket, and jeans so ripped, it looks like his boxers grew sleeves.

"Now *that's* cool," Stu says, admiring them.

They walk by us, like we're a couple of trees. Cameron doesn't even give me an extra glance, even though he and I shared a table at the club.

"Hey, Luke," Stu calls out, waving.

Luke keeps walking. After they leave, Stu and I sit down on the curb by the grass in the courtyard. The sun bounces from the trees and illuminates the disappointment on Stu's face.

"Why do you want to be a part of the water polo team again?" I ask.

"It was my only identity," he says, pulling a weed from the grass next to us and frowning at it in his hand.

I nod, feeling that. In Beijing, my friends knew me to be

funny. That all went to quicksand when I got here. I think about how hard it's been for me to build it again.

I look over at Stu.

"It's not your only identity," I offer.

He glances up, hopefully. I bump my shoulder lightly with his.

"You're also a nerd, remember?"

He gives me a toothy smile.

39
Serene

READING LIAN'S EMAIL, I feel awful about lunch. I should have asked him to stay, and not been so worried about what he might say to my friends.

And I should have gone to Chinese Club. Instead, I decided to go to Pinkberry with Quinn, thinking that we could talk about Cameron, just the two of us.

"So I don't understand, he was jealous of your *dress*?" Quinn asks, holding her frozen yogurt cup.

We're in line for toppings. I point to the cut-up strawberry mochi.

"No, he was just mad," I say. "Said it was too revealing."

Quinn rolls her eyes. "Yeah, but it's *couture*."

I smile at her, grateful for the words.

"So you liked it? The spread?"

"I thought it was . . . dope!" she says.

She takes so long saying "dope" that I wonder. If this

were *her* in *Teen Vogue*, I'd be so hyped, Pinkberry would have to get ten pounds more of mochi.

"What's wrong?" I ask. We take our froyos and sit down at a table outside, under the shade.

"Nothing," she says. "Just . . . you could have warned me. I told my dad the reporter plastered you with alcohol. And in the piece, you said you talked to him because you were mad at your mom. Sounded like you knew exactly what you were doing."

Wow. Can't she just be happy for me that I smoothed things over? I always pictured that one day, when I'd climbed to the apex of some undeniably high mountain—like *Teen Vogue*, for instance—that the dynamics would change. Quinn and I, we'd finally be equals. Real best friends. Instead, Quinn still makes everything about her.

"First of all, I never asked you to tell your dad that."

"You were freaking out. You needed my help. What was I supposed to say?" she asks.

"Not that!" I blurt out. "Did you know I obsessively googled the reporter for a whole year, just to make sure he didn't get fired? That his career didn't go up in flames because of what happened?"

Quinn scoops a big spoonful of frozen yogurt. "It *should* go up in flames. Lying to you like that, telling you he was a fashion student!"

"But he didn't plaster us with drinks, is my point," I tell her.

"Whatever," Quinn says. "I did what I did."

"And I'm grateful. Really grateful." I look down at the soft mochi pieces hardening next to the freezing yogurt. "But . . . I also felt like I owed you. For an entire year."

Quinn stares at me, yogurt dripping from her spoon.

"We're friends," Quinn reminds me.

"Sometimes, it feels like you're the headliner and I'm just standing around, trying to scalp a ticket," I confess quietly.

A couple of girls in their tweens walk inside Pinkberry. They have *Teen Vogues* tucked under their arms.

Quinn points to the girls. "Not anymore."

I take a deep breath and lean in. Here goes.

"Then I need you to accept something. I don't think I like Cameron anymore," I tell her.

Quinn puts her fingers to her temples like she's having a massive brain freeze. "Nooooo," she says. "You guys are breaking up? That's gonna be *so* complicated for me and Luke. . . ."

I give her a look. Quinn stops agonizing over what this will mean for her.

"So what? You like someone else?" Quinn asks.

I nod.

"Please tell me it's not your new club president," she begs, putting her hands together.

I feel my skin grow hot. "So what if it is?" I ask.

"It'd be social suicide. You'd go from headliner to pitching a homeless tent in the parking lot." She puts a hand up, correcting herself. "I'm sorry, an unhoused tent. You wouldn't even be able to scalp tickets."

It stings, hearing her put it like that.

"It's not *me*, Serene," Quinn says. "It's Sienna Beach. I didn't make up the rules."

I stab my spoon into the yogurt, wishing she weren't right. Wishing Sienna Beach weren't so merciless.

"You gotta ask yourself, is it really worth it?" she asks.

"Serene." The sales team calls for me later in the office.

I zap myself from replaying Quinn's words and get up from my desk. All week, the team's been running social media ads and behind-the-scenes pics of the shoot, capitalizing on the momentum of my piece. I walk over to the sales team desks.

"Everyone wants that dress! But it's couture—it's one of a kind! What do we do?" they ask.

I think about what Mom said about diffusing couture to street wear.

"Design meeting in forty-five minutes! Let's figure out how to diffuse the tulle!" I call out.

"No offense, but we usually do our design meetings on Fridays," Jonathan says.

I raise an eyebrow. "Oh. Well, that's OK, you can just sit back and listen. We can have the junior designers lead this time."

Carmella smiles. Later, she comes up and thanks me. As

all the designers go back to their desks, I ask her if she'll show me how she uses software to realize concepts digitally. I notice the junior designers do most of their design work digitally, whereas my mom still sketches by hand.

"'Course, no problem!" Carmella says.

She makes space for me next to her desk, and I watch as she works magic with her mouse and keyboard to craft patterns, graphics, and designs, and even fit them to 3D virtual models. What usually takes my mom hours takes mere minutes.

"So cool!" I exclaim. "Can I try?"

"Sure!" she says, handing me the mouse. She teaches me how to sew and drape fabrics over the avatars.

"It's just like real sewing," she says. "Except if you make a mistake, you don't have to throw the whole piece away."

"This is mind-blowing," I say as I play around with the tools. And *such* a game changer! Stitching is my greatest weakness. I hadn't quite inherited my mom's flawless touch. But with these tools, I can finally sew without fear!

"It's what got me through fashion school," Carmella says. "The other students, they were always buying all the nicest fabrics and outsourcing their designs to professionals who would sew everything. Meanwhile, I was staying up all night sewing whatever scraps of cloth I could find."

I look over at Carmella. I had no idea things were so unfair in fashion school.

"My mother was a single mom too. A cook in a taqueria,"

Carmella says. "She thought I was crazy wanting to go to fashion school, but I told her I needed to follow my dream."

Carmella opens a file and shows me some of her personal designs, not just for dresses, but for swimwear and even shoes.

"Carmella! These are incredible! Do you ever think of starting your own line?"

"Maybe someday," she says. "After I pay off my student loans. That's why I'm here working at Lily Lee. She's one of my heroes, your mom. The fact that she did it all on her own . . . as a POC woman . . . it gives me hope that one day, I can too."

We both turn to look at my mom through her office glass. She's sitting at her desk, sketching. There's something wrong with her hand and she accidentally knocks over a bottle of water on her desk.

"I'll be right back," I tell Carmella.

I walk inside Mom's office. She's holding her right hand in her left, massaging it, staring at the spot on her carpet where the spilled water pooled.

"You OK?" I ask. "Don't worry, we'll clean it up."

I start walking to the door to get Marcia, but Mom gestures to me, *No.* "Close the blinds." She points.

"What's wrong?" I ask as I pull the blinds closed. She lets go of her right hand, which starts to tremble slightly.

"It's been like this all day. It started with tingling, but

now it's shaking. I can't stand it," she says. "How am I supposed to draw, to design?"

I walk over and take her hand in mine, trying to steady it.

"Mom, you can totally still design. You can use the computer, Carmella was just showing me—"

"No, I'm done," she says. "I won't be tortured this way by the chemo. I'd rather live the rest of my days to the fullest."

To my horror, she takes the chemo pills Dr. Herman gave her and chucks them across the room. They hit the carpet and spill all over. As if that wasn't bad enough, Mom gets up from her desk, walks over, and crushes them with her stiletto heel. I scream.

"Mom! Stop!" I plunge to the carpet and try to save the precious pills. "What are you doing?"

"It's *my* life," she says, grabbing the pills out of my hand and throwing them away. "*I* get to decide what goes into my body. Give me those."

I scoot away from her, clenching the pills tightly in my fist. How can she say that? Doesn't she understand it's not just her life, it's mine too? She'd be giving up on *me*.

Tears drip onto the carpet. I collapse, a hysterical mess.

Mom joins me on the floor and tries to calm me. "Honey, I'm sorry! But years is just *one* way to measure life. I can live on through my designs."

"No you can't!" I fire back. I get up and run to her desk

and start ripping up her design book.

"Stop!" Mom commands.

I ignore her. "Will these designs attend my graduation? Or walk me down the aisle at my wedding, because Dad sure as hell won't!"

With every rip, Mom cries as though her heart is being ripped open. But I don't care. Mine already got shattered a long time ago when one parent walked out. I'm not about to lose a second.

40
Lian

SERENE FINALLY CALLS me that night. I'm making last-minute changes to my set and I immediately close my laptop.

"Hi!" I answer, putting a chair in front of my bedroom door and walking into my bathroom so we can talk in private. "Did you get my email? I'm so sorry."

"I'm sorry too. I overreacted. It's just . . . I've been going through a lot lately."

"You don't have to explain. I way overstepped."

"No, but I do," she says, taking a deep breath. "My mom . . . ," she whispers. "She has cancer."

I sit on the cold floor, taking it in.

"I'm so sorry," I say. "How long have you known?"

"About a month now," she says. There's a tremor in her voice as she says, "It's stage three pancreatic cancer."

Oh *fuck*. I lean my head back against the shower door.

It's so unfair this has to happen to Serene. And for a whole month, she's been going through this?

I think back to all the times she's been at Chinese Club. I have no idea how she held it together, how she's being strong. I would be a complete mess. Despite all my complaints about Mom, if anything *actually* happened to that porn-bashing, rose-scented madwoman, I'd be on the floor bawling for at least a century!

"Serene . . . ," I say.

Quietly, Serene starts to cry. It breaks my heart hearing her weep.

"Meet me at the beach. Point Sienna. Ten minutes," I say.

It takes a Herculean effort to sneak out of the house. Mom wants to know whether I'd finished *Little Fires Everywhere*, and what I thought of it. I want to talk about it with her but not now.

"It's a great book," I say. "I liked all the class and race themes."

"Me too!" Mom says, pulling up a chair. I could tell she was eager to get into the book with me. I look anxiously at the door. Serene's probably already on her way.

"You know what I like? The mothers in the story."

"Yes, each one trying so hard to protect child," Mom says.

"Yeah. But they also gave their kids space," I point out. I glance at the clock on the wall. I have seven minutes to get to Point Sienna.

Mom crosses her arms, catching my drift. "Where you wanna go, anyway?"

I make something up off the top of my head. "I left my graphing calculator at Stu's house when I went over there to eat bad Chinese food."

Mom puts both hands over her cheeks. "Graphing calculator so expensive! Yours color! Go go go!" she cries.

I dash out and jump in the car. I speed toward Point Sienna, the windy beach halfway between my house and Serene's. It's a small beach, off the map to tourists. I like it because it's so windy, the seagulls look like they're flying in place on a treadmill.

I wait in the parking lot, staring up at the stars. Serene steps out of her car minutes later, wrapped in a blanket. As she takes off her flip-flops and walks onto the soft sand, I run over and give her a hug.

"I'm so sorry," I say as she leans in.

Her soft tears press against my shirt as the ocean wind blows goose bumps on our arms. We walk until we get to the edge of the dry sand, where the waves have lightly patted the surface. She takes the blanket and offers half to me. We sit side by side, her head against my shoulder, snuggled together.

"Why didn't you tell me earlier?" I ask.

She shrugs. "Have you ever kept a secret for so long that it just, I dunno, becomes a part of you?"

I nod. I've been doing it with my parents my whole life.

"Can they do something? Surgery or chemo?"

Serene punches the sand with her fist. "My mom's decided she doesn't want to do chemo. It's too much for her." In the moonlight, I can see her chin quivering.

I wish I could do something to stop this pain. She shakes her head, her wet tears falling into the ocean mist.

"You know what she said to me today? She said it's *her* life," she says. She hurls the words at the waves. "Like it has nothing to do with me, whether she takes that little pill or not. Like I haven't been spending every single waking second of the last month taking care of her."

Her voice breaks as she says that last part, and I hold her as she sobs.

"You know what the worst part is," she mutters, in between the cries, "I can't even get mad at her. The cancer stole that too. . . ."

"Yes you can," I say.

Serene laughs. I smile, glad I can make her laugh even during this shitty night.

"Sure you can. Get mad, right here." I turn to the navy waves, bathed in moonlight. "Here, watch me." I jump up and scream into the waves, "FUCK YOU, CANCER, YOU TURTLE EGG RAT BASTARD—LEAVE SERENE'S MOM THE FUCK ALONE!"

Serene runs into the water and joins me. "YEAH, FUCK YOU, CANCER! I HATE YOU. YOU'RE A PIECE OF SHIT!"

The two of us take turns shouting into the void. I cheer Serene on as she lets out a scream so piercing, it fills the night sky.

Afterward, the two of us stand in the moonlight. The waves purr beneath our feet. Serene reaches over and takes my hand, wrapping her fingers tightly around mine, while my heart thumps. She looks so beautiful in the moonlight. I want so badly to kiss her. But I remind myself she doesn't need that from me right now. What she needs most is a friend.

And so we stand, hand in hand, watching the ocean and listening to the waves, and letting our hands do all the work of saying the words we can't just yet.

41

Serene

I'M FALLING IN love with Lian.

The thought swallows me like a sneaker wave as I drive home. He's the only person I can show my shit reel to. Who can make me laugh even when I'm at my most rock bottom. Who doesn't judge me and understands instinctively what I need.

He's my rock, just like I'm Mom's. The one person it's OK to show the threads tattering at the edges.

Walking back into my house, I try and hide the joy on my face as Mom sits at the dining room table, staring at a glass of Ensure. She eats so little now, she's had to resort to the supplemental drink for old people. It makes me feel guilty that I'm falling in love while my mom's chugging liquid dinner.

But maybe Lian's right.

Cancer doesn't hold all the cards.

I think of the two of us screaming at the waves. It felt so good to let it out.

"Hey," Mom says. "Where've you been?"

"Nowhere," I say, heading up the stairs. I'm still so mad at her for stopping the pills, I can't bring myself to talk to her.

"Oh, Dr. Herman called," she says.

I stop, and look over at her hopefully. "He convince you to get back on chemo?"

"No. He wanted to talk to you. Your genetic results are back."

I clutch the staircase railing. *Fuck*. Just when I finally found someone I really like. Just when I've managed to stop thinking about the BRCA thing. I put my arms protectively in front of my chest, look down at my two girls, and shake my head.

"I don't want to know anymore," I say.

"What?"

I toss Mom back her line. "I've changed my mind. It's *my* life, right?"

"But you've already done the test—"

"What do you care? You were against me getting it in the first place!"

"That was before I knew how shitty this thing is. I don't want you to have to go through it. Especially . . ." She puts a hand over her mouth, but it's too hard to contain her emotions.

I fight the tears in my eyes.

"Especially when you're not around," I finish for her as I walk quietly up the steps.

Back inside my room, I close the door and lie on the ground. I listen to the waves crashing, slamming one curveball after another onto my shore. I want to laugh out loud at the absurdity of me thinking maybe I can actually have a normal life and find love and joy. For thinking cancer doesn't hold all the cards.

That night, I tap open WeChat and write to the private detective.

Thanks for your offer to help. I'd love to find my dad Li Jin. Can we start by going to this address and seeing if the people who live there now might have any leads?

I copy and paste my relatives' address and my letter to them.

Lian's right. I don't have time to wait for snail mail to arrive. Not when I have a BRCA result hanging over me.

I send the message, then forward my *Teen Vogue* piece to the 271 Li Jins I find on WeChat.

And I wait.

I picture my dad opening his phone in the morning, seeing the notification. Clicking on the link. Spending the rest of his morning staring at my picture, trying to compose the perfect email to send back to me. What do you say to a long-lost daughter you've never met? It's gotta be as terrifying as contacting a long-lost father.

Somewhere between one a.m. and two a.m., I drift asleep. In my dream, I meet my dad and together, we open my BRCA result. It's positive. I'm one of the 1 percent of people with a 65 percent chance of developing breast cancer and a 70 percent chance of ovarian cancer. I have a ten-fold risk of developing pancreatic cancer. I turn to my dad, wanting a hug. But he shakes his head. He can't bear the thought of losing me again. So he walks away.

I wake up in a panic, gasping for air, sweat dripping off my pajamas. I immediately grab my breasts, feeling around for lumps, pressing at my armpits. I have no idea what I'm doing. I squeeze my boobs like oranges.

Finally, when I have poked and probed my entire body to nearly bruising, I fall back against my pillow.

For the rest of the night, I lie awake obsessively checking WeChat—my dad hasn't replied—and wondering what I do if the result is positive. Will my dad still want to get to know me?

42
Lian

I RUN ONTO campus the next day and grab Stu. "HEY, NERD!" I shake him. "Guess what? We held hands!"

"Fuck, yeah! THAT'S GREAT!" He gives me a high five. "What'd her hand feel like?"

"It was amazing." I smile. I close my eyes, trying to remember the softness of her skin, the urgency of her fingers as we held on to each other, looking out at the thundering waves.

"Well, was it well lotioned? Did it smell like coconuts?" he asks. "C'mon, give me some details!"

Cameron rolls by with his skateboard, nearly knocking over Stu. "Get the fuck out of the way, loser."

"Hey!" I call after him. "Who are you calling 'loser'?"

"Yeah!" Stu chimes in. "You're about to lose your girl-friend!"

Cameron jumps off his skateboard and I freeze. I pull

on Stu's arm, for him to shut his trap, and we bolt for the library.

Inside the library, I spot Serene by the Business aisle. I ditch Stu to go and talk to her. She's wearing a loose, baggy pullover sweatshirt and wide-legged pants. She's practically swimming in it and yet, she still looks gorgeous. She can literally wear a plastic bag and still look amazing.

I smile at her. "Hey!"

"Hey! You get home OK?" she asks, taking a book called *Capital Structure and Corporate Governance* off the shelf and putting it on top of another thick book, *The End of Fashion*.

"Whoa. That's some heavy-duty reading there," I say, pointing to her book.

Serene looks down. "Someone's gotta disrupt the industry," she says.

"Here, I have something for you," I say. I dig into my pocket and pull out a small plastic rectangle.

"What is it?" she asks, gazing down at it.

"It's a backspace key. I got it off my keyboard." I turn it around and show her. "See, I scratched out the word 'delete' and wrote in 'FUCK CANCER' with a permanent marker. Now you can pound on it every time you delete something. . . ."

She throws her arms around me before I even finish the sentence.

"I love it!"

Cameron walks by the library window and glances in.

He sees us hugging, but Serene doesn't seem to care.

"You have no idea how much I needed this today," she says.

"What's wrong?"

She doesn't reply. I wonder if it's just the stress of everything. A fun idea pops into my head.

"Hey, you wanna help me go shopping?" I ask. "I need something cool to wear to my stand-up audition on Saturday."

"Of course! I'd *love* to," she says.

We make a date to meet at the mall after her work, at six thirty. And I spend the next six hours trying not to smile like an idiot in class, while dodging Cameron's icy glares.

We meet at the Grove in the evening. I beam when I see Serene. She's wearing a short, flowing dress—she must have changed at the office.

"Did you make that?" I ask.

"Yes! I'm learning how to design from Carmella in my office," she says. "Did you know you can cut a dress online and there are these avatars that will walk down a virtual runway in it?"

"I can believe it. Pretty soon, we'll all just be sitting around in our houses naked," I joke. "Wearing virtual clothes."

Serene laughs and taps me on the stomach lightly with her hand.

We walk upstairs to 7 for All Mankind. According to Serene, all I really need to look cool is the perfect pair of jeans.

"And confidence," she says. "That's how Beyoncé can rock a metal corset."

"Oh, I can rock a metal corset," I fire back.

Serene bursts out laughing. Then her face falls a little.

"What's wrong?" I ask.

"Nothing . . . just this test I took." She shakes her head.

"What test?" I ask.

"I'm about to get a label . . . a private label," she replies quietly.

I figure it's something for her company—I bet she'll rock the label. Serene turns her attention to the jeans stacked on the table, grabbing enough to fully clothe a denim marching band.

Most of the jeans she picks out are "distressed" in some way.

"You know we can just rough these up for free, right?" I ask her as she pushes me into the changing room. "All we have to do is tie me to the back of your car and go off-roading at the beach!"

"Get inside." She rolls her eyes.

Five minutes later, I come out in a pair of ash-gray jeans with more holes than a golf course. "What do you think?"

"Wow," she says. "That looks *amazing*."

"Whoa—that is a strong word. Are you sure you want to

use it right now? You might want to save it, you know, for the metal corset."

She giggles.

I glance at the mirror. "Not bad," I say. As I'm checking out the perfectly distressed holes on my pants, Serene tells me she's reached out to the private detective.

"Really?" I ask, surprised. "What'd he say?"

"He's going to hand-deliver the letter to the address!" she says, lifting her crossed fingers.

"That's amazing!" I jump in the air, a little too enthusiastically (I might have ripped another couple of holes).

Serene laughs and tells me I've probably just made the pants more valuable.

After I change out of the pants and pay for them, we walk outside. It's a beautiful night, and I wish I could take her to dinner.

"Do you have to go home?" I ask.

"I have some time," she says.

"Great! Want to grab a bite?"

"Sure, where were you thinking?" she asks. "Din Tai Fung in Century City?"

"Oh, if you want dim sum, there's only one place. . . ." I grin. "C'mon, I'll show you."

That night, under the shiny mini disco ball hanging from the ceiling of our private karaoke room, Serene and I feast on delicious homemade dumplings. There's a parade of food in delicate bamboo baskets as Lizzo and Shawn Mendes serenade us over the karaoke speakers.

"How'd you find this place?" Serene asks.

I grin. "It sounds depressing but I literally googled 'dim sum and karaoke' one day. I used to go to KTV a lot in Beijing with my friends."

"And you come here by yourself?" she asks.

"No . . ." I flush. "Yes." I have come here by myself to practice my sets. It's the only place where I can get an actual mic and a private room.

Serene smiles. "It's OK, I sing in the shower too."

Hearing this, I toss her the mic.

She looks down at it for a second, then wipes her mouth and grins. She takes the karaoke remote and finds a song.

As Serene sings "Good as Hell," dancing along to the music, I lean back on the couch, smiling at her. She lets her hair down. When she gets to the part in the lyrics, "If he don't love you anymore, just walk your fine ass out the door," she points to me.

I put my hand over my heart, pretending to be crushed. "Just so you know, I'll never walk my fine ass out the door," I joke with her.

Serene finishes the song, then sits down next to me. "Really?" she asks. "What if I'm not always like this?"

I study her eyes. "What do you mean?" I ask.

She hugs her knees to her chin on the leather lounge.

"Like if there's something about me that has to

change . . . ," she whispers.

I shake my head, not following. "Why would you have to change?" I ask. "You're perfect, just the way you are—"

"There's this test," Serene finally blurts out. She covers her head with her arms. "It's called BRCA. And it's for cancer."

"So?"

"So I took it. And I'm scared. I'm worried about finding out my result later this week."

I reach for her hands. "Listen to me, you don't have cancer."

"Not now. But if it's positive, I will. It's only a matter of time," she says, hiding her head again. She mutters from underneath her arms, "I have like a seventy percent higher chance of getting it."

"So? You know what the increased risk of earthquake is living in Los Angeles? Ninety percent. Or wildfires! Or Sienna Beach falling into the ocean?" I ask. "We have a higher chance of becoming toasted algae than you getting cancer."

Serene peeks out at me.

I look firmly into her eyes. "And yet there's nowhere else I'd rather be."

"Even if I have to get a fake boob bra?" she asks.

"What are you talking about?"

"I might have to do preventative surgery. Like Angelina Jolie, and cut off my breasts. And I'll have to get a fake boob bra and it'll look like there's a boob growing out of my neck or something."

I put a finger to my chin, picturing this. "That actually sounds kind of sexy. Can I help pick it out?"

Serene smacks my arm lightly with her hand.

"No, but seriously . . . ," she says. "I might have to start taking estrogen pills. Go into teenage menopause."

"You're not going into teenage menopause."

"But what if I do? I'll lose all sexual desire. I'll look like an old lady!"

"I love old ladies."

Serene chuckles. "Are you sure you're not freaked out by any of this?"

"Why would I be freaked out?" I ask.

She bites her lip, looking down. "Because it's cancer?"

I can tell how much this has been tearing her up inside, and I put a hand to her chin and lift her gaze to mine. "I'm not freaked out." Just to prove it, I grab the remote. I scour the list and pick a song.

As "Just the Way You Are" by Bruno Mars comes on, Serene throws her head back and laughs.

"Oh, her eyes, her eyes," I sing to Serene. "Make the stars look like they're not shinin' . . ."

Serene blushes as I sing.

When I get to the refrain, I throw my whole body into it, kneeling down on the floor and staring into Serene's eyes. "When I see your face, there's not a thing that I would change. 'Cause you're amazing, just the way you are!"

Serene puts a hand over her heart.

"That was . . . ," she says when I'm finished, at a loss for words. We both laugh. "You're *really* good."

"Thanks." I beam. "You should see some of my friends in Beijing. They're next level."

She grins. "I'd love to meet them."

"You will," I say, sitting down next to her and reaching for some water. She bumps her shoulder lightly into mine.

"Did you ever go with your girlfriend?" she asks teasingly.

"I didn't have a girlfriend," I tell her. She looks surprised. "I know it's hard to believe, what with my ridiculously irresistible voice and all."

She laughs.

"What about you? You ever go karaoking with Cameron?" I ask.

"No way," she says. "I'm pretty sure he thinks you need a passport to go east of the 101." She adds, "It's over between us, by the way."

"Really?" I try to rein in the delight on my face.

The song "Shallow" comes on. Serene jumps up.

"Hey! We should sing a duet!" she suggests. She pulls me up eagerly.

"Shallow?" I ask.

"C'mon!" she begs.

As the screen turns to Bradley Cooper and Lady Gaga

falling in love, we put our heads together, singing into the mic. I feel the heat rising in my body as we lock eyes. Somewhere between the third "In the sha-a-llow," I put the mic down.

Leaning in, I ask Serene if I can kiss her.

43

Serene

WE KISS. A slow and tender kiss that makes the world disappear . . . and it's just us. Our foreheads touching. His thumb caressing my skin as my fingers reach up. I feel his hair at the base of his neck and as our lips touch, all my worries melt. The cancer, my dad, the BRCA test, everything. All I can think about is how perfect this moment is.

"I've waited so long to do that . . . ," Lian whispers, looking into my eyes.

I lean in and kiss him again. He's gentler than Cameron and I savor the taste of his mouth, the caress of his tongue, our lips moving in perfect synchrony. I want the kiss to never end.

But then the phone rings. His caller ID says it's his mom.

"Where you?!" a voice demands. It's loud enough that even I can hear.

"Uhhh, I was at the library studying with Stu, like I told

you. And then I got hungry and stopped to get a bite to eat."
Lian gestures for the remote. I turn the music down.

"The library? It's nearly nine o'clock!"

"They had really great appetizers," Lian says.

"Which restaurant."

"Denny's," Lian lies. He makes the *I dunno* gesture at me
with his hands. I look at him, confused. Why's he lying to
his mom?

"Denny's, aiya! Why you eat that fake, plastic, butter-
fried junk when you can come home and eat mapo tofu?"
his mom asks.

I laugh at her hysterical description of Denny's. Lian
looks at me in alarm and puts a finger to his mouth, *Shhh!*

"Who that?" his mom asks. "You with a girl?"

"No, Mom! That's just Stu," Lian insists, pacing the
small karaoke room. "He has a really feminine laugh."

I gawk at him. *What's happening? Why does he keep lying?*
Sorry, he mouths.

"Put me on video," his mom demands. "I wanna see for
myself."

I gesture to the phone and mouth *Should I just introduce*
myself? He shakes his head and waves his arms through the
air: *ABSOLUTELY NOT!*

Lian takes the phone, goes into a corner, and all but
screams into it, "THERE'S NO GIRL, MOM!"

"Put me on video!" his mom repeats.

Lian exhales in exasperation. Then he mutes the call and

turns to me. Putting both his hands together, he asks, "You mind if I head out early?"

"Wait, you're leaving?" I ask, struggling to cover the disappointment in my voice.

"It's just my mom . . . she's kind of intense."

"No, sure, I get it." I nod, even though my mouth still feels hot from our kiss. "Do what you have to do."

"OK, great, I'll call you," Lian says. He leans over and kisses me goodnight on the cheek, then he *runs*. Legit takes off, tearing outside.

He forgets his jacket and I chase after him to give it to him. I see him outside giving his mom a 360 video tour of the karaoke bar's back parking lot. As he turns his phone, he gestures for me to duck to not be in the frame. And as depressing as it sounds, I do. As Lian continues FaceTiming with his mom, I crawl back to my car.

I don't know what to think. All I know is for all my years hiding bits and pieces of my heritage and identity in Sienna Beach, I've never had to duck for a guy before.

Cameron's waiting for me on the steps of my house when I get home. I groan as I turn off the car. *I so do not need this right now.*

"What are you doing with Belt Bag?" he asks.

I ignore him and continue walking toward the house. Mom's car's not in the driveway. Is she still at the office?

"I saw you guys in the library," Cameron continues,

following me inside. "I have a right to know."

"Oh you do?" I ask, putting my bag down and kicking off my shoes. Cameron ignores my no-shoes example and continues wearing his sandy flip-flops into the dining room, which I find massively annoying.

"You sent me nudes, I think that qualifies me to a certain amount of intel!"

I turn away, the regret hitting me like high tide.

"I should have never sent those to you," I fume.

"But you did!" he says.

He flashes the nudes I sent him. *How dare he!* I try to grab his phone from him, but he holds it away.

I try to keep calm, weighing my options. Should I tell him we're still together? Would that make him calm down and agree to delete the photos? Or should I unleash the full force of my anger now? I decide to go with the latter option.

"You better fucking delete them," I say, the rage in my voice even louder than waves crashing behind me.

"We'll see," he says. "First I wanna know why. I was so nice to you. I even listened to you drone on and on about cancer. And to cheat on me with the foreign exchange student? Jesus, Serene, couldn't you have picked someone better?"

I fight the urge to push him against the glass wall, into the ocean.

"He's not a foreign exchange student! His name is Lian Chen! And he's ten times the guy you'll ever be!"

Cameron's nostrils flare. "Fucking hell he is," he says. "He's a pussy. Just look at the way he walks."

I take a step toward Cameron. "Oh, I love the way he walks. I love the way he kisses me. The way his hand presses my back," I tell him.

"Stop."

With every step I take, I tell Cameron other things I love about Lian.

"I love running my fingers down his shirt—"

"FUCKING STOP, YOU BITCH, OR I'M GONNA SEND THESE PICS TO THE WHOLE SCHOOL!" he shrieks, holding up his phone.

I freeze. My blood drains to the cold marble floor.

"How's your new boy gonna feel about that?" Cameron smirks.

"Don't you dare. . . ."

"Maybe I'll send it to his mom too."

I charge toward the door, swinging it open. "Get out," I scream. "Get the fuck out."

Cameron holds his gaze on me. I stand as strong as I can, the ocean wind blowing at my chest. He finally leaves, but not before muttering, "You're going to regret this."

Cameron jumps in his car and speeds off, leaving me in the dust. I grab at the sky. If he actually does leak the pics, what am I going to do?

Frantically, I text Mom.

Mom, where are you? I really really need to talk to you. PLEASE MOM, I NEED YOU.

Regret pools inside me as I think of the pics. How could I have been so stupid? I wriggle and twist, disgusted with myself. The feeling rises in me like dirty tub water on the verge of overflowing. I pace in the kitchen, staring at Lian's contact on my phone.

I want to call him so bad. Instead, I grab a piece of paper and start writing the Chinese characters Lian taught me, tracing them over and over. I finally find solace in the Chinese character for "regret," which I look up on Google. I see that it's made up of the radical for "ocean," *hai*. As I trace the character over and over again, I hope and pray that like the ocean, this wave will eventually retreat . . . that my mistake won't cost me everything.

44
Lian

I SHOULD NEVER have picked up my mom's call. I should have thrown my phone into the ocean before I even went shopping with Serene. I should have not let anything interrupt our magical first kiss, not even a raging wildfire!

"UGH!" I scream to the ocean waves as I drive home with the window down, wanting so badly to get back there. To feel Serene's pillow-soft lips again. The scent of her as my cheek touched hers. The quickening of her breath as I pulled her in closer, and closer.

It's enough to make me try to climb the tall gates of the Cove, sharp steel spikes and all!

I text Serene as I drive—**are you ok?**

She doesn't reply. SHIT! She hates me. It's official. I might as well sign up for the army now.

When I walk back into my house, Mom is standing over the stove. She takes one look at me and throws the bamboo spider strainer down dramatically. I glance at my sister, who looks up quietly from reading a book about a ballerina, like *Oh, you're gonna get it.*

"This is how it starts. You come to America, stay out all night. Join gang, sell liver for crystal breath?"

"It's not crystal breath, it's crystal meth," I correct, squeezing my eyes shut. "Never mind. Mom, I told you, I was in the library. I was on my way home." I grab at my hair in frustration. Dad looks up at me from sketching a snowy mountain on his iPad and shakes his head.

"Don't give us that," Mom says. "We not born yesterday."

She takes out her phone and puts it on the table. There on her screen is the picture of Serene in *Teen Vogue*. My face turns ashen white. *How does she know about us?*

"Auntie Sarah sent it to me. This a girl at your school!"

Ohhhh, thank God. She doesn't know about *us*. Amy puts her book down and peers curiously at Serene.

"I think she looks nice," Amy says.

Mom makes a face. "Only one type of girl go in underwear for magazine."

I grit my teeth at what Mom's saying about Serene.

"She's not in her underwear, she's in a dress," I correct.

Amy adds, "I think she looks like a dancer!"

"She looks like a *slut*," Mom fires back.

"You don't know anything about her!" I say in Serene's defense.

Amy gives me a curious look as Mom kneels down beside

my sister. "Amy, you must promise me, you must never *xue huai* like this."

Xue huai means "learn bad" in Chinese. It's the number-one fear of Chinese mothers—that their kids will be corrupted by America, a fate worse than death. As my sister nods slowly, Mom mumbles to me, "As for you, we see if already too late."

I clench my jaw as she spoons out twelve dumplings with her spider strainer and sets the plate down in front of me. As horrible as my curfew-skipping ass is, I'm still not beneath feeding.

"I'm not hungry," I say, and go to my room.

My sister creeps into my room later that night.

"So where were you *really*?" she asks, closing the door behind her and doing a pirouette to my desk.

"Go away," I tell her.

"Oh, c'mon. Not like I'm gonna tell," she says, plopping down on the floor beside my bed. "I'm the one sneaking to dance every week, remember?"

My phone rings. Amy jumps up and sees Serene's pic flashing on my phone before I can turn it over. "Oh my God, that's the girl!" Her eyes go huge. "You know Underwear Girl?"

"Don't call her that!"

"Are you guys like *dating*?" she asks. "Mom's going to freak."

"No, we're not!" I blurt out, then put a finger to my lips. Are we? Is it official now? "I'm not getting into this with you. Now get out of my room!"

I reach to take the call but Amy silences it and crosses her arms, not in any rush to leave. "If that's who you were with tonight, you're gonna need my help."

"Why am I gonna need your help?"

"Because she's way out of your league!"

I balk at the absurd suggestion.

Amy pulls up Serene's gorgeous pic in *Teen Vogue* on her own phone. "I mean, just look at her! She's in a national magazine. Wearing no underwear!" Amy says. "You are in the middle of nowhere. Clearly wearing underwear."

I look down at my pants.

"You want her, you're gonna have to go big or go home."

I furrow my eyebrows at her. "How?"

She picks up the remote in my room and switches on Netflix. "Guys are always making big, grand gestures in American movies."

I grab the remote from her and shoo my sister out. "OK, OK, I get your point!"

"THINK BIG!" she hollers as she scurries back to her room.

After my sister finally leaves, I try Serene (but she doesn't pick up) and put my stand-up sets aside to study how to get a girl to fall in love with you. I watch three romantic comedies back-to-back. First of all, whoever mislabeled them as chick flicks has clearly not seen *Love & Basketball*. These are not chick flicks—these are *all* flicks. And from them I've learned three things:

1. I need an eccentric best friend. (Which I've already got. Stu, check.)
2. A really great rain scene. (That's gonna be tough. It's LA. We're always in a drought.)
3. My sister is not wrong. I need to make a grand gesture.

In every single one of these movies, there is always some kind of grand gesture that the guy makes. And it's usually around the time of the epic first kiss!

There is *not*, however, an epic first kiss where the guy receives a call from his mom and walks out. *Shit*.

I lie awake the rest of the night thinking about what kind of grand romantic gesture I can do to make it up to Serene and get that amazing moment back. It's gotta be something big and unforgettable, not just a silly keyboard gift. It has to be ten times better.

(By the way, I am super encouraged that the guy in these movies is *not* the ridiculously good-looking guy. HALLE-LUJAH FOR NERDS!)

45

Serene

IT'S LATE BY the time my mom finally comes home.

"Sorry, I went for a walk in the mountains," she says. "I didn't have any reception. What's wrong?"

She sits down next to me on the couch. I tell her what happened with Cameron.

"Oh, my bao-bier," she says, holding me in her arms. "I'm so sorry."

I cling to my mother, relieved she's not mad. Relieved that she can undo so much pain with just one word. One look. One hug.

"What if this gets out?" I ask. "What will my friends think? The people at work—"

Mom shushes my concerns. "It's not going to get out. If it does, he'll be looking at a lawsuit on his hands."

"But it'll be too late. It'll already be *out*," I tell her. As if we didn't have enough other battles going on without adding a lawsuit to the mix. "I can't believe I sent him the pics."

"You're seventeen. You're allowed to make mistakes!"

I look up at my mother, appreciating her empathy, but nauseated by my stupidity. She didn't get to where she is by making mistakes. She got to where she is by being in control. Never letting a weak moment get the best of her.

Mom gets up and goes to her room. "I want to show you something."

She returns with the framed sketch from her desk. It's a picture she drew of women in the Victorian era wearing various lavish, colorful dresses and evening gowns. I always thought she was paying tribute to *Little Women*, one of our favorite movies. But Mom tells me, "See those colorful dresses? Before the Victorian era, it was extremely expensive to dye fabrics. But then one day Walter Henry Perkin Jr. accidentally mixed oxidized aniline with wine. That's how synthetic dye was created.'"

Mom puts a hand to the picture.

"I keep this on my desk to remind myself, it's OK to make mistakes. Some of the best innovations in fashion came as a result of designers daring to experiment."

My eyes crinkle. She has no idea how much her words mean to me.

"See, this is why I need you around," I whisper, putting

a finger to my eye to dab my emotions. "To tell me stuff like that."

Mom gazes down.

"You already know everything I have to teach you," she says. "It's all right there." She points to my chest. "You carry me inside you, bao-bier."

I shake my head, not wanting to carry her around like some jade pendant. I want to hug her in real life. I want to laugh with her, get mad at her, take goofy selfies with her, and eat too much cake with her, sit on the couch and cry about guys with her. Before I know it, I'm full-on bawling. And Mom scoops me up in her arms, and whispers to me, "Even if I didn't have cancer, we never know what the future holds. We have to just take it one step at a time."

And I nod, wanting to believe her words.

That night, while Mom sleeps, I compose an email to Cameron.

Cameron—

Please delete the private pictures of me on your phone. They are private, sent to you in a moment of ~~complete BRCA panicking~~ total trust. They were for your eyes only. I thought (and still hope to believe) that you would respect my privacy and not violate my trust in you. Which is why I shared my most intimate photos with you.

I'm so sorry things didn't work out between us. We have so many great memories together at the beach and hanging out with our friends. I'll always treasure them. But now I just don't feel the same way about you that you feel about me. I hope you understand.

I'm sorry if I hurt you in any way. You have every right to be angry at me. If you want to talk, I'm here for you. But please don't hurt me in this cruel and irreversible way. Delete the photos. I'm begging you.

Serene

I tried to write the email in as nice a way as I could. I hate that even when a guy threatens to do something totally demeaning, a girl still feels like she has to be nice in order to get the guy to not do something illegal.

I press Send.

As I wait for Cameron to respond, I open WeChat. There's a message in my in-box! It's the private detective! I sit up excitedly. I could use some good news. "Please," I whisper as I open the message and use WeChat to translate:

I'm so sorry. I went to the address. The people who live there—Mr. and Mrs. Fung—do not know you, your mother, or your father.

A stone drops to the pit of my stomach. I power off my phone. Turning to my Chinese calligraphy again for solace,

I start drawing. This time, I draw the Chinese character *dan da* (be brave) as boldly as I can.

Highlighting each radical in a different color, I stare at every little clue my ancestors gave me to stay strong, even in the face of my most mortifying fears.

46
Lian

MY PRINTER GROANS and grunts like an old man.

"C'mon, c'mon," I mutter as it slowly prints the Great Wall brick by brick.

It's all part of my grand gesture to Serene—I'm taking her to Beijing. Well, sorta. I'm re-creating it in my room. So far, I'm already twenty-five pages into the Great Wall. I'm going to cover all four walls of my room with the posters. Then tomorrow, after the audition—which will hopefully go well thanks to my golf hole pants—I'm going to invite her over.

Mom and Dad and my sister will be at Hsi Lai Temple over in Hacienda Heights praying for my good ECEP results. It's perfect.

Next to the majestic beauty of the Great Wall, which once protected the Ming dynasty during a period of great turbulence and impending threat, she'll see she has nothing to fear when she opens her BRCA results. And then I'll tell her how much she means to me in a speech that'll sweep her off her feet, and then—

My sister tap-dances in. She's been learning more and more styles of dance at her dance academy.

"Mom wants to know what kind of snack you want to bring for the test tomorrow—" She stops mid-sentence when she sees the Great Wall in my room. "Whoa—what's *this*?"

"Nothing. Just pictures."

"Cool!" my sister says, reaching for the color printouts and the tape. "Can I help?"

"Don't touch it!" I snap. "You'll smudge it and it won't look perfect!"

"What's it for?"

"I'm just . . . redecorating." I shrug. "I miss Beijing. Don't you miss Beijing?"

"Not enough to turn my bedroom into a Pinterest!" she says.

I turn her around and start leading her out. "OK, that's enough for you. Tell Mom I don't care. Anything! I'm not even going to eat it."

Amy looks at me funny. "Why not? Isn't the test like hours?"

The only hours I care about are how many it's gonna take for my slow-ass printer to spit out the rest of the eighty pages or so I need. At the rate it's going, I'll be up all night, and the last thing I need is to fall asleep at my audition. I suddenly remember. "Oh, by the way, when you guys are at the temple tomorrow, can you get Mom and Dad to . . . take their time?"

Amy scrunches her face. Then a hyper, almost delirious look takes over as she pushes me back into my room, closing the door behind her.

"Spill the beans! What are you up to?"

"Nothing," I tell her, trying to act as casual and normal as I can. But the printer betrays me and makes a sharp beep. While I dash to put more paper in, Amy lunges for my computer.

"Seventy-five more pages?" she asks, reading the printing commands. "Are you making some sort of mural?" She gasps, putting her hands over her mouth. "Is *this* your grand gesture for Serene?"

I am disturbed by how quickly my sister figured it out. *She* should be going to MIT.

"Is that why you want us to take our time at temple? You know Mom will kill you, right?"

Of course I know my parents will eventually find out I bailed on the ECEP when my test results come back with a big fat zero. But hopefully by that time, I'll have gotten the audition and killed it at the show. And we'll finally have an honest conversation, in which they'll listen to me about what I want to do with my life and not what they or Highway Robber want me to do.

My sister continues talking with her hands, slicing them violently through the air. "I mean like murder you in your sleep, or worse—tell other Chinese parents about you," my sister continues. "Your name will be an urban legend, like on one of those milk cartons, except it won't be for a missing kid." Her pupils flash. "It'll be for a disloyal kid."

I grimace. Sharp needles of guilt jab into me. "They'll get over it," I tell her.

Amy shakes her head from side to side.

"You're their firstborn son. They'll never get over it," she says. "You'll be breaking their wok if you do this."

"You're the one skipping SATs every week!"

"That's different. I'm *twelve*," she says. "Besides, it's not like I'm gonna skip the actual test!"

"Look, will you help me?" I ask her. "Just keep them at the temple until I text you? I'd do it for you."

Amy reluctantly agrees. "Fine." She grabs a sharp letter opener from my desk. "I better go start digging."

"For what?" I ask.

"For a spot to put your decapitated body," she replies.

I take the letter opener back from my sister and set it down next to my half of the jade pendant. I hope this works.

47

Serene

"SERENE, COME IN," Dr. Herman says.

I look up from my WeChat, trying to mask my disappointment. The private detective tried five other places he thinks could give us some leads, including my mother's old university, but they all came back with nothing.

And out of the 271 Li Jins, five replied, but they were all too young to be my dad. I silence my phone and walk into Dr. Herman's office. Mom offered to come with me for my BRCA result but I told her I could handle it. Now, entering the cold, sterile office all alone to learn my fate, I wonder if I should have taken her offer.

"Thanks for coming in," Dr. Herman says, gesturing for me to take a seat. "I have your genetic results right here—"

"Actually, would it be possible for me to open them later? By myself? I'm sorry, it's just, it's a lot. And I'm going through some stuff right now."

I look down at my hands, thinking of Cameron and the inevitable bomb that's going to drop at any second. So far, there's still no reply to my email.

Dr. Herman holds his hand up. "No need to apologize." He hands me the sealed envelope. "You can open it whenever you want. No rush." He points to the results. "I'm here to talk anything over with you. But take your time."

I give him a small smile, taking the envelope. I'm relieved I don't have to do this right here. I can do it in the privacy of my bedroom, where I can eat an entire box of artisan chocolates, punch Lian's FUCK CANCER button 879 times, play the *Friends* theme song "I'll Be There for You," and think of my dad.

In a cautious voice, I ask, "Actually, now that you have my genetic result . . . is there a way to see if any of my relatives . . . match with me?"

He looks up. "You mean like an ancestry service?" he asks.

I nod.

"Certainly we can submit it to something like 23andMe for you," he says. "Are you trying to see if any of your relatives have BRCA?"

"I just want to know them," I say. "Especially my dad."

Dr. Herman nods, and makes a note of it in his file. "Absolutely. We'll submit it right away."

I thank him and place the envelope into my purse, astonished at the information level of science. Why didn't I start with genetic testing first? Then it hits me why: I would have known my BRCA sentence earlier. I stuff the envelope lower into my purse.

"How's your mom doing?"

I tell him she's been feeling a little better, not so nauseous anymore since she's stopped the drugs. "Did she tell you she threw away the capecitabine?" I ask.

"She did email me," he says. "I have to say, I was disappointed to hear that."

That makes two of us.

"I know the drugs are hard to tolerate, but actually, we just got her latest blood work back and her cancer marker came back lower. So they were helping." He shows me on a piece of paper.

I want to jump up and hug him. The first glimmer of hope since this whole thing started!

"So it's working!" I exclaim. "Does she know? We have to get her back on it!"

"I did call her," he says. "But she felt strongly that the quality of life without chemo was going to be better." He sighs. "In some patients . . . the side effects are more pronounced." He walks around his desk and takes a seat next to me. "Now there is something else I've been experimenting with. I've seen good results with low-dose continuous applications of a combination of chemotherapies."

I sit up. "Really?" I ask. "And you've seen good results?"

He nods. "With the right combinations and low doses,

yes. And the side effects seem to be less harsh."

"Then let's try it! What are we waiting for?" I ask.

"But here's the thing. She'd have to come in more, take them continuously. There won't be the typical rest periods. It's not the normal standard of care. . . ."

I smile. "That's OK. My mom's never stuck to the standard, in anything. She wouldn't be here if she had."

That gets a smile out of Dr. Herman.

"She'd have to agree to it. And judging by her email, she seems set on never touching the stuff again."

"I'll talk to her." It's the best news I've heard all day, and I thank him profusely.

"Great. And let me know, after you read those results," he says. "They're nothing to be afraid of. You have your whole life ahead of you."

I nod. Easy for him to say.

Lian emails me as I walk outside of the office. The subject of his email is: YOUR BRCA RESULT.

I tap open his email and read:

You're perfect just the way you are.

Smiling, I call him. He answers on the first ring.

"Hey!" he greets me.

"Got your email. I'm walking out of the doctor's office as we speak," I tell him, unlocking my car.

"What'd he say?"

"I don't know, I haven't opened the result yet." Then a

wild thought occurs. "You wanna open it together?"

"Hell, yeah!"

I glance down at the envelope in my purse, feeling my fear shrink a little.

"How's tomorrow?" Lian asks. "After my audition?"

"OK!" I clutch the paper, squeezing the fear out as I nod into the phone as bravely as I can.

48
Lian

MOM ROAMS AROUND the house like a nervous mother hen on Saturday morning, grabbing last-minute granola bars, water bottles, No. 2 pencils, and throwing them into my bag.

"Mom, I'm good! I have enough snacks to climb Everest twice!" I tell her.

"You can never be too prepared," she says. "Everything you worked hard for boil down this moment. Just think, in a few months, you could be at MIT!"

More like in a few hours, I'll be onstage at Laugh Club. I swallow hard.

"This is your one chance," Mom says.

"No," I say, trying to comfort myself more than Mom. "If I screw up, there will be other chances."

"Other chances are for white people," she replies. "We only get one."

She's probably right.

"He's going to do well," Dad says. "He always does."

With that, he proudly holds up a gorgeous completed illustration of his Yosemite mountain range masterpiece. He's finally done with it!

"Wow, Dad, that looks amazing!" I say, admiring the colors and details.

"Thanks," he says, handing me his picture. "I know how hard you been working on this test. And today, you will enjoy the fruits of your labor."

Mom smiles. "For dinner, I'm making your favorite. Roast duck. Dad and I going to Monterey Park after temple to pick up the duck."

"Great! Take your time!" I tell them, glancing at my sister.

Amy chimes in, "Can we stop at the shaved ice place after?"

"Sure!" Mom says. "I can pick up some mango pudding for all the aunties. I'm hosting Bragathon next week!" She smiles at me. "They'll all want to know how the test went."

My hand twitches and I grab the car keys.

"All right, gotta go!" I dash out the door, desperate to get out of here before I lose my mind from the guilt.

I jump into the car and speed out of the driveway. I pull over after a few blocks, to catch my breath.

The anxiety pools in me. It's 7:04. The exam starts in an hour. I can still make it, if I wanted. I can tell the Laugh

Club manager I'll meet him another time. I don't have to blow off ECEP. What if Mom and Dad are right, and the comedy thing doesn't work out? Or worse, what if I'm actually not funny?

The self-doubt ticks inside me.

I try to count the number of Asian American stand-up comedians out there. There's Ken Jeong, but even he was a doctor first before he became an actor. He worked for Kaiser Permanente. He was still pressing down on old ladies' stomachs, asking them where it hurts, when he got his first movie. Am I being crazy brave or crazy stupid, thinking it can happen to me, that I should go for my dream full throttle?

Then I think about my dad and how he gave up his dream of being an artist. Without ever really trying. And now, he always sighs when he draws, because he'll never know if he could have made it. I want to know, I decide. Even if I fail. I want to tell my kids I gave it my all.

And so, when the clock ticks 8:05, and my parents' car passes me on their way to San Gabriel Valley, I officially ditch the exam that I've been studying for, for the last two years.

I drive to Hollywood, where I choose courage. And I choose purpose.

It's go time.

49

Serene

LIAN'S ONSTAGE AT Laugh Club when I walk in. I didn't tell him I was coming, but I knew I didn't want to miss his performance for the world. Quietly, I take a seat in the back.

"The thing about Asian parents, you gotta understand, is it's not personal. They just have good money sense. They want a good return on their investment. You're like a car to them," Lian says into the mic.

I laugh.

Lian looks up, sparks of surprise in his eyes.

"They know, the minute they have you, you go down in value," he continues. "That's why they always look so disappointed."

He mimics an Asian parent, letting out a heavy sigh in the mic.

"And no matter what you do, you're never going to get

back to the *day* before you were born. When you had promise. When you had potential. When you had *no* opinions."

The club manager bursts out laughing. Lian is killing it,
as I knew he would. I hold up my phone to snap a pic. I'm
so proud of him!

When Lian's done with his set, I clap wildly as he walks
down the stage.

"Great job," the club manager says. "That was funny!"

"Really?" Lian asks.

"That stuff about Asian parents—I was dying back
there!"

"Me too," I say. Lian looks up at me in surprise.

"You think you can squeeze me in?" Lian asks the manager.

"Let's see. How's Tuesday?" He glances at his calendar.

"Tuesday's great!" Lian blurts out. "And do you mind
if my girlfriend . . ." My pupils go wide at the word. Lian
blushes. "I mean my friend! Can she film me for this competition?"

I smile.

"'Course," the manager says. "Be here at eight, ready to
perform!"

Walking out, Lian takes me into his arms and spins me
around in the lot.

"Can't believe I got a slot!" he exclaims.

"I can believe it!" I laugh. "You were on fire!"

"It was so nice of you to come, by the way," he says, his shy eyes smiling behind that mop of hair of his.

"Are you kidding? I wouldn't miss it!" I say to him.

I can tell he's on cloud nine. And it temporarily lifts me from my somber mood.

"What's wrong?" Lian asks.

I glance at him. How is he always able to read me?

With a deep breath, I tell him that my mom still refuses to go back on the chemo, even the low-dose option that Dr. Herman suggested. She axed the idea when I told her last night.

"I was up the whole night begging her. Explaining to her how it's going to be different," I tell him. "But she won't listen. She just wants to do what she wants to do." A stray tear falls.

"Come here," he says, pulling me in for a hug. "I know what's going to make you feel better. Follow me in your car."

I drive with the window down. As the ocean breeze whispers through my hair, I decide I'm not gonna live in fear of losing my mom. I take the BRCA paper in my purse and crunch it up into a ball. I'm going to *live* and I'm going to love. Because joy is a revolution!

I step on the gas and follow Lian to his house.

50
Lian

I WISH I could describe Serene's face when she walks into my room and sees the life-sized mural of the Great Wall. It makes the sleepless night listening to my printer grunt and moan worth it.

"OMG, you *made* this?" she asks, spinning around.

"Told you I'd take you to Beijing," I say, walking up and hugging her from behind. As we look out at the glowing sunset just above the Great Wall, I nestle my head on her shoulder.

"How long did it take you to do all this?" she asks.

"Nine hours to print everything," I tell her. "And a life-time to find the girl."

Serene turns, her eyes melting. Cue grand-gesture-moment soundtrack in the background. Time for my speech!

"I'm totally in awe of you, Serene Li," I tell her. "I think you're the coolest girl in the world, and not just because you have purple hair or you're in a magazine rocking a dress that's missing half the fabric."

Serene laughs.

"You're awesome because you care about people. You're kind and you take chances, like showing up today for me at Laugh Club and walking into random Chinese Club meetings and actually staying even though I was spewing nonsense about Cheetos. You actually want to get to know who people are inside. Do you know how rare and powerful that is?" I put my hands on her arms. "And nothing can ever change that."

Tears stream down Serene's face when I'm done with my speech.

"You're pretty powerful yourself," she says. "These last few weeks, I've been living with this terror. . . ." Her lips quiver slightly. "But you. You made it bearable. You made it fun."

She interlaces her fingers with mine. "I think I'm falling in love with you," she whispers into my ear.

They're the most thrilling words a guy can ever hear. But to hear them from your best friend, the person you most enjoy talking and laughing with . . . I'm blind with joy, flying high above the Beijing skyline.

"I'm in love with you too," I whisper back as I lean in and kiss Serene. Her lips tremble under the heat of mine. Her mouth tastes so good. I wrap my fingers around her neck and look into her eyes.

Serene, just as breathless, gazes over at the crumpled ball in her purse. "You ready to do this?" she asks.

"Ready." I nod.

She reaches for the paper with one hand and starts uncrumpling, then pauses. "Are you sure we should open it now? Maybe we should open it later. What if it's a mood killer—"

"It won't be. Just open it!" I tell her.

"OK," she says.

Carefully, she tears open her test results.

51

Serene

"IT'S NEGATIVE! I'M BRCA negative!"

Lian grabs me, and we're both jumping up and down as I wave the test result in the air.

Then we fall into each other's arms and kiss. Slowly at first, then passionately, the sweetness of relief mixing with the headiness of promise. Of life! The worries and anxieties I've been carrying about my mom, about the company, Cameron, everything dissolves as our bodies touch. We start tearing each other's clothes off. My hand reaches inside Lian's shirt, exploring his body. I want to feel every inch of him. I guide him to his bed, while he lays me down, his hands caressing my face, traveling down to my neck. My shoulders . . .

And then he stops.

"What's wrong?" I ask. Our foreheads touch. I can feel his breath, short and shallow, like mine. I want him so bad.

"I don't have a condom," he says.

"I have one in my purse," I tell him. He looks at me, surprised. "My mom makes me keep it in my purse, just in case . . . but I've never used it."

Lian grins, tenderly kissing my breast. "That makes a first time for both of us."

I reach over for my purse. As I hand him the condom, he starts unwrapping it, then locks eyes with me. "I just want to make sure you're ready," he says. "I know today's a really emotional day. Is this what you want? We can totally wait."

I shake my head. Fuck waiting. After everything that's happened, I want to live!

"I'm sure," I tell him. "Are you?"

"Yes . . ." He moans as he kisses me again, his tongue stirring up whimpers of anticipation. As Lian puts on the condom and I take my shirt off, I gaze into his eyes, feeling the ecstasy building inside me as our breaths mingle. Our bodies are bathed in the sunlight. I run my hand down . . . touching him. I cannot wait to feel him inside me.

Then we hear a noise downstairs. We freeze.

"Lian?" a voice calls.

"Shit!" Lian exclaims, jumping up. He throws on a pair of boxers as the door swings open.

It's Lian's mom!

She screams! I scream! She covers her eyes with her hand as I grab for the sheets, trying to cover myself.

"You're having sex? You blew off ECEP for SEX!" Lian's

dad and sister come flying into the room too. His dad's jaw plunges. Lian's sister, Amy, takes off her *Born to Dance* sweatshirt and hands it to me. I quickly put it on.

"How long this been going on?" Lian's mom asks.

Nervously, I extend a hand. "Hi, Mrs. Chen, I'm Serene Li—"

"I not talking to you!" she snaps. Then, a look of recognition crosses her face. "You the Underwear Girl!"

My face flushes. Lian glances at me apologetically, while Amy quietly mouths, *I thought that dress was sick!*

"You *sleeping* with her?" Mrs. Chen asks.

"Mom, I can explain . . . ," Lian says.

"I can't even look at you right now," Mrs. Chen says. "You lied to us! What's worse, you taught your sister to lie too! Kevin at 888 called us in the car—she hasn't been going to SAT for weeks!"

Lian's sister turns to her brother, biting her lip. "I'm sorry. She made me confess everything!"

"We know what you been up to. Smart Immigrant Kids Exchange—it doesn't exist!" Mrs. Chen continues, shouting.

"We googled it," Lian's dad adds.

"You been lying to us. This whole time!" Mrs. Chen says. "You know how hard we work for you to have good future? How much we sacrifice so you can go to good school and see Highway Robber? How can you trick us like this, telling us you're taking test when really, you're home screwing Underwear Girl?"

"Ummm, actually we were in Holly—" I mumble. Lian pokes me with his elbow, and we lock eyes. He shakes his head, *No, not now.*

Mrs. Chen lets out an earthquake of a sob. Lian's dad turns to me and says, "You better go."

I gaze at Lian one last time for a sign, some signal that we're going to be OK. We're going to be OK, right? I just need a glance, a word. A touch.

But Lian doesn't take his gaze off the floor.

I pick up my pants and BRCA result off the floor and edge out of the room.

52
Lian

MOM'S ANGER LEAVES tremors of aftershock that shake the posters of the Great Wall off my walls. After forty-five minutes of screaming her head off, she's moved on to the silence phase, thank God. I am unworthy of her words. But she lets her disappointment be known with every clang of the dishes, and every slam of the drawers.

I creep down the stairs and peer into the kitchen. Mom's doing the dishes while Dad's sketching on the iPad.

"Mom, I just want to say . . ." I put my phone down on the counter and cautiously take a seat.

"Bi zui," she tosses back, "shut up" in Chinese. "You don't get to talk. You earn your words after you reschedule test and cut off contact with that girl."

"I'm not going to do that," I tell her.

She looks up from the dirty dishes. When I was little,

one look from my mother was all it took. No matter how much I wanted to keep playing with my friends, I'd drop my toys and leave with her. It became almost a game, testing how obedient I was. My mother loved that she always won. I was the most obedient of all the kids. There was never anything you could put in front of me that I couldn't walk away from.

Today, I stare back defiantly.

"I'm not going to stop talking to Serene," I tell her. "I'm sick of you guys controlling my life. I'm not some flower you can pluck and trim. I have my own plans. It's *my* life. And I don't want to be an engineer. I have no interest. I want to spend my life doing what *I* want to do, with the person I love."

Mom is dumbfounded. Dad's iPad stylus falls from his hand. They both don't say anything. For a second, I think I've won. Until Mom reaches over and grabs my phone from the counter with her dishwashing gloves.

"This is mine now," she says.

I try and level with her. "C'mon, Mom. I need that. You really want me driving around without a phone?" I eye my precious phone in her soapy hands.

"You not driving anywhere," she says. "From now on, I drive you to school. Straight there, straight back. You do all homework in front of me, then I take your computer and turn off Wi-Fi."

"Hey!" my sister protests.

Mom shoots her a death stare, and she retreats back up the stairs to her room.

"Break the rules and we go back to Beijing."

The air constricts in my throat.

"Dad," I start to say. I glance at my father. *Do something!* But Dad gets a work call and has to take it.

"Are we clear?" Mom asks.

I grip the countertop, jaws locked, fighting the fury inside me.

"You know the thing that hurts the most?" Mom asks, sniffling. "I thought when you borrow that book from library that you finally *care* about your immigrant parents. What we going through. I thought when we talked about the book, you finally wanted to understand."

"I do want to understand. But you never want to understand *me*!" I fire back.

"Oh, I understand you. She pretty. She sexy. You body changing. You can't control—"

"No! She's a talented fashion designer—that's why she was in *Teen Vogue*!" I say, frustrated. "You're so fixated on what she was wearing, you didn't even read what she was saying!"

"I read she's a student. And so are you," Mom reminds me. "And now look at you. This isn't the Lian I know. If I had known this was going to happen, I would have never brought you here." With that, she takes my phone and tosses it into the sink full of water. "Now go to your room and give me your computer!"

I want to scream at my mom—this is insanity! I can't be trapped in here like an animal. But I hold my tongue, biting it until it bleeds, for I cannot be sent back to Beijing.

53

Serene

HANDS SHAKING, I reach for my phone to text Lian from his driveway. I have no idea how my legs managed to carry my mortified body out. I can't believe the way his mother talked to me. And he just stood there! Quinn texts me.

Have u seen it? I told Luke if this is Cameron, that's it. He's dead to me, Quinn texts.

Seen what? I ask.

Your nudes. They're all over Snap!

My breath chokes in my chest. This isn't happening. This *cannot* be happening!

I swipe over to Snap and Insta. Sitting in Lian's driveway, as his judgy mother frowns at me through the window, I stare at my naked body on Snap. Unable to move. Unable to look away.

I ram my phone against the steering wheel so hard, the screen cracks.

Driving home in LA weekend beach traffic, I call Cameron. He doesn't pick up. I leave five voice-mail messages—*TAKE THEM DOWN, YOU FUCKER, HOW COULD YOU?*

I text Lian through Siri.

Hey . . . I need to talk. Call me! It's urgent!

An "UNDELIVERABLE" message appears. What? He blocked me? My heart plunges. Has he seen the nudes? Is he furious?

I try texting Lian back a few more times, and each time I get the same "undeliverable" message.

Fuck! I pound on my steering wheel, screaming into the void as my car beeps. "UGGGHHH!" My phone dings with an email from Lian.

Hey—

I'm so sorry. Are you ok?

My mom took away my phone. She's gonna take away my computer in a second too. I just wanted to let you know I'm really sorry. I won't be able to see u for a while. We have to cool it for my parents. They're threatening to disown me. Hope u understand.

Love,

Lian

As Siri reads the email to me, I think, *Oh God. He's going to be offline for a while? What if I can't talk to him after he sees the nudes?*

Can I just call u for two secs? I email back.

He shoots an email back half a second later.

This is killing me too! But we have to 忍 (ren).

He writes a Chinese character I've never seen, and I pull over and use Google Translate to look it up. It means "to endure." I grip the steering wheel—he wants me to *endure*?

I need to see you in private, I write back.

Maybe next week. This weekend I'm 🔒 🔗 . P.S. See how the character ren is made out of a knife over a heart? That's how I feel rn.

Well I can't just ren! I email back, flipping over to Snap and staring at the comments flooding in.

Whore.

Ewww so disgusting and inappropriate.

Left boob supremacy.

Huuuurrrl 🗿

I wish I can unsee this twice

HOT DAYUM

Baby girl, would you like a sugar daddy?

Can I have a booty call?

You look cold 😬

Face burning, I can't tap Delete fast enough. Finally, I delete Snap and Instagram altogether from my phone and tap back into my email. There's no response from Lian. Shit! His mother must have grabbed his computer.

I trace the Chinese character for "endure," going over the "knife" with my finger. The most infuriating part is even in this painful moment, Lian still manages to find a way to be romantic.

"Mom?" I ask, walking inside my house when I finally get home.

"I'm in my study," she calls back. I find her at her desk, working. Ever since she stopped the chemo, she's been designing like crazy. The pen drops from her hand when she sees my tears. She rushes over to me.

"Talk to me," she says.

"Cameron," I say, choking on the words. I point to my phone. "My pics."

I plunge into the leather sofa chair and throw my head back. What are Lian's parents going to think of me now?

"Don't worry," Mom says, reaching over for her own phone. "I'm going to make some calls. He's not going to get away with this."

As Mom walks out of the study to talk to her lawyer, I get up and go to her desk. I look down at Mom's designs. She's working on a pair of baggy silk print pants. I admire the careful way she draws every line. I wish I'd paid the same attention to detail in my own life. Maybe then I wouldn't have made such a grave mistake trusting Cameron. Or I would have noticed Lian's mom's terrifying grip on her son earlier, or the fact that he was lying to her about where he was this entire time.

"Isaac, hi, it's Lily Lee . . . ," Mom says on the phone

outside. "I've got a bit of a delicate situation, with my daughter."

She walks down the hall with her phone.

As Mom talks to Isaac, I tap open her computer and click on the fashion design software. Maybe if I focus on work, it'll help me forget. In the application, I start drawing the word *ren* over and over again, except this time, I put it on the back of a T-shirt.

As I'm working, an email pops up in Mom's in-box. It's from Julien. The subject line catches my eye: NOTES ON YOUR LATEST DESIGNS.

I open the email.

Hey Lily,

We took a look at your latest designs. Love the bold silks and the colors. And I get that you're trying to pay homage to Chinese street fashion—I've seen the vids on TikTok too. But with all due respect, it just looks too ethnic. So we're gonna pass on going into production on this. We can't afford to rock the boat right now, hope you understand.

Best,

Julien

"Too ethnic?" I say out loud.

Mom comes back in as I'm reading the email.

"Isaac says since you're still a minor, Cameron can be

breaking child pornography laws," Mom says. "Is he over eighteen?"

I shake my head.

"Well, he still distributed it," Mom says. "I'll set up a meeting with Isaac tomorrow."

"Would I have to go to the police?" I ask.

"Let's meet with Isaac first, and take it one step at a time," Mom says, reaching for my hand. "Don't worry. It's going to be OK."

I smile at Mom, grateful.

She walks around her desk to look at the design I'm working on.

"Oh, I like that!" she says. "Very cool!"

"Thanks," I say, then fall quiet a little. I wonder if I should mention the email from Julien.

Mom's already scrolling through her phone, checking her messages.

"Hey, Mom, I'm sorry about what Julien said . . ."

"What'd he say?" she asks, still wading through her avalanche of emails. She finally finds his and taps on it. Frowning, she says, "Well, that's a bummer."

"But that doesn't mean you can't make it, right?" I ask her.

She flips through her design pad and shows me the high-waisted pleated miniskirts with knotted buttons that just got rejected.

"Oh, those are *gorgeous*!" I tell her.

"I know," she sighs. "But it's expensive to take a design from concept to runway. It takes money. And Julien, Chris, well, they control the money."

"No, the *customers* control the money," I remind her. "I'm so sick of these guys telling us what to do and getting in the way. It's *your* name on the door!"

"Might be my name on the door, but I only own fifteen percent of the company," Mom reminds me. "After Julien and the others invested, I wasn't able to buy more shares. If I refuse to follow their recommendation, they can throw me out at the next board meeting and find a new CEO. Then where would we be?"

I stare at her design pad, wishing there was an easier way.

"Look, I want to show you something." Mom opens her drawer and pulls out a bunch of papers. "These are all the designs of mine that never made it into production." I peer down at the beautiful designs—lace-trimmed skirts and metallic shirts. One-shoulder fringed dresses that practically beg for you to dance in them! Jackets that pop with color!

"Mom, these are some of your *best* work!" I tell her.

Mom gives me a sad smile. "Thanks," she says. She walks over to her closet and pulls out a delicate hand-stitched top I've never seen. "Just because they didn't make it into production doesn't mean they didn't make it into this world." She smiles at the cropped, ruffled top. "I sometimes wear this one to sleep."

"I don't get it, though. If there's already a sample, why can't we sell that on our site today?"

Mom puts the top back. "Sadly, that's not how it works. The investors are only interested in a sure bet."

What's a sure bet in life? I think of my own crumpled-up result. Even though I'm negative, it doesn't mean I won't still get cancer.

"By the way." I look up at my mom. "I got my results from Dr. Herman."

"Really?" Mom freezes. "And?"

"It's negative," I tell her.

Mom runs over from the closet to give me a hug. "Oh, *bao-bier*, that's the best news ever. I'm so relieved."

I smile as I hug Mom.

"Guess your dad wasn't completely useless," she laughs. "Gave you a good set of BRCA genes."

A small smile escapes me as I leave Mom to her work. I go to my room, settling in for a long night of waiting for Lian to email me. And wondering what the entire school is saying about me on Snap.

I work on my new shirt to pass the time, adding in tiny drops of blood to the character *ren* where the knife lies over the heart. I think of all the ways Mom and I have endured. All these years, I thought I was the only one making concessions at school, chipping off pieces of myself to be accepted. Now I see all the ways my mom's had to compromise her vision, shave off pieces of herself, too. The blood we both shed, without anyone ever noticing. The smiles we've faked to survive.

I'm sick of just surviving.

When I'm finished, I send my design to Carmella. One way or another, I'm making this shirt.

54

Lian

THERE'S AN EERIE silence at school on Monday, like everyone knows something that I don't. I haven't seen the blue sky in two days, except through my window. I am pissed, horny, depressed, and scared shitless my relationship with Serene is over. But as I walk onto campus, I don't understand why everyone else is staring at Serene.

"Dude, did you not hear?" Stu asks. "Serene's nudes are all over Snap!"

I almost trip on my shoelaces.

"Did you say nudes?" I ask.

Stu pulls out his phone to show me, and I immediately grab it and confiscate it. I don't want him looking at that stuff. Or any of my classmates. I get so angry thinking that's what all these fools were doing last night, staring at and violating Serene's body that way. I tear off running.

I race up and down the halls, looking for her. I search

the library, the gym, and the arts center. I finally find her crouched on the floor by the water fountain behind the empty science labs. She's in an oversized hoodie that hides her eyes.

"Hey . . . ," I whisper as I sit down beside her. "I'm so sorry." I open my arms and look into her eyes.

She has every right not to want to speak to me again. But to my surprise, she hugs me back.

"Did you see?" she asks. Heat rises from every inch of her.

I shake my head. I want her to know emphatically that I don't care.

"I was just messing around—" she says.

"You don't have to explain," I tell her. "He did this to *us*."

Surprise mixes with relief as she reaches for me with her hands. We kiss. Hungry, stolen kisses that make the world disappear and everything right again. I close my eyes, savoring the taste of her lips. The smell of her. It's the only thing that got me through the weekend.

Her breath hitches as her lips linger on mine, and she stares into my eyes.

"Your parents—"

"They never have to know," I promise her. "I won't tell them."

She shakes her head. "They're going to find out. I think I should just explain to them."

I start sweating. "You don't understand Chinese parents."

Serene furrows her eyebrows. She looks offended. "My mother's Chinese."

I grasp at my hair. In my frustration, I blurt out, "Yeah, well, she's different. She gives you a condom to put in your purse."

Serene's eyes jump as soon as I say the words, and I regret them with all my heart. But it's too late.

"I can't believe you're judging me!" She grabs her purse and gets up.

I jump too and try to beg her to understand. "No! I'm just saying, your mom is reasonable. My parents would never do that."

"Well, they should!"

"I know! They should do a lot of things. But they don't!" I fire back. I kick the water fountain in between us. "They would never give me a condom because that would mean they accept that I'm having sex. And that would never happen in Chinese culture." Serene stares at me blankly. "They would never let me go to Laugh Club because that would mean that they accept I have hopes and dreams outside theirs. They would never even let me go to an American house party because that would mean that they accept that I am capable of turning down alcohol and drugs without their presence."

As I call out my long list of "they would nevers," Serene

337

looks into my eyes, her anger softening.

"So why don't you just tell them?" she asks.

"It's not that easy. They'll never listen."

"Have you even tried?" she asks.

I look down.

She shakes her head. "No, you didn't. Instead, you let them think that I somehow lured you away on Saturday. Instead of the truth—that you were out there, trying to make it. Pursuing your passion."

Like that'll make one iota of different to my parents. But clearly it does to Serene. I swallow hard, begging her with my eyes. I'm so worried I'm going to lose her. And petrified of what she's asking. That I open up the rawest part of me to my parents and hope they don't stop loving me.

"I just can't, OK?" I say to her. "Not yet. I'll do it later. After I perform and submit my video and win the competition—"

"And how are you going to do that now that you're grounded?"

Fuck. Somehow when I was locked in my room all weekend, picturing Serene and wondering how I was going to apologize, I hadn't even thought about my big performance at Laugh Club tomorrow!

"I'll figure out something," I say, racking my brain for possibilities. "Maybe if Stu calls my house and tells my mom there's a group project at his house. . . ."

"So, more lies." Serene crosses her arms.

Before I can respond, Serene shakes her head and starts walking down the hall.

"Serene, wait—"

But she doesn't turn around. She's sick of my lies. And, quite frankly, so am I.

55
Serene

I STAY CROUCHED in the back of my hoodie, trying to disappear in class the rest of the day. The teachers don't seem to know what's going on, thank God. Cameron talks obnoxiously loud—he *definitely* knows what's going on. The sound of his laughter makes me want to violently rip his hand from his wrist, so he can never text again. I try to drown out his jokes with his friends in the back of French.

After school, I drive to the beach and run into the water, trying to wipe the glares off me. The waves drown out the whispers in my head.

The thing that hurts the most is I can't even hug Lian. I want our relationship to be solid, not something we have to hide. But he says we can't because of his traditional Chinese parents. I may not know every Chinese character and custom yet, but I know a few things—honesty and family. Those are Chinese values I know and live by every day.

I pull out my phone and call my mom as I watch the waves. She doesn't answer, so I text her.

Hey any news from Isaac?

When she doesn't text back, I get in my car. It's not like Mom to not respond. I head over to the office.

Julien's in Mom's office with her and Isaac when I walk in. I frown at Julien. What's *he* doing here? Isaac looks up at me when I walk in and does a little wave. He's an older white man in his sixties, always dressed up in a bow tie and a button-down shirt, no matter how hot it is.

"Hi, Serene," he says, gesturing me into the conference room. "I'm sorry about what happened. Can you tell us more about the boy?"

I tell them about Cameron and how it all started. How he came over the other night and threatened to release the pics.

"Did anyone hear him threaten you?" Isaac asks.

I shake my head. My mom was out that night, unfortunately.

"But it was at our house, right? Maybe the Ring cam got the footage," Mom suggests.

"Brilliant!" Isaac jots down notes in his notepad. "Let's go to the police with that, and any other evidence—"

Julien holds up his hands. "No police."

"Why's he here?" I ask, turning to Mom, hugging myself with my arms.

"*I'm* here because everything concerning the company concerns me. Unfortunately, that includes everything you do," he mutters.

I try to shake off the judgment.

"Well, if we can't go to the police, we'll have to resolve this privately," Isaac says. "Any idea what Cameron's parents are like?"

"I can try and talk to them," Mom offers.

"It's probably best coming from me," Isaac says.

I shake my head profusely.

"You guys. This is my life. Don't I get a say?" I ask. "Why can't we go to the police, if it's clearly against the law to distribute pictures of minors?"

"Because it's much more likely to attract attention and wind up in the news cycle if we do," Julien answers. "And what are people going to think? Even if you're the victim, the fact remains, what the hell were you thinking sending it to him? Clearly your judgment is flawed. You need to stay out of this and let us handle it!"

I look to Mom, but she doesn't say anything. I shake my head and storm out of the room. I head straight to the Business Affairs office, ignoring the looks of pity as I walk across the office. God, everyone knows.

"I want everything there is on Julien," I say to Lilian, head of BA. "Credit card bills, investor contracts, all of it. It's for . . . my mother."

Lilian picks up the phone. "Can I call her to confirm?"

"She's in a meeting," I say to her.

As Lilian puts all the information together, I tell her I'll be right back, and head to Starbucks. Carmella takes the elevator down with me.

"I heard about what happened. I'm so sorry," she says.

"Thanks," I say. "It royally sucks."

"What are you going to do?" she asks.

I shield my eyes from the blinding sun when we get out of the office building. Up and down the street, people are walking, hustling from one end of Santa Monica to the other. Whenever one of them looks down at their phone, my body tenses, wondering if they're on Snap looking at my nudes. I realize if I ever want that feeling to go away, there's only one thing to do.

"Hey, do you want to go somewhere with me?" I ask. "Do you have a few minutes?"

"Sure! Where are we going?" Carmella asks.

I lead the way past Starbucks to Olympic Drive, where I push open the doors to the Santa Monica Police Department.

In the police station, the officers take down my statement. They're extremely patient and sympathetic as I explain what happened. I sign into my Snap with Carmella's phone and show them the pics.

"I want to assure you that in California, sexting with a minor and possessing and distributing any explicit images of a minor is illegal and will be punished by law," the police officer says. "It doesn't matter how this image got out. The fact that he has it on his phone is a violation of the law."

I exhale a giant breath when I hear him say this. I had been worried that Cameron will claim he didn't post it.

"Now we're going to need some more information on this boy. Do you have his address?" the police officer asks.

I nod. As I give them Cameron's address and details, my phone rings. It's Marcia.

"Hey, Marcia, I'm kinda busy," I answer.

"Serene? Your mom's in the hospital," she says breathlessly.

"WHAT?"

"It just happened. She collapsed in her office. We called her doctor and he told us to take her to the hospital immediately," she says. "The ambulance just took her. She's at Cedars-Sinai."

"Oh my God. I'm on my way!"

I jump up and tell the officer, "I'm sorry, I have to do the rest later, by phone. My mom's in the hospital."

Carmella and I bolt for the door.

I gasp for air as I speed toward Cedars-Sinai, my knuckles white as I clutch the steering wheel. Carmella stayed back at the office to hold down the fort. I rev the engine.

Please, God, please . . . let her be OK!

I shake my head, riddled with regret. I shouldn't have

left the meeting with her and Isaac. I should have stayed. I pound on the steering wheel, honking the horn as I wait on the 10 Freeway.

"C'mon!" I scream.

But the late-afternoon traffic grinds to a halt. And as I sit on the crowded freeway, I grab my phone and try Mom. *Pick up, pick up, pick up.*

She doesn't answer. I tell Siri to text her.

Mom! Are you ok? Hang on, I'm on my way! Call me back!

I try her two more times. I try everyone else I can think of—Marcia, Dr. Herman, even Julien. But it all goes to voice mail. As I sit in traffic, the thought that loops in my mind is, *Please God, I need more time. I'm begging you. I'm not ready!*

Thirty minutes later, I rush inside the hospital and tell the receptionist my mother's name.

"Lily Lee, here we are, room 628."

"Thank you!" Tears blurring my eyes, I glance at the elevator, but it's currently all the way up on the eighth floor. I can't wait that long. I run up the stairs, two at a time, grunting, panting.

Cameron texts me, **What the fuck! The police just called me.**

GOOD! I block him and scream in the stairwell, a primal, thundering echo that leaves the wall shaking. I push forward, fueled by the worry, the hope, that if I can just get to my mom, if I can just see her, there might be a way. There might be another day.

But when I get to her room, she's surrounded by doctors and nurses. She's lying in bed and her eyes are closed.

"Mom!" I exclaim.

The doctors look up from examining the various beeping machines and monitors on her. I spot Dr. Herman.

"Let's step out to the hall and talk," he says, guiding me out.

We walk into the hall. Julien and the others are all standing around by the vending machine. I lean in closer so Dr. Herman can talk to me privately.

"She had an acute liver failure from the cancer," he fills me in. "The team was able to relieve some of the pressure on her brain."

"On her *brain*?" I ask. The entire hallway starts to spin, the strong fluorescent lighting blinding me as my head throbs. "So the cancer's spreading? Is this because she stopped chemo?"

Dr. Herman responds with a sigh. "It's very hard to tell, but with cancer this advanced . . ." His voice drifts off.

"But she was doing so well. She seemed to have more energy!"

"So did the cancer. Sometimes a gap is all it needs to gain an edge at this late stage."

I close my eyes, clenching my teeth to try to keep it together.

"Can I talk to her?" I ask.

"She's on very powerful drugs, but she should come around in a few hours."

I thank Dr. Herman. "Oh hey, I got your results back from 23andMe," he says. "They're in my office. No direct relative matches, I'm afraid."

I struggle to process the disappointing news as Julien walks over. He's with Chris, another one of the investors.

"Serene? Can we talk to you?" he asks.

I walk back into Mom's room, ignoring them. I sit down on the chair across from Mom and reach for her hand.

"I want to be alone with Mom," I say to them.

"This is kind of urgent. We need to talk about what to do with the company," Chris continues. "We need a functioning CEO, and obviously your mom . . . well. She no longer fits that bill."

I shoot them both a look. Really? Do they have to do this right now?

"I really need a moment," I repeat.

They back off. I wait for them to walk fully out the door before turning to Mom.

"Please, Mom, if you can hear me . . . you need to wake up." I tug at her frigid hand, but her eyelids remain closed. A tear rolls down my face and onto her IV drip. I glance up at Julien and Chris through the window, torn between getting the nurse and telling her I got Mom's IV wet, and letting Julien and Chris see me cry. I wish they weren't here. If they weren't here, I'd climb into bed with Mom and hold her.

I decide, fuck it. Next to the beeping machines, I move Mom's wires out of the way and climb into bed with her. We lie together, mother and daughter, just as we've done a hundred times.

If I close my eyes and drown out the beeping sounds, I can almost pretend we're on my bed when I was little. And Mom's just drifted asleep after telling me a bedtime story. A story of how the two of us are going to take over the world, and no one can stop us.

I cling to this memory of better times, blocking out the vultures circling, and venom spreading outside, as I snuggle my mom.

56
Lian

BEING COMPLETELY CUT off from Wi-Fi is like being put under for surgery. Blood is being spilled, insertions made, people are talking—but you have no idea about what. Is Serene's sext leak getting better or worse? I have no idea. All I know is Serene's right. I have been scared to tell my parents my dreams. I've dismissed the possibility of them ever listening to me based on a mathematical probability, not certainty. I've been having conversations with them only in my head and not in real life.

I muster up all my courage and walk downstairs to the kitchen.

"Hey, Mom." I take a seat at the table as calmly as I can. "Can we talk?"

Mom looks up from the big bamboo steamer of hot mantous. She turns off the fan on the hood, but not the heat. She throws mushrooms into her pork shoulder stir fry. The wok crackles with the sizzling oil, which shoots and lands on my arm. But I press on.

Mom reaches for the soy sauce, and I hold it out of reach to get her attention. Without soy sauce, nothing is possible in Chinese cuisine.

"Hear me out," I tell her. My mom finally turns off the gas.

"I'm sorry I lied." I take a deep breath. "I should have told you and Dad the truth. The reason I skipped ECEP was to go and audition at a stand-up comedy club."

Now Mom's eyes are more depressed than the mushrooms in her wok. Confessing to an Asian parent you want to be a comic is like confessing you want to join a motorcycle gang. Still, it's not about her acceptance, I tell myself. It's about speaking my truth.

"I don't want to be an engineer."

Mom doesn't lift her gaze from her wok. It's like we're having a conversation through the mushrooms.

"You want to be a comic," she repeats.

"Yes. A stand-up comic," I confess to the mushrooms. "I want to write jokes that are so honest and hilarious, people choke on their drinks."

"I choking right now." Mom looks up and frowns at me. "This Underwear Girl's idea?"

"No. It's mine." I stand up tall. "And by the way, she's not Underwear Girl. Her name is Serene and she's my girl-friend."

My face beams with pride, even brighter than the man-tous, as I describe everything that Serene means to me. Mom responds by flicking the fan on *loud*.

I try and shout over the fan. "She makes me happy, Mom! She believes in my dreams!"

Mom takes the soy sauce from me, adds the pork, and finishes off the dish. "You think just happy, that's enough? You know what real life like? Especially in entertainment industry? Constant rejection. People booing you off stage. You judged every minute."

"Well, good thing I have some experience in that," I mutter.

Mom throws her spatula down, offended. "No you don't. You just a kid. You have no idea what it's like to fight every day for a seat at the table, like your father does at his com-pany. To have to flail your arms, just to prove you exist."

"Actually, I do . . . ," I say to Mom.

I reach to turn off the fan. As the steaming mantous cool, I finally tell her what this year's really been like for me. Not the glossy sweet soy version, but the real version. I tell her about Cameron and Luke, how everyone in my school calls me the wrong name. Even my best friend, Stu, I got from letting him cheat off me. *That's* what moving to Sienna Beach has been like for me.

My mom is speechless. "Why you didn't tell me earlier? We could have gone to Irvine, more Asian."

"I don't want to move schools. I like it here."

"Because of Serene."

"Yes. She inspires me—we inspire each other!" I try and level with her. "You're always talking about these American schools. Harvard. Yale. Stanford. You know what they all have in common?"

"They expensive?"

"No. They all have a liberal arts education. Liberal *arts*. So people can explore and find out what they're really passionate about and go *do them*. Like you did . . . with your flower shop in China. Mom, I saw the way you lit up every day." I reach for her hands. "That's what I want too. That's all I'm asking. For the chance. For me to decide my own fate. To live my own life. Isn't that why you brought me here?"

As I wait the agonizing minutes for her to respond, I stare at the steam dissipating from the mantous, trying not to hope, but hoping anyway that my mom will finally get it. Hope is such a dangerous thing in Chinese culture. That's why there's a "scarf" radical in the characters . . . too much and it can choke you.

Finally, Mom speaks.

"Fine. You wanna follow your heart, follow your heart," she says. "But you have to choose. Comedy or Serene. You can't have both."

"You're making me choose between my passion and my love?" I ask, putting my hand over my stomach.

Mom chops the air with her hands. "If you serious about

comedy, you can't be distracted by anything or anyone. You have to love it above all else," she says. "Even then you might not make it."

"Oh, I'll make it."

"Then prove it to me. Choose. We will support you in whatever you decide. But you can't have both."

57

Serene

IN THE HOSPITAL room, I nudge Mom, trying to get her to stir, while outside, Julien and Chris plot and scheme what to do. I can hear them talking through the door—*sell, take over, merger, bid.*

"Mom, you gotta wake up," I say.

There's a knock on the door and Julien and Chris walk inside.

"How's she doing?" Julien asks.

"Fine, she's just resting," I say. I reach for the cup and pour my mom some water from bed, as though she and I were just chatting over tea.

"We just talked to the doctor," Julien says. "He thinks a medical leave of at least four months, if not more, is in order. Without a real successor, we're going to free-fall. All potential buyers and offers will disappear. We'll be left with nothing. We have to talk next steps."

I glance at Mom, lying there helpless. She'd be livid if she heard. "We're not selling. My mom will be fine. When she wakes up, we'll start her on the new course of chemo, and she'll be all better—"

"Listen, Serene, I know this is difficult, but this is what your mom wanted," Julien says. He takes a seat on the plastic-y sofa across from me. "From day one. The goal was always to sell, she knew that. She wanted to make sure you'd be taken care of. But we have to act now. Every minute we wait, the landscape changes."

Chris pleads with me. "Do you really want to see us go through layoffs and the rumor mill? Have to get restructured and owe debts, and have our biggest accounts walk? Because that's what's going to happen."

My head spins with all the terrifying scenarios they're throwing out.

Julien adds, "This way she's preserved. Her brand will forever be protected and secured. She'll join the likes of Kate Spade. It's the best way to protect your mom's legacy. Isn't that the goal here? Isn't that what you want?"

"Yes, but—"

"So let's make it happen. As her daughter, you have power of attorney. Isaac's on his way down here now."

I shake my head. It's all happening too fast. I grab on to Mom's hand, trying to find my anchor.

As Julien calls Mom's attorney, Mom's eyelashes flutter open.

"*Bao-bier . . . ,*" she mutters.

"MOM!" I cry.

"Lily . . . thank God, you're OK," Julien puts down his phone, feigning relief. "How do you feel?"

He exchanges a nervous glance with Chris.

"What's going on?" Mom asks, wasting no time at all in getting back to boss mode.

Chris clears his throat.

"We're just trying to figure out what to do. Given the situation, you clearly need a medical rest. And without solid leadership, the company's value will plummet."

Julien walks over and takes Mom's hand. He leans in close to her.

"It's time to think about next steps, Lily," Julien says. "LVMH, PVH, they're all still interested. I just spoke to them. But if we wait, they walk."

"Why?" Mom asks. "The company's not sick, *I'm* sick."

"A company's only as good as its leader."

"But Apple—"

"We don't exactly have a Tim Cook," he says, throwing me a glance.

My face burns. I plunge my gaze to the cold hospital floor.

"This is our last chance. Everyone can see the writing on the wall. . . ."

Mom closes her eyes and pushes her eyelids with her fingers.

"I need a moment alone with my daughter," Mom says.

Julien and Chris nod and start making their way out. "I'm going to call a board meeting for tomorrow. Let's get everyone together as soon as we can." He closes the door.

I turn to Mom. There's so much I want to say to her. But before I can, Mom reaches for a pen and a piece of paper.

"Go home, go to my safe. Here's the code." She jots it down. "Find the company incorporation papers and the investment contracts. If things get ugly, I'm gonna need them. And call Isaac!"

I look at the numbers she scribbled. It's the only code in the house I don't know. "Right now?" I ask. "I'm not leaving you. What if something happens?"

"Listen to me. I won't be strong-armed into selling my company. We have to fight them with everything we got. I won't let them take this from us. Everything I've ever done is for you, Serene."

I swallow hard. How do I say to my mom, right now, all I really want is for her to be OK? I don't care about the company, about the sale. It's awful and sad, but we've held on for as long as we possibly can, and now it's killing her. Can't she see that? If letting them win means I get to keep her for one more day, then fine. THEY WIN.

"Mom, we can't fight two battles at the same time—the cancer and the company," I plead with her.

She kisses my hand and pushes me toward the door. "Which is why I have to do this. I already know I'm going to lose the other."

I shake my head, fighting the tears, as I throw my purse over my shoulder and head home to grab the papers.

58
Lian

I CHOSE SERENE. It was a no-brainer. She's the girl who first believed in me. Told me my dreams are valid. I'll suck it up and go to four years of engineering if I have to. But I won't be able to live with myself if I know I ditched the girl of my dreams. Mom walks into my room as I'm about to dial her on the home phone.

"Give me the phone," Mom says, grabbing it from my hand.

"What do you mean? You said you'd support me, no matter what I decide!"

"That was before I read about *this* in ParentSquare," Mom says, showing me the email blast that went out about Serene's pics.

Oh nooooo.

"Your new girlfriend has naked pictures of herself on the internet!" she says. "You know what that mean? It mean they stuck on the internet. FOREVER! Like durian smell in refrigerator. Cannot remove!" Mom shakes her head with profound disappointment. "Doesn't she know that?"

"This isn't her fault!" I say in Serene's defense. "Cameron leaked the pics! She was violated."

"Of course her fault. She the girl! No girl with good jia jiao would ever send naked pictures of herself to boy."

My blood boils. *Jia jiao* means "family upbringing" in Chinese. It's the most important thing a person can have. My hands ball into fists at this sexist and unfair accusation of Serene.

"Will you stop?" I ask, eyeing the car keys sticking out of her pants. I've got to get out of here. "This is madness! Enough!"

"I agree," Mom says, fuming. "Enough. You're not going to keep seeing her."

"Oh yes I am!" I tell Mom.

"Even after this? *Why?*"

"Because she doesn't make me choose between two things I love, she accepts all of me! That's what love is, it's not expecting perfection and punishing flaws. It means being for them *always*."

With that, I make a lunge for the car keys.

Mom screams as I grab them from her pants. "Ah! What you doing? Where you going?"

I bolt down the stairs without answering.

"If you leave, I'm calling China Airlines right now," she warns.

"Go ahead. Take me to Beijing in chains. But every minute I'm in the US, I wanna be free," I call back, dashing out the door and jumping in the car.

59

Serene

I KNEEL IN front of my mom's safe, punching in the combination she gave me. As a kid, I spent hours in her closet, trying to guess the code, while my imagination ran wild about what was inside the mysterious box. In the end, the code is simply a combination of our birthdays—7-5-2-3.

Half a dozen manila envelopes fall out when I open the safe. There are old pictures and immunization records. Every single birthday card I ever gave her. I smile, looking through the memories.

I start combing through the manila envelopes, looking for the company incorporation papers. I find birth certificates, bank statements, and the house deed, but no company investment contracts. Finally, I find all the company stuff, buried under a bunch of house repair receipts.

"Yes!" I exclaim, shoving the papers into my purse.

I start to put all the manila envelopes back. My phone

rings—it's another call from the Santa Monica Police Department—but I silence it. I have to get back to the hospital. As I'm trying to close the safe, an old envelope jams the lock. I pull the letter out, examining its yellowed, aged edges. That's when I see the name—Li Jin. It's a letter from my dad!

I rip it open.

Lily:

I trust that you are settled and well in America. I am of course equally sorry that things played out the way they did. We all make mistakes, but some mistakes you never stop paying for.

I've deposited the amount into your account. I hope you use it for a fresh start. As you have already agreed, we will have no further contact after this. I wish you and Serene well in America.

Best,

Jimmy Li Jin

Hands shaking, I turn the envelope around and stare at the date. I was three months old. My dad's address is on the back, clear as day. All this time, my mom lied. She knew exactly where my dad was. She just didn't want me talking to him, because she'd already sold her silence.

My eyes cloud as I see the receipt for the wire transfer: $250,000. I dig around for more letters, but there are none. I reach for the company investment papers from my purse. Under "individual initial investment," I see a bunch of names and how much they put in. I find Mom's:

Lily Li, founder—$250,000

"Nooooo!" I bite on my lip until it bleeds. I suck on the wound, drinking the sour, metallic taste of having been traded for a company.

Julien and Chris have already gone home for the night. I carry the papers into Mom's hospital room.

"Oh good, you found them," Mom says. "Isaac just left. There's going to be an emergency board meeting at the office—"

I thrust Dad's letter in her face. I don't give a shit about the board meeting.

"What is this?" I ask.

Her face turns to ash as she registers the letter. I can't stand to look at her. Can't stand to see the guilt, riddled with awkwardness, most of all her *regret* at not having hid the letter better.

"You *lied* to me! Have you been talking to him all this time?" I ask.

"No! Of course not! It's not like that. . . ."

"Then what is it like?"

Mom tries to look away, but I move so she can't dodge my gaze. I want my mom to see, to *feel* the extent of my pain, what she's taken from me all these years.

"I know you're angry," she says, trying to sit up. One of her wires comes undone and starts beeping, and instinctively, I reach to reconnect it. I hug my arms to my chest, pissed at myself for *still* caring. For still loving. She abused my love.

"The mistake he's talking about." I point to the letter. "Is that me?"

"No!" she's quick to say. But I don't believe her. She tries to take my hand. "You have to understand. We loved each other very much."

"Then why does it say don't ever talk to me again?"

"It's complicated. It was never going to work out."

"So you decided to cut a deal?" I whisper, the words too ugly to say any louder.

"It's not like that!"

"Then what was it like?" I ask.

More machines start beeping and Mom starts gesturing through the window to the nurse. I know what she's trying to do. It's what she does every single time I try to bring up my dad. She shuts the conversation down. Well, not this time.

"Mom!"

"He was *married*, OK? It was an affair. His wife found out. That money was hush money, to get us both out of the picture!"

I take a step back. No, no, no, no, no. "You're lying. You said I was born out of love. This can't be happening!"

"You wanted to know the truth. . . ."

I shake my head furiously. I refuse to accept it. My mother didn't come to America to flee some scandal. She came to pursue her dreams. My mom's not a mistress, she's a boss!

"Your father comes from one of the wealthiest families in Asia. At the time, two hundred and fifty thousand US dollars was a lot of money—"

"And you took it," I mutter.

"Damn right I took it," she says without flinching. It disturbs me she says it so proudly. "I used it to provide us the life you deserved. *We* deserved."

She still doesn't see it. The deal she made, the deceit keeping it from me, that's not love. It's a transaction!

"I love you so much, bao-bier," Mom says. "Can't you see I did it for you?"

"No, you did it so you could have this massive company."

A tear rolls down her withered cheek. Her voice cracks. "That's not why I did it. All I wanted was to give us a better life. That's all I ever wanted."

I toss her precious investment contracts on her bedside tray and walk out of the hospital room. "Well, you didn't."

60
Lian

I WAIT FOR Serene on her steps under the foggy moon. I followed a FedEx truck to get inside the Cove. My neck cranes whenever a car drives by, hoping it's not Cove security, here to bust my ass.

At last, I spot her Volvo SUV coming up the road. She jumps out of the car when she sees me.

"You're here! How'd you get in?" she says. "What about your parents?"

"I told them everything!" I say. "I'm so sorry. You were right! I should have done it sooner!"

We fall into each other's arms. I kiss her in the moonlight.

"I'm so sorry for everything," I tell her. "Are you OK?"

"Lian! I don't even know where to start." Tears stream down her face.

I hug her tight. "Everything's going to be OK." I run my

hands up and down her bare arms. She's frozen. "Here, let's get you inside. Have you eaten?"

She shakes her head as she searches for her keys. "I've been in the hospital all day." She tells me her mom's at Cedars-Sinai for liver failure.

"Oh my God," I say as she unlocks the door. "Is she OK?"

Serene doesn't reply as we walk inside. She shivers in the breeze, reaching for a throw blanket. The ocean wind comes burrowing in from one of the open windows. I walk over and close them and turn on the fireplace. Serene takes a seat on the couch, staring into the fire while I go to the kitchen to make her some warm honey-and-ginger water. I put some rice in the rice cooker too, using my thumb to measure the water like my mom, in case she's hungry.

Walking back into the living room, I hand Serene a warm mug. She takes a small sip.

"Thanks," she says.

"It's honey and ginger. I don't know if you like it," I say.

She looks at me shyly. "I like that you're here," she says.

The fire crackles in front of us. "I like that I'm here too." I smile.

Serene looks at me curiously. "So what exactly did you tell your mom?" she asks.

I sit down beside her. "That I love you. That you're important to me. That I want to live my own life and pursue my own dreams."

"And what did she say?"

"Doesn't matter. I can't live my life searching for her approval. She may understand after a week. She may never understand. But just saying the words, man, it felt good."

Serene smiles. "I'm proud of you," she says, touching my arm.

The feel of her hand on my skin is electrifying. I reach over and kiss her. Her soft lips melt into mine. Her breath hitches as her lips linger on mine, and she stares into my eyes. There's a burning desire in me to just lift her from this couch and carry her upstairs to her bedroom. But I can tell something else is bothering her.

"What is it?" I ask.

"It's my dad," she says. "I finally found his address in the safe."

She tells me everything.

"She's been lying to me all this time," Serene says, burying her head into her hands. "My mom, whom I trusted more than anyone else in the world. Pimping herself out to a sugar daddy. *That's* how she got her start in fashion. God, if anyone knew."

"That's not the way I see it," I say to Serene, prying her hands away to look at her. "I see a woman in a hard position, trying to make the right choice to protect her child. A mother who bravely crossed over to the US, where she didn't know a single soul, so she can start over."

Serene peeks back at me.

"I'm not saying what she did was right, keeping this from you—I definitely don't think that was right. But people make mistakes. And sometimes a secret . . ." I swallow. "Just grows."

"Well, now it's ruined everything," Serene says, lying on her stomach on the couch and kicking her feet up. She stares into the fire. "You know what hurts? I hate this feeling. Hate that I can't believe her anymore . . . can't root for her anymore. I miss her."

I put a blanket over Serene and lie down next to her on the floor.

"You can. It just takes time."

"She doesn't have time."

The nakedness of her words hangs in the air. We both fall quiet, letting the waves carry our unsaid fears to and from the shore.

Serene's phone rings. "It's the woman from Business Affairs in my mom's office," she says. "I have to take this."

"No problem," I tell her, getting up to go to the kitchen to check on the rice. "I'll make us something to eat."

As Serene takes the call, I open the fridge. There are a million leftover dishes organized in Tupperware in the fridge. I start pulling them out, recognizing Serene's neat handwriting—*chicken pot pie, broccoli chicken, meat loaf.* They're all dishes she's made for her mom. I smile at Serene's thoughtfulness. I wonder when's the last time someone's cooked for her.

I pull out sugar snap peas and chicken from the fridge. Years of watching my mom in the kitchen and I don't even have to look up the recipe. As I pour the oil into the pan, Serene walks in.

She puts her phone down, takes a seat at the counter, and reaches for a raw snap pea.

"So fancy," Serene says.

"Nah, just some good home cooking," I tell her.

Serene nods. "I'm excited. It's been so long since someone cooked for me."

"You should come over to my house sometime. My mom's an amazing cook." I pause, wondering. Hoping that one day, we'll all sit around the table: me, Serene, my family, and her mom. That my mom will get to know Serene. I think if she gets to know Serene, she'll see how much she has in common with her. They're both strong women who like to say "I love you" with food.

Serene smiles.

"So what did the Business Affairs person say?" I ask.

"She told me some stuff. There's gonna be a board meeting tomorrow. They're gonna decide whether to sell the company."

"But won't your mom still be at the hospital?"

"She could dial in," Serene says. "But . . . she told Isaac to vote whatever I decide."

"Wow," I say, turning off the heat. I stare at Serene. "If that's not total trust, I don't know what is."

Serene walks over to the rice cooker and starts scooping the rice into bowls. "Still doesn't undo the pain."

"I know."

"Maybe I should just sell it. It'll be so much easier," she says, setting the bowls of rice down. "I won't be reminded every day of my dad's hush money. That's gotta be the most humiliating way to finance a company."

"So what?" I ask, setting down my plate of stir-fried chicken and peas. "Who cares how it started? You and I started with some goofy after-school club."

"Hey, that wasn't goofy! I learned some amazing Chinese characters in that class," she says, holding up her phone to show me her latest shirt design with the character *ren*.

"Whoa! Now *that's* incredible!" I beam at Serene. "Has anyone ever told you you should be a fashion designer one day?"

Serene grins. "I do love it."

"So if you really love it, don't give up on it," I say. "Even if it's hard. You'll figure it out."

I pop a sugar snap pea in my mouth, lean across the counter, and kiss-feed it to her.

61

Serene

LIAN SLEEPS OVER that night. We fall asleep in each other's arms, and though my stomach's still in a tight knot over the shareholders' meeting, it helps to nestle my head between my pillow and his shoulder. Lian's arm drapes over my stomach. Every few hours, he pulls me in tighter and I inhale his scent.

At half past five, when the first light is coming up on the ocean, I tiptoe out of my bedroom and go into my mom's office. For the next hour and a half, I work at Mom's desk.

A knock on the door finally pulls me from my zone.

"Hey." Lian walks in sleepily. He's wearing his jeans from last night, but no shirt. I gaze longingly at his ripped abs. "We have to go to school."

I glance at the clock. It's nearly seven a.m. I groan. School. Ever since my pics leaked, it's been agony sitting through my classes. I tell myself to forget about the pics and focus on the goal. In exactly ten hours, at five p.m., the shareholders' meeting will decide the fate of the company. My plan's either going to work or fail spectacularly.

"You should come," I invite Lian, then remember. "Oh shoot, your comedy set's tonight."

I register the disappointment on his face. "I can do that another time," he offers. "I'll text Phil, the manager."

"Really?" I ask.

He nods. "Absolutely. Besides, I want you there. You have to film me."

I know how much the comedy set means to him, so I appreciate him rescheduling so he can be there for me tonight. "Deal."

"Should we start getting ready?" he asks.

"Actually, it takes about five minutes to get to school from here." I smile at him mischievously, reaching out a hand. "We have . . . a little bit of time."

He grins as he walks over. With one swoop, he picks me up from my desk. I scream and laugh as he carries me down the hallway. He finally sets me down in my bedroom and I strip out of my robe in the pink morning light. Lian lies on the bed and takes me in.

"I want you so bad," he says.

I walk toward him. "I want you too," I whisper, climbing into bed and kissing him. I reach for a condom and start peeling his pants.

As the ocean breeze drifts from the window, Lian and I

have sex for the first time. I gaze into his eyes, feeling the ecstasy building inside me as our breaths mingle. Our bodies rise and fall together, bathed in the powdery, pastel light. The waves ripple through me as we come together. And I want to cry because it feels so good.

Later, we walk into school together holding hands. People stare at me and I don't care. Let them stare. I know what they're thinking and I hold my head up high. Last night, I decided only *I* can control my destiny. The nudes, my dad's letter—they only hold power if I let them.

I glance over at Lian, calling his parents from my phone.

"Hey, just wanted to let you guys know, I'm at school," he says. "I spent the night with Serene. We were careful, don't worry. I'll be home soon. I love you guys."

I put a hand to his back, knowing how hard it was for him to make that call. And how necessary. He leans over and kisses me and I feel my knees go weak.

I never used to understand why people called it making love. Wasn't sex just people hungrily grabbing at each other, sweaty bodies on rumpled sheets, lips parted? But as I gaze into Lian's gentle brown eyes, I feel my heart glow with love.

We kiss in front of the whole school. We don't care. We're in our own private universe.

The principal, Dr. Timothy Daniels, runs up to me. He stands by awkwardly, waiting for me and Lian to stop kissing, then clears his throat.

"Serene, I want to assure you, we're going to find and take down every last picture. What Cameron did was illegal. The police have already been to his house. He's been suspended, awaiting expulsion procedures," he assures me.

"Thank you," I tell him. "I appreciate that."

"And if anyone says anything to you," he says, raising his voice to all the students, "I want to know about it immediately. This is a safe environment for all our students, and we want to keep it that way."

As Dr. Daniels walks back to his office, I look around and spot Quinn, who rushes over.

"Oh my God, Serene, how are you dealing?" she asks. "I want you to know, Luke and I are behind you one hundred percent. We haven't talked to Cameron. I'm glad the police are involved."

"I hope he goes to jail for what he did," Lian says.

"It's so good you have Lian here to help you deal," Quinn says. "I was thinking—"

Lian's eyes do a double take. "Excuse me, did you actually call me by my real name?"

Quinn turns red.

"Lian Chen. Good to meet you." Lian extends a hand.

Sheepishly, she takes it. I muffle a laugh at Quinn's face.

"I'm sorry," she mumbles. "I knew that, of course. I just . . . I don't know."

I tuck my hands into Lian's hip pocket, amused. It's kind

of fun watching Quinn squirm awkwardly.

"Anyway, so I was thinking maybe we should host a party for you at my house. A post-sex-pic party, you know, so we can reinvent you?"

I think about the offer. It's the kind of thing the old me would have jumped at. The new me? Not so much. "No thanks. I don't need to reinvent myself." I smile at Lian. "I like me just the way I am."

"Me too," Lian says, kissing my nose.

Hand in hand, we start walking away.

I can hear Quinn shouting from behind me, "You just gonna Kim K this thing? That's cool too!"

Lian and I share a laugh as we tune Quinn out. I don't know why it took me so long to do that.

At the board meeting later at Mom's office, I breathe in deep. The room is filled with all of Mom's investors and board members—some of whom I've never met. Thirteen men and four women sit around the table. The tech guys set up the phone in the middle of the table so Mom can listen in. She's still in the hospital recovering. And even though she can totally vote remotely, she still insisted on giving me the right.

I'm sorry for everything, she had texted. **Whatever you decide, I'll support.**

Carmella walks over and I whisper to her, "Are we ready?"

"Ready," she says.

I glance over at Lian in the back of the room. He's holding my phone, which I gave to him while I do the meeting. As the tech guys finish setting up, Julien walks over and tells Carmella and Lian to step out.

"Board members only, I'm afraid," Julien reminds them.

"Oh no, they're with me," I say.

"But this is a private meeting," he says, confused.

Before Julien can get into it with me, the tech guys patch Mom through and tell everyone they're ready. Julien gives up on Lian and Carmella and calls the meeting to order.

"Thanks for coming, everyone. As you're all aware, we're here to discuss the next steps of the company in light of Lily's deteriorating health. I think we can all agree that no matter what happens, the most important thing is that the company not only survives, in the event of the founder's death, but thrives. With that in mind, I'd like to present two potential acquisitions offers from LVMH and PVH, both extremely lucrative offers."

Julien passes out the deal details in glossy, thick folders. There are murmurs of surprise and approval around the table as everyone opens the folders and digs in.

"PVH seems like it would have the most synergy with our brand," one of the investors, John, says. "It already owns Calvin Klein and Tommy Hilfiger. They have the scale and can crank up the production."

"But LVMH—we're talking Fendi, Dior, Celine!" one of the other investors adds.

I clear my throat and move my chair to stand up. All eyes turn to me.

"Hi. I'm Serene Li. Many of you know me as Lily's daughter. But I've also been working at this company this year, learning the ropes, understanding the business from the bottom up. And I believe that acquisition is not our one and only path forward."

Julien rolls his eyes.

"Here we go—" he starts to say.

"Let the girl speak," one of the women investors, Marisa, says.

"While all these offers are no doubt exciting," I continue, "what makes us unique is that women, real women, see themselves in our clothes. They see themselves *represented* in our dresses. Our clothes mean something—whether it's the one-of-a-kind daring couture dress that frees a woman's body, or the ready-to-wear collection that pays homage to the great female writers of the nineteenth century. These aren't just clothes to be mass-produced and sold for the highest profit margin. They're pieces of art. Political. Inspirational. Meaningful."

"And there's currently no one to continue that art," Chris points out.

"That's not true," I say, nodding to the hardworking designers outside the glass conference room. "See those talented men and women? They're the real heart and blood of the company. This whole time my mom's been ill, we've not missed a single deadline. A single buyer's meeting. Or marketing opportunity. We can totally continue to grow this company, without selling it. We can execute my mom's vision, just as Apple has done without Steve Jobs."

"And who do you propose we install as CEO?" Julien asks. "You?"

A few of the investors chuckle.

"No offense, but you don't exactly have the best judgment," Julien adds.

I stiffen, trying hard not to let his comment derail me.

"Actually, no one," I respond. "I propose a new model, where the duties of CEO are shared among the designers. A system where there's total transparency and employees feel real ownership of the company. Without having to go through a complex hierarchy, I believe we're also able to respond faster. Case in point."

I pick up my laser pointer and nod to Carmella. She clicks on the wall-mounted projector and my entire collection of shirts flashes onto the screen for all the investors to see. I was up early this morning designing not just the ren T-shirt, but five other ones. And thanks to the software, Carmella and I were able to put real shirts on real models. As the models walk down a 3D runway, Julien looks at me, confused.

"You went into production without our approval?" he asks.

"Not exactly. I wanted to test something out. You said

the WeChat shop wouldn't work. Well . . . this morning, we uploaded these shirts to the company WeChat shop, which we revived."

I nod to Lian, who flashes our WeChat account onto the screen. Incredibly, we see the sales numbers jump in *real time*. It's five p.m. in California, which is nine a.m. in Asia. The presale number on the screen begins to climb—8. 13. 32. 49. 79. 107.

Five seconds later, the number jumps to 349 for the ren shirt.

"All those are actual orders coming in?" a board member asks.

Lian pulls up the tab that lets us see not just how many orders, but how much *money* is coming in. Everyone gasps as the amount soars—$5,000. $10,000. $35,000. I hold my breath. I always knew China was a big market, but I had no idea it was *this* big.

"That money's already in your WeChat account," Lian tells the investors.

"And with it, we can confidently go into production without worrying about losing a cent," I tell the investors. "It's a sure bet and a radical new way of doing business, releasing products preproduction, so our *customers* can decide."

Carmella pulls up a projected profits slide she and the team made. When the investors see how much more money we can make using the new model, a few investors clap.

"I think it's bold," Marisa says. "Very impressive. I like it."

She looks around the room, but the other investors' eyes are still glued to the WeChat screen. They can't seem to tear their eyes from watching our new collection take off. I smile at Lian. I'm so glad he came; I couldn't have done this without him. Lian uses my phone to take a video of their shocked faces.

"All I'm asking for is a chance," I say to the board. "When my mother sewed the very first Lily Lee dress in our one-bedroom apartment, she didn't do it to try to crank out product. She did it because she wanted her dresses to mean something. To say something. And what you're watching right now, in real time, is her legacy living on. My mom succeeded because she always had her finger on the pulse of society. She knew what women wanted. What they were going through. Clothes were her language to communicate to the world, not only to reflect it but to change it. And that's what we do here every day. That's what we do better than a large corporation. *That's* how we'll deliver you record-breaking return on your investment. So I ask you humbly, dear board, to please vote no to the sale."

My heart pounds as I wait for the investors to deliberate. As Julien calls the vote, anxious, nail-biting seconds pass. One by one, the investors vote.

"I vote yes sale," Julien starts.

"Yes," Chris adds.

"No," I say emphatically.

382

Tense moments pass as I wait for the other investors, praying to the fashion gods. Finally, the other investors speak.

"No."

"No."

As the nos keep coming, I look to Carmella. It's working! Carmella walks over and we both hold hands. *Is it possible? Did we actually save the company?*

"I agree with Serene, it's too soon. I want to see how this new corporate structure plays out. It's gonna be a no for me," Marisa says.

"Tell LVMH they can kiss our couture ass!" another investor hollers.

I laugh. Julien scowls, throwing his acquisitions folder down dramatically on the table. But I'm too busy counting all the fifteen Fuck No We're Not Selling!

Afterward, Julien walks up to me.

"I hope you know what you're doing," he hisses, dumping all his offer folders in the trash. "It's one thing pulling a publicity stunt. But it's a whole other thing running a company."

"I know," I respond with a confident smile as Lian hands me back my phone. "I've only been watching my mom do it my whole life. Oh, and by the way, the next time you try to expense a personal trip to Cancún, you might want to think twice."

I forward him an email I got from Lilian in Business Affairs of all the times he's charged personal expenses to his corporate card, like his Porsche lease and countless Tinder dates.

I glance down at the conference phone, wondering if Mom's still listening.

"Mom?" I ask.

The connection fizzes, disconnecting. I head out of the conference room, thanking Carmella and the team and telling Lian I'll call him later.

There's one last board member's vote I have to hear with my own ears.

62
Lian

I LINGER IN the foyer of our house. It's hard to go from the exhilarating high of watching Serene kick corporate ass, to bracing for the shitstorm of son-bashing I'm about to receive. But it has to be done. And if today's taught me anything, it's that sometimes the most difficult conversations can surprise you.

"Mom?" I ask.

"In here," she calls from the kitchen.

I see Dad in the kitchen with Mom. He's home early. My parents are looking at the video of Serene's incredible speech on my mom's phone. I forwarded it to her. I know I wasn't supposed to record it, but I just couldn't resist. I wanted to show them the girl I've fallen in love with. Not the tabloid version but the real, authentic version.

"Hey," I say nervously, taking a seat next to them.

Mom puts her phone down. Dark circles surround her

eyes. She was probably up all night worrying about me.

"I'm sorry I walked out last night," I tell them.

"You made your mother cry," Dad says.

"I was so worried. You no phone!" Mom wails.

"Because you drowned it in the sink," I mutter.

Neither of us says anything. Mom fiddles with the fallen petals of the roses on the table.

"What did you think of the video?" I ask quietly.

They nod.

"And?"

There's a long spell of silence. Then, finally, "Her speech very moving."

I look up, hopeful.

"She's clearly a smart girl," Dad says. "Pretty, too."

Mom tosses him a look.

"Still shouldn't have lied to us. And ran off like that," Mom says.

I nod. "You're right. I'm so sorry."

"We're your parents. We deserve to know the truth," Mom continues.

"But sometimes when I tell you the truth, you still don't accept it," I say. "You just want me to do what *you* want me to do. But I'm seventeen now. I'm going off to college soon."

Mom starts tearing up.

"I know," she cries. "What am I going to do, after you're gone?"

"You have to let go and let me make my own decisions." I reach for Mom's hand. "And trust you raised me well."

"But what if you go down wrong road?" Mom asks, reaching for a tissue.

I think about the question long and hard. "I don't think there are any wrong roads. I think there are just roads," I answer. "Not everything's gonna be smooth for me. I'm sure there's gonna be all kinds of bumps ahead to being a stand-up comic. But I kinda think the bumps are what's interesting."

"Like coming here," Dad agrees, patting my back. "Today, I got an interesting offer. My boss saw my art in my office. And now he wants me to supervise product design."

"That's great, Dad!"

"It won't be easy," Dad says. "I don't know much about product design. But I figure if my son can waste eight hundred sheets of paper making the Great Wall in his room and risk getting disowned from his parents to go after his passion, maybe I can give my passion a chance too."

I smile. Mom leans over and asks, "Have you eaten?"

"Have you eaten" in Chinese culture is as close to "I love you" and "I forgive you" as you can get.

"Not yet," I tell her, my stomach rumbling.

She gets up and walks around the counter. As she takes the lid off the pot of steamed ginger pork ribs, the aroma of the succulent pork fills the room.

"Smells good," Dad compliments.

"Much better than my snap peas I made yesterday for Serene," I say. "Hey, can I invite her to dinner next week?"

Mom takes her time answering, pouring the ginger broth into four bowls.

"Only if she bring her mother. I want to ask her how she started her business. I've been thinking maybe I get back into being florist again. In America this time."

"That's a great idea!" I hug my mom.

"Maybe I find cheap shop in San Gabriel Valley. I want to ask her how to get loan." She pauses for a second. "Also I want ask her how she raise such a strong daughter."

I beam. I'd like to know that myself. She really is something. I realized today that I don't need to make a grand gesture to impress Serene. Just showing up for her, when she needs me, is the grandest gesture I can make.

Dad gets up to help Mom with the bowls. "Maybe Serene can give me some public speaking tips. I have my own board presentation next month!"

As Mom calls my sister down for dinner, I put my arms around my parents, for it means so much for them to finally accept me.

"Thanks, you guys," I say. "I love you so much."

63

Serene

MOM'S ASLEEP WHEN I walk into the hospital room. I take a seat next to her bed. The nurses tell me she's been sleeping for most of the day. I wonder if she heard my speech at the board meeting.

Mom's frigid finger touches my cheek hours later. I didn't realize I'd fallen asleep.

"Mom." I sit up. She smiles at me, her lips pale and cracked.

"Didn't mean to wake you," she says. "You must be exhausted after your big speech."

"You heard?"

"Of course," she says. "It moved me to tears. I thought to myself, even if I die right now—"

I shake my head. I'm not going to let her start. "Don't say that."

Mom nods and sits up, reaching to move a bunch of wires

out of the way. She moves closer to me.

"I'm so sorry I hurt you," she says. She starts coughing and I tell her it's OK. "No, I need to say this. I messed up. You and I are a team. I should never have kept this from you all these years. You deserved to know the truth."

She takes a deep breath.

"I was ashamed. I thought you would look at me differently. My family, all my brothers and sisters, when they found out, they all wanted nothing to do with me. They were ashamed of what I did. That's why I left China. I didn't want the circumstances of your birth to follow you."

I look away. Every time I think about the "deal," it stirs up an uncomfortableness not even those naked pictures of me can rival. I keep imagining my father out there, living this double life. Having a parallel family, other children. Do they know about me and my mom?

"Your father, we loved each other very much. I want you to know that," she says. "We'd known each other for many, many years. Your grandmother made suits for his family. And he would always come along and watch me in the back, sewing."

"So why didn't you guys . . . ?"

"It was out of the question. I was just a seamstress. His family wanted him to marry someone from a more prominent family," she says.

"So you came to America to prove them wrong. . . ."

Mom shakes her head. "I came to America to prove to

myself. To wash away all those feelings of inadequacy. All those long nights wondering why . . . if we were madly in love, why that wasn't good enough. The minute I stepped on American soil, I stopped needing the approval from his family. I stopped needing to prove to someone else I was good enough to be loved. I *am* enough. I deserve to be loved."

My heart weeps listening to Mom tell the story.

"That's why I never sent back a postcard or an email. Instead, I tried to love you as ferociously as I could. I thought I could shield you. But now I see I've hurt you, the one person I'd die to protect. . . ."

The lump hardens in my throat as Mom puts her hands together.

"Will you please forgive me?" she asks. "I am so sorry."

"Mom," I cry. "All this time I wanted to get in contact with Dad, so he can see. So he can know how amazing you are. *We* are. That's all I wanted."

"I know."

"But if you don't want me to—"

"No. I want you to do what you need to do, sweetheart, to complete this missing piece of you. I'm here to support you. And just because my relationship with your father was hard, doesn't mean yours has to be. I'm sending you all his contact info."

I hold my breath as Mom taps on her phone.

A notification pops up on mine a second later.

Dad's contact info—
Jimmy Li Jin Tao
jjtli@163.com
Tel: +86 591 929 3833 (cell)
+86 591 456 8109 (home)
+86 591 881 8203 (work)
33A Central Park Apartments
6 Chaowai Avenue, Chaoyang
Beijing, China 100000

I stare at the information in wide-eyed disbelief. Cell, home, *and* work? I can't believe that when I finally get his number, I'm suddenly flooded with information.

"Thanks, Mom," I tell her.

She gives me a weak smile as she closes her eyes. I leave my mom to rest. Standing outside her room, in the hallway, I tap on Compose Email.

Dear Dad,

I close my eyes, trying not to disintegrate into a puddle of tears, as I type the words. I've waited so long for this moment. I think about all the times I've stared out into the ocean, wondering if he's OK out there. Wondering if he's thinking of me back. Being mad at Mom for changing her last name to Lee, so he can never find us. The birthdays where I ran to the mailbox, hoping this was the year he'd send me a card. Only to slam the mailbox shut, skulk back inside, and tell myself it's OK—when I finally make contact, it'll all be worth it. I'm going to blow him away with my words.

In the end, all I can manage is:

Can we talk?
Love,
Serene

It's hardly the beautiful, eloquent prose I always pictured I'd write, the kind of email that would make him regret the excruciating wait of getting to know me, his long-lost daughter.

But as I lean against the hospital wall, I think of Mom's words.

I stopped needing to prove to someone else I was good enough to be loved. I am enough. I deserve to be loved.

And I press Send.

Lian waits with me at the hospital over the next few days after school, as Mom gets strong enough to be discharged. I so appreciate him being there, supporting me every time my phone dings with a new email and the air in my lungs freezes at the thought that it's my dad.

But they're just emails from Carmella and Ali, or Marcia, letting me know the latest preorder numbers or factory update. Things are going really well at the office. My plan of giving the team more ownership over the product is working. Morale has shot up significantly, and so have profits.

I spot Dr. Herman in the hallway.

"Dr. Herman, how's she doing? Can she come home yet?"

"A couple more days, I'd say. Oh, and Serene, I was very happy to hear your mom's willing to give the low-dose chemo a try. . . ."

"She is?" I ask in surprise.

He gives me a rare smile. "The next few months . . . are gonna be tough," he says. "But working together, I think we can get through them."

I nod, trying to be strong. Lian puts his arms around my shoulder.

"How much time would you say she has left, Doc? How many good months?"

"Define good," he says.

I struggle to reply. "Good, you know. Where she's herself and she's able to laugh and smile, and be . . ." The words choke in my throat. "My mom."

Dr. Herman puts a hand on my shoulder gently and looks into my eyes.

"Then I'd say she has forever," he replies. "I see a lot of patients, and Serene . . . the bond between you and your mother, it's special. Nobody's ever gonna take that away."

I nod and thank him. The words mean more to me than he'll ever know.

My phone dings with a notification. As I look down, my pupils flash. It's him. The email I've been waiting my entire life for. I glance over at Lian, who understands instinctively.

"Excuse me, Dr. Herman," I say. "I'll catch up with you later."

I leave Lian and Dr. Herman and walk all the way over to the end of the hallway to find a quiet place. Taking a deep breath, I open the email.

Dear Serene,

I was so happy to receive your email. How are you? I hope you are well and that your mother is well.

I have often thought of you over the years and wondered how you are.

After you emailed me, I searched for you on Google and found your magazine interview. Clearly, your mother has done a great job raising you, though it must not have been easy by herself.

I don't know how much your mother has told you about the way we parted, but know that it was not an easy decision. I'd like to talk to you more about it.

Will you come and visit me in Hong Kong? I live and work in Hong Kong now with my family. Please let me know and I will have my personal secretary arrange the details.

Warmly,

Jimmy

My eyes drink in his offer. He wants to meet me! In Hong Kong! It's more than I ever hoped! I take a second to take it in, this quiet moment of euphoria. I finally got my answer. My dad's thought about me too all these years. I wasn't just a footnote on a lost page.

"You OK?" Lian asks, walking over. I nod. "What'd he say?"

"He wants to meet me," I tell him.

"Oh my God, that's great! In Beijing?"

"In Hong Kong," I tell him.

Lian gives me a hug. He knows how much this means to me. As Lian goes to get us celebratory sodas from the hospital cafeteria, I push open my mom's hospital room door to tell her. I pull my phone out nervously, not sure how my mom's going to react. She puts on her reading glasses as I show her my dad's email.

"You should go," she says when she's done reading.

I gaze up in surprise.

"This is what you always wanted. A chance to restart and rekindle," she says.

I'm grateful for her blessing. It means so much for her to accept this other part of me. To allow me to pursue this, even though it's fraught with painful memories for her. I now know that that's the real definition of love. I start to think about Hong Kong, feeling the stirrings of excitement. But then I look down at my mother, and the wires and monitors beeping around her.

"Maybe later," I say.

"No, now. He's inviting you. Go before he changes his mind! I'll bet he'll fly you first class and put you up at the Four Seasons! You could go over fall break."

Fall break's in a couple of weeks. No. How can I leave her?

Mom gives me a stern look. "Serene, you can't wait around for my cancer. You have to go out and live your life."

"This is my life," I tell her, putting the pills she has to take into a paper cup. If I leave, who will remind her to take her pills? To reheat her food? To tell her she's beautiful even when she's sick? "I want to be here with you."

Mom takes my hand. "Are you not going because you're afraid?"

"No. I'm not going because we're a team. You said so yourself. And right now you need me."

Mom takes off her reading glasses. "Oh, Serene."

"I'm not giving up on Dad. But if and when I do restart with him, it'll be on my terms. On my time," I decide. "He can wait."

She leans in to hug me. As the wires beep and the IV drips wobble, we cling to each other.

"Spoken like a true boss." Mom smiles through her tears.

64
Lian

Three months later

I'M LATE. I pick up the pace, sprinting across the campus to the auditorium in the back of the school. It's the third and final day of the school-wide talent show—my sister performed yesterday at the elementary school and she did GREAT. As for me, I'm just trying not to sweat through my underwear.

I get to the auditorium and squeeze in from the back. All around me, dancers, musicians, and other acts are warming up backstage. I peek out at the sea of judge-y, frowning classmates, well, except Stu, who bet Oliver twenty bucks that I'll win.

A voice calls out to me.

"Lian! You ready?" Serene asks. I turn around. Her beautiful smile fills me with confidence.

"Ready," I say.

"You're going to do great! I'm sitting in the front with

your parents!" She kisses me and wishes me good luck. I smile. A little over a month ago, when Serene's mom was finally starting to feel a little better, we had our first dinner together. And just as I predicted, Serene and my mom bonded over moo shu pork.

I peek out from the curtain at my parents—they look as nervous as I do, especially my mom, who waves to the book club parents awkwardly. The principal calls everyone's attention.

"Welcome, everyone, to the sixteenth annual Sienna High Talent Show!" he says. "First up, we have Lian Chen, who's gonna get things started with a little stand-up. Take it away, Lian!"

I walk out. The spotlight beams on me and for a second I am fully blinded. Then, as my eyes adjust, something magical happens. I forget about the fact that I'm in a high school auditorium where half the back is texting and there's a couple full-on making out. Or the fact that my mom is inching so far in her chair to take a video of me, she's about to fall over. Or the fact that my dad's discovered the stale cookies the administration put out and is gobbling them up like he hasn't eaten for days, and Serene is clutching her half of the jade pendant so hard, it might break.

I let everything go as I grab the mic. And I become . . . an entertainer.

"Hey, everybody, I'm Lian Chen, and I'm here to perform

a set I wrote for you guys. It's called 'Asian Boy Lands in Suburbia.'"

Serene whoops.

"Suburbia is an interesting place. I never thought I'd ever move to a place where the yards are this big. And the diversity this small . . . ," I say, pinching with my fingers.

My dad chuckles.

"Seriously, guys. I am like the only Asian guy most of you guys know. Look around you, everybody else here is white." I pause. I see a lot of nodding heads around the auditorium. "That's like having one color of Post-it, for all your subjects—it just isn't enough."

My classmates laugh. I relax my shoulders as I continue my set. When my five minutes are up, I put the mic back and peer out at the audience. A second passes. Then another. I roll on the balls of my feet as I wait for a response. A reaction. *Any* reaction—I'll take even a hiccup. The auditorium is so quiet, I can hear the buzzing of the air conditioning in the back.

Then Stu jumps up and starts clapping. He claps wildly, I mean, like he's trying to generate electricity with his hands. And one by one, my classmates join in. The claps swell toward me like a tidal wave. I glance at my mom, who stands, shell-shocked. And I laugh, in gleeful disbelief, as I receive a standing ovation from my peers.

Afterward, Serene runs up to congratulate me.

"That was amazing!" she cries. I put my hands around

her neck and kiss her.

Stu walks over and high-fives me. "You kicked ass up there!"

A few of my classmates walk over and say to me, "Great job, Lian. You're a really funny dude."

"That's my best friend!" Stu calls back proudly.

It fills me up with joy that my classmates finally *see* me, even more than winning. (The trophy, in the end, went to a girl who sang the shit out of "Chandelier" by Sia while twirling a baton. And rightfully so. "Chandelier" is a really hard song to sing.)

I hug Serene and scroll through the many, many DMs and messages from my classmates about my set, glowing with pride. But the post that makes me the proudest is on WeChat. My mom uploaded the video of my performance onto her WeChat, along with the caption:

Asian Boy Surprises Parents <3

65

Serene

WATCHING LIAN PERFORM and put himself out there, I'm in awe of his presence onstage. He's a born star, there's no doubt about it! I'm so proud of him for going for his dream, just as I'm going for mine.

I arrive at the Santa Monica Pier the next day, where I'm holding my first ever fashion show. Fresh lilies line the pier, courtesy of Lian's mom's new flower shop. I had the idea to turn the pier into a runway, having models arrive on eco-friendly scooters. Mom laughed when I first told her, but as the first models arrive and the fans and photographers go wild, she cheers from the front row. I'm so grateful to Dr. Herman for the low-dose chemo. Even though she's had to slow down—these days she doesn't go out much—she's still with us.

The ocean wind blows in her hair and she struggles to keep her scarf in place. I look around for an extra scarf, but

Mom decides to release the hand holding her scarf. As her scarf floats out to sea, she smiles at me, and shrugs.

As the music plays and the lights flash onto the "runway," Carmella sets up a mic at the end of the runway. It's all part of my surprise—the reveal of my very first couture piece. It's a dress I've been working on for months. Even my mother hasn't seen it.

And here's the kicker—*I'm* going to be wearing it. As I quickly change into the dress, I gaze down at my creation, almost afraid to breathe. It's a dress made entirely of paper—tiny pieces of Chinese fortunes that hug me against my waist.

I can hear Lian in the back with his family, cheering as the spotlight hits me and I walk out onto the runway.

"Queen!" Carmella yells.

I blush as I reach for the mic at the end of the runway and gaze out at Mom. I tap on the mic and the music fades.

"I'm Serene Li, and thanks for coming to my first collection," I say into the mic. "I'd like to dedicate this dress to my mom." I look down at my dress and continue, "This dress represents all the little pieces of me . . . pieces that I'd been hiding, pieces that I'd been searching for. And pieces I didn't even know existed."

As I spin around, I explain to the audience what this year has been like for me—finding out my mom has cancer. Trying to prove I can fill her shoes at her company, while trying to create my own footprint. Finding my dad.

Falling in love. I smile at Lian.

"Life is not about just collecting the good fortunes, but taking the good with the bad," I say, my fingers traveling up and down the fortunes stitched to my dress. My mom dabs her eyes from the front row. "It's about accepting all the pieces of you, however complex and hard. I used to want so badly to fit into a neat box. Now I know there is no neat box. I'm a composite of all my identities . . . and my fortunes."

The fans clap from the back. As I thank the audience and pose for pictures in my couture dress, I see a Chinese man squeeze through from the press section. He exchanges a few words with my mom, then walks toward me.

The emotions choke in my throat as I recognize his face.

"Dad?" I ask, trembling as I take in the real, walking version of the man in the pictures. He reaches out to me with his hands.

"Your mom emailed me," he says. I walk into his arms and we hold each other for the first time in my life. "I'm so proud of you and everything you've become."

As my dad hugs me close to his chest, I feel the tide soar, the years rolling up like waves as my two oceans finally connect.

Author's Note

On Oct 5, 2020, my world got turned upside down when my mom called me with the most shocking news—she was turning yellow.

She was in Hong Kong at the time and I was in the United States. She first noticed it in her skin and thought she was just getting a little tanned. But when she went to see her doctor, he suspected pancreatic cancer. I was shocked. One minute, she was perfectly healthy, eating Chinese cabbage and doing tai chi in the park. The next minute, she's in the emergency room, fighting for her life.

The ensuing few months were the most intense, dramatic months ever as her body wrestled with the cancer, and I wrestled with the very real possibility that I might lose my mom. I jumped on the first flight back to Hong Kong. Hong Kong had one of the world's strictest quarantine orders at the time, and I sat through mandatory hotel quarantine for fourteen days with my son while my mom was undergoing the Whipple procedure, one of the toughest operations on the planet. I was not allowed to leave my hotel room. I had to wear an electronic wrist monitor. I could see her hospital from my hotel—I was just steps away, *so close*. Every day, I'd put my hand to the window, hoping, praying that she'd still be there by the time I came out. All I wanted was to hug my mom again.

Finally, they let me out of the hotel. Tears streamed down my face when I finally got to hug my mom. She had survived the surgery!

Then the other shoe dropped—during the surgery, they discovered she had one of the rarest and worst types of pancreatic cancer, one associated with a very poor prognosis. My heart sank when I heard this. Like Serene in the story, my mother is my best friend. She's the first person I call when something good happens to me. She's the only person who knows how I'm feeling with just a look. She's my rock. And the idea of not having her anymore . . . not having my *rock* . . . terrifies me beyond words.

But I wasn't giving up. And neither was my mom. I researched doctors and on the recommendation of an old classmate, found the incredible oncologist Dr. William Isacoff in Los Angeles, who had a reputation for thinking outside the box. He told us to come to LA for chemotherapy. It was not easy convincing my mom to come back to the United States with me in December 2020, let alone to move to Los Angeles, the epicenter of Covid at the time. There were no vaccines available yet. I'd be taking my mom, who was extremely weak and vulnerable after the surgery, from a place with zero Covid cases to a place with almost 20,000 per day. But I felt it was the best chance we had of surviving this thing.

And so, on that cold, dreary day, December 13, 2020, I boarded the aircraft back to California with my mom, dad, and daughter, Nina. I left the boys with my husband, who was still working in Hong Kong at the time. As a mother, the decision to separate from two of my kids during a pandemic was one of the hardest decisions I had to make. But I was also a daughter, trying to help save my mom's life. And I knew that having all three kids with me, without my spouse, and no in-person school, would make it very hard for me to focus on my mom.

So we said our goodbyes. That day at the airport, we all wept as my son Tilden hugged his lao lao and pleaded with her to still be alive by the time he came over to the US again. We didn't know when that was going to be. We genuinely did not know whether we were all going to see each other again.

Somehow, we made it onto the flight and moved to Los Angeles. The next six months were a grueling roller-coaster ride of good news, bad news, chemotherapy, immunotherapy, CT scans, blood tests, genetic sequencing, and many, *many* trips to the doctor. I threw myself into the process, going to every doctor's meeting, researching every drug, thinking if I just worked hard enough, I could somehow control it.

But cancer's not like a character in one of my books. I can't control it.

Cancer has a mind of its own.

Just like love.

And that's when Serene and Lian came to me. Writing this love story, about bravery, about not giving up even when you're facing life's most terrifying storm, about a complicated but unbreakable mother-daughter bond, helped me get through this terrifying time. Helped me be the rock to my mom that she's been to me my whole life, through the ups and the downs. Helped us both find the laughter and the joy, again, and celebrate each day as it comes—which is the best way to live life, cancer or no cancer. That's what this whole journey has taught me.

As I write this, it's been a year since my mother's diagnosis. She's doing well, and she's still in treatment. I do not know what her prognosis is, and neither does she nor anyone else. But we're all living life to its fullest, and that's what matters. The rest of my family finally joined us in Los Angeles in the spring and summer of 2021. And Tilden finally got his wish—we all clung to each other in the most joyous hug.

Sometimes when you're in the eye of the storm, the best thing to do is hold each other and hang on tight.

Thank you for reading the love story that helped heal my heart.

For more information on pancreatic cancer and to understand the warning signs, please visit the Pancreatic Cancer Action Network at pancan.org.

For patient stories about living and thriving with pancreatic cancer, please visit Let's Win! Pancreatic Cancer at letswinpc.org.

To donate to the funding of scientific and clinical research of pancreatic cancer, please visit the Lustgarten Foundation at lustgarten.org.

Kelly hugging her mother after getting out of hotel quarantine, Hong Kong, November 2020

Tilden, Kelly's son, hugging his grandmother before her flight to the US, December 2020

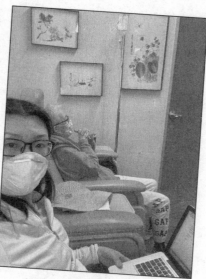

Kelly writing *Private Label* in the doctor's office while her mother gets chemotherapy, March 2021

Kelly with her mother in Los Angeles, November 2021

Acknowledgments

I'd like to thank the following people whose unwavering faith in this book made it possible: Tina Dubois, Ben Rosenthal, and Katherine Tegen. Thank you to the greater Harper team: Jacquelynn Burke, Lena Reilly, Laura Mock, Amy Ryan, Shannon Cox, Audrey Diestelkamp, Kathryn Silsand, and Julia Johnson. It is an honor and a privilege working with you every day! I'm also incredibly grateful to Marcos Chin for his stunning cover! Thank you for bringing Serene and Lian to life!

To my greater team at ICM: Ava Greenfield, Alicia Gordon, John Burnham, Roxanne Eduard, Tamara Kawar, Alyssa Weinberger, and Hirsh Bhatt. Thank you for believing in me and championing my work! Many thanks to Richard Thompson, my lawyer, for your wise counsel.

More than anything, I am grateful to my mother's medical team, led by Dr. William Isacoff. When my mom was first diagnosed with pancreatic cancer, I thought it would be a death sentence. However, thanks to the extraordinary care and groundbreaking ingenuity of Dr. William Isacoff and his team, including Dr. Simran Sekhon, Shadea Okhovat, Afag Murad Ali, and Faye Purcell, and a successful Whipple surgery, performed by Dr. S. T. Fan at the Sanitorium Hospital in Hong Kong, my mother is alive and thriving.

In going through this journey with my mother, I've come to better understand this mysterious disease. *Pancreatic cancer does not have to be a death sentence.* I've gotten to know 10+ year survivors who are living their best lives. They include Diana Roth, Diane Ronnau, Laurie MacCaskill, and many others. Hearing their stories motivated my mom to get through chemo, and me to keep writing. These strong women truly are an inspiration to the human spirit!

For anyone going through this journey, please know you are not alone. Keep advocating for yourself, don't give up, reach out to others, and keep fighting, because medical advances are being made every day. I'm especially grateful to organizations such as Pancreatic Cancer Action Network (which connects patients with survivors), Let's Win! Pancreatic Cancer, and the Lustgarten Foundation. My sincere gratitude to Dr. Daniel Von Hoff at the Mayo Clinic, as well as Dr. Janine LoBello, at Ashion. We still have a long way to go and I hope that this book raises awareness for this terrifying diagnosis, as well as the importance of finding a cure!

Finally, as with anything—writing a book, getting through cancer—it always helps to have family support, and I'm so grateful to mine. A big hug to my three kiddos Eliot, Tilden, and Nina for being so patient with me while I was writing this book. To my dad, for driving my kids while I took my mom to the doctor every week. To my husband, who listens to me talk about pancreatic cancer endlessly every single day. Most of all, to my mom, for inspiring this story.

Thank you for never giving up on me, Mom. I will never give up on you.